Bombshell

a Whiskey Dolls novel

Jessica Prince

Copyright © 2021 by Jessica Prince
www.authorjessicaprince.com

Published by Jessica Prince Books LLC

All rights reserved.
No part of this book may be reproduced in any form or by any electronic or mechanical means, including information storage and retrieval systems, without written permission from the author, except for the use of brief quotations in a book review.

Discover Other Books by Jessica

WHISKEY DOLLS SERIES

Bombshell

HOPE VALLEY SERIES:

Out of My League

Come Back Home Again

The Best of Me

Wrong Side of the Tracks

Stay With Me

Out of the Darkness

The Second Time Around

Waiting for Forever

Love to Hate You

Playing for Keeps

REDEMPTION SERIES

Bad Alibi

Crazy Beautiful

Bittersweet

Guilty Pleasure

THE PICKING UP THE PIECES SERIES:

Picking up the Pieces

Rising from the Ashes

Pushing the Boundaries

Worth the Wait

THE COLORS NOVELS:

Scattered Colors

Shrinking Violet

Love Hate Relationship

Wildflower

THE LOCKLAINE BOYS (a LOVE HATE RELATIONSHIP spinoff):

Fire & Ice

Opposites Attract

Almost Perfect

The Locklaine Boys: The Complete Series Boxset

THE PEMBROOKE SERIES (a WILDFLOWER spinoff):

Sweet Sunshine

Coming Full Circle

A Broken Soul

Welcome to Pembrooke: The Complete Pembrooke Series

CIVIL CORRUPTION SERIES

Corrupt

Defile

Consume

Ravage

GIRL TALK SERIES:

Seducing Lola

Tempting Sophia

Enticing Daphne

Charming Fiona

STANDALONE TITLES:

One Knight Stand

Chance Encounters

Nightmares from Within

DEADLY LOVE SERIES:

Destructive

Addictive

Whiskey Dolls Playlist

Want to know what the Dolls dance to?

"Toes" by Glass Animals
"Kill Of The Night" by Gin Wigmore
"Ex's & Oh's" by Elle King
"Never Say Never" by Cole Swindell and Lainey Wilson
"Youth" by Glass Animals
"Set Fire to the Rain" by Adele
"Elastic Heart" by Sia
"Heat Waves" by Glass Animals
"Chandelier" by Sia
"Gooey" by Glass Animals
"Shame" by Elle King
"I Feel Like I'm Drowning" by Two Feet
"Sweater Weather" by The Neighbourhood
"Lovely" By Billie Eilish with Khalid

Chapter 1
Marin

"Welcome to Cooking Solo," the tall, reed-thin woman at the front of the room announced in a voice that rang with so much cheer, it screamed of bullshit. "A class designed for singles, such as yourselves, who want to learn the art of cooking for one."

And this is what my life has become, I thought glumly, *being passive-aggressively judged by a stick figure with a carat-and-a-half rock on her ring finger.*

There should have been some sort of disclaimer when I signed up for the class online stating the instructor was a "happily married mother of three."

If you were going to be teaching people to cook for one because they were painfully and glaringly *A-L-O-N-E*, the least you could do was be single yourself.

But oh no, Chef Jodi—a title she'd undoubtedly christened herself with and insisted we call her by—couldn't stop talking about her loving husband and precious babies.

I kind of hated Chef Jodi. Chef Jodi was an asshole.

"Now, we're going to start off simple, because the last thing any single man or woman probably wants to do is waste time in the kitchen cooking up some complicated dish just for themselves, am I right?" She let out a condescending laugh. "I'm sure you'd rather be on one of those Tinder apps or on a blind date or whatever it is you single people do nowadays to try to meet someone."

I was going to smack the shit out of this woman with my handy little spatula the next time she came around to my station.

"So tonight, I'm going to teach you to make one of my husband's favorite meals—"

The vibe in the room was growing more hostile the longer she rattled on, and something told me Chef Jodi was going to be getting some pretty nasty reviews on Yelp.

"For the love of God, Jodi," a woman who looked to be in her sixties, one station across and back from mine, declared. "We *all* know you and your family. Your husband spends so much time in his damn recliner doin' a whole lotta nothing that his ass is permanently flattened. Those *sweet little angels* you're goin' on about nearly started a forest fire last summer with a bunch of illegal fireworks, and everyone in town knows you lock yourself in the bathroom with a bottle of wine and sleep in the bathtub at least once a week just to escape the chaos. So you can get the hell off your high horse, already."

The laugh I tried to swallow down came out as a snort as the room filled with snickers from all directions.

With Jodi properly put in her place, she managed to go about teaching the rest of the lesson without any more insults, and we were able to go about making our rosemary chicken without the commentary on how much her husband loved it.

I wasn't a very good cook, so for the past few months I'd been living off cereal, boxes of powdered mac and cheese, and soup from a can—another reason I'd stupidly thought signing up for Cooking Solo was a good idea.

By the end of the class, I'd succeeded in making a passable dish that didn't smell like charred feet and was only slightly rubbery, so I was feeling pretty good about myself as I cleaned my station and packed up to head home. Then I turned around and lost my breath at the sight of the man at one of the stations near the back of the room.

Pierce Walton: the sexiest man in existence, successful lawyer, single father of what had to be the cutest little boy on the face of the planet, world-class prick, and the older brother of my abusive asshole of an ex-boyfriend.

Well shit.

My feet were rooted to the floor for the several seconds it took my brain to reengage after short circuiting—because that was the kind of effect the man had on pretty much everyone, men and women alike.

Before he could look up and spot me, I ducked behind a group of fellow singles and booked it for the side exit as my heart beat wildly, attempting to escape the confines of my chest.

As soon as I rounded the corner, I plastered my back to the wall, breathing like I'd just run a mile at a dead sprint. I chanced a quick peek, unable to help myself where Pierce was concerned. From the very first moment I'd met him, the man had some kind of crazy power over me. Inappropriate as hell, given that I'd been in a relationship with his little brother at the time. But it couldn't be helped. There was just something about him, he was a freaking wizard or something.

A few people passed by, giving me strange looks, but I couldn't bring myself to care. I tried to be as inconspicuous as possible as I leaned farther for a better look. Just another inch . . . and there he was. God, the man still took my breath away.

It really was too bad we hated each other.

In my defense, my hatred of him was solely reactionary. He'd hated me first, so I figured it was only fair I hate the stupid sexy jerk back. I'd have been fine with the guy if he hadn't decided within the first half hour of meeting me that I was somehow seriously lacking for whatever reason.

Bombshell

I'd been dating Frank for six months when he'd taken me to meet his family for the very first time. I was standing in his mother's kitchen, helping with the last-minute preparations of the very lovely dinner she'd made, when the back door suddenly opened and a Grecian god came waltzing through.

I was stunned into immobility at the mere sight of him. In his expensive-looking suit and well-polished shoes, he looked like he belonged on the glossy pages of a magazine, modeling men's designer clothes, not stepping into a small, countrified home in a small mountain town. Then I looked down to the little toddler holding his hand, a near spitting image of the dark and dangerous man who'd just come in, and nearly swooned into a puddle of goo.

The only way I could describe how I felt in that moment was *dazzled*. I was completely dazzled by this gorgeous stranger while standing in the kitchen of my boyfriend's childhood home.

He looked up at me with eyes so blue they glinted like glaciers in the middle of the sea, and for a beat, he seemed almost as flummoxed as I was. There was something in his penetrating gaze that I wasn't able to read, but whatever it was, it had warmed me to my core. It made me fidgety and antsy. I wanted to dive in and get to know him at the very same time a tiny voice in the back of my head was telling me to run away because this man was Dangerous with a capital D.

We stood there, staring at each other in surprise for what felt like an eternity before Mrs. Walton cleared her throat and broke the spell. Then he smiled a smile that rattled me to my very core.

"Well, hello there," he said in a velvety smooth voice that had just the right amount of delicious rasp to it. "I'm Pierce." He extended the hand not attached to the adorable kid, and the instant his long, thick fingers engulfed my hand, goosebumps broke out across my whole body. "And who might you be?"

His mother jumped to introduce me when it became obvious the power of speech had failed me, and as soon as the words, "Frank's girlfriend" left her mouth, a switch flipped. The man who'd nearly knocked me on my ass just a minute earlier with nothing more than a smile was suddenly giving me the deep freeze.

Every encounter after that was downright chilly. Every forced conversation felt layered with frost until I eventually just gave up all together.

Frank used to bad mouth his brother constantly, always going on about how arrogant and condescending he was, how he thought he was better because he'd gone to law school and worked in the city. The colder Pierce acted toward me, the easier it was to understand Frank's animosity toward his big brother, and eventually, Frank's animosity became my own.

Once again my breath caught in my throat as I

watched him. With the sleeves of his expensive button-down rolled to mid-forearm, I was able to stare, transfixed, at the cords and muscles flexing and straining beneath his golden-tanned skin as he wiped down his prep station.

The last place I'd ever expected to see Pierce was at a cooking class. It was a complete contradiction to the callous man I knew him to be.

His hair flopped down over his forehead as he leaned over, adding a boyish element to the man's hard, chiseled face that managed to somehow soften his granite-like features just a bit. I hadn't thought it possible for the man to ever look soft. He always seemed to be in a bad mood. In the three years I'd dated his douchebag of a brother, I'd only been around Pierce a handful of times and, with the exception of that very first encounter in his mom's kitchen, I'd never seen the man smile.

On top of hard, brooding features, he had the most incredible icy blue eyes I'd ever seen. They had the ability to freeze a person to their core with just one look. I knew that for a fact, considering after each run-in with the glacial man I felt like I had frostbite.

Still, as much as it irked me, I couldn't help being fascinated by him.

"Uh . . . everything okay here?" I jerked up, whipping back around so fast my hair slapped me in my face when I turned to the woman standing a few feet away. She lowered her voice to a conspiratorial whisper as she looked off in the direction I'd just been staring. "Do you need me to call the police or something?"

"What? No! Oh God. No. Sorry. I just—" I stopped myself mid-ramble and held my hands out, palms up. "No, sorry. Everything's fine. I just spotted someone I know, and I didn't want him to see me, so I'm hiding."

Oh great, Marin. Because that admission totally doesn't make you sound like a wackadoodle.

Her brows climbed higher on her forehead. "Why didn't you just leave then?"

I gave a small, self-deprecating laugh. "Well, because I didn't want *him* to see *me*. But *I* still wanted to see *him*, you know?" Realizing how that sounded, I quickly added, "But not in a weird way! In a totally normal, non-creepy kind of way."

I'll take Things Stalkers Say for a thousand, Alex.

If anything, the woman looked even more convinced that she needed to call the police.

I pulled in a slow, steady breath in an attempt to calm my nerves that had been firing like crazy since I saw Pierce, and explained, "He's my ex-boyfriend's older brother."

Understanding lit her eyes, and the panicked look of *I'm standing here talking to a psycho* drifted away. "Ah. I see." She joined me at the wall and peeked around with me to get a better look. "Wow," she breathed. "He's very good looking."

"Yeah," I said with a defeated sigh. "The stupid jerk."

Bombshell

She looked back to me, a quizzical brow arched in suspicion. "Sorry. It's a long story. I should probably get out of here before he notices me. Is he looking this way?"

The woman glanced back. "No—wait." She watched for another second before whispering, "Okay, go!"

"Thanks," I whispered back, pushing off the wall and scuttling down the hallway.

"Have a good evening. See you next class," she continued to whisper-yell.

"Yeah, you too," I returned, waving over my shoulder.

Half an hour ago I'd been so sure I was done with Cooking Solo and that snooty Chef Jodi. But then I saw him. And even though I couldn't stand the guy, I knew that if it meant I'd get another chance to gawk when he wasn't looking, I'd be returning for the next class.

Because I was nothing if not a glutton for punishment.

Chapter 2
Marin

Every light in the house was on, making it glow like a spotlight on the quiet, sleepy street. I could hear pandemonium from inside as I climbed the porch steps and knocked on the front door.

I waited patiently as a blood-curdling scream erupted from inside. A second later my older sister pulled the front door open, looking harried and exhausted. Glancing back over her shoulder, she shouted, "Erika Marin Allen, if you don't knock off that screaming *right now*, I'm gonna shave your head in your sleep!"

"It's not my fault!" my eleven-year-old niece shouted back from somewhere upstairs. "Matt let his stupid rat out of its cage again!"

"Tubby's not a stupid rat!" my nephew decreed loudly, as full of indignation as a nine-year-old could possibly get. "He's a guinea pig, and he needs his exercise!"

"He wouldn't need exercise if you didn't overfeed him and make him fat!"

"He's not fat!"

"Enough!" my sister boomed in her loud, shrill *mom* voice that had both her kids going silent. "Matt, put Tubby in the plastic ball if you want to give him exercise. Erika, chill out. You're losing your mind over nothing. And *both* of you. Stop. *Screaming!*" she screamed.

"Did I come at a bad time?" I asked as I stepped across the threshold.

Tali rubbed at the space between her eyebrows as she pushed the door shut and started for the kitchen, leaving me to follow after her. "Nah, just another night in the Allen household," she muttered as she rounded the island toward the sink stacked high with dirty dishes.

Instead of pulling up a stool, I came up beside her and started loading the dishes she'd rinsed off into the dishwasher, trying to lighten the load she was quite clearly carrying on her shoulders. She turned to give me an appreciative grin, and I noticed she looked even more tired than usual. Purple half-moons bled out from beneath her eyes, and her normally dewy complexion looked ashen.

"Hey, you okay?"

"Yeah. Just beat. I've been fighting off a migraine for a few days now, and the damn thing isn't giving up without a fight."

"Where's Nick? Why isn't he in here doing this if you don't feel well?"

My sister let out a snort chock-full of derision as she scrubbed even harder at the plate in her hand. "Where do you think he is?" she asked bitterly. "He's still at work. Another late night," she said in a low, mocking voice that I could only assume was supposed to sound like her husband. "It's the third late night this week."

I took the plate from her before she snapped it in half, and loaded it in with the rest of the dishes before closing the front of the dishwasher and starting it.

"I thought you said his hours were supposed to go back to normal once he got that promotion."

"I thought so too," she grumbled, drying her hands on a hand towel before grabbing a glass of wine that had been sitting on the counter a few feet away. She quickly downed the contents and reached for the uncorked bottle. She held it up and gave it a little wave. "Want one?"

"Sure," I answered, moving around the island and hopping up on one of the stools while she grabbed a second glass from the cabinet and proceeded to fill both of them three quarters full.

She took the stool beside mine, sliding my glass in front of me while taking a healthy gulp from her own. "Things were supposed to get better after he got that stupid job, but if anything, they've only gotten worse," she lamented. "He's at the office more than he's home. He's even going in on weekends now. He missed one of Matt's baseball games and Erika's choir recital."

I spun the wine glass by its stem, studying Tali's profile as she stared off into space. "Have you said anything to him about it?"

"I would . . . if he was ever home long enough for me to instigate the conversation. Most nights he doesn't get home until I'm already in bed, and on the nights he's actually here at a reasonable time, he's so damn tired he crashes right after dinner. Even when he's here physically, he's not present, and it's starting to affect the kids. Matt's starting to cling to me like he's afraid I'm going to up and disappear like his dad. And Erika's acting even more dramatic than usual, and she developed this attitude almost overnight. She jumped into that pre-teen emo phase a whole hell of a lot faster than I expected. She's so damn moody all the time now. Everything I say or do is wrong."

"Ah, I remember those day," I lamented, sipping at my wine.

"Yeah, I do too," Tali mumbled, "and I'm dreading the day she gets her first period."

I leaned over, bumping my shoulder into my sister's. "If she's anything like you were when you got your first period, I'd maybe up the policy for fire damage."

I finally got a smile out of her. Granted, it was a small one that didn't come anywhere near her eyes, but it was still something.

She let out a defeated sigh while propping her elbow on the island and resting her chin in her hand. "We used to be good, Mar. Nick and I were a team. I don't know when it changed, but I feel like I'm a single parent here, and I didn't sign up for that."

"I'm sorry, Tal." My heart ached for my big sister. I'd have given anything to make things better for her, but unfortunately, that wasn't up to me. That responsibility fell to Nick, and I hoped like hell he got his head out of his ass before it was too late. "I'm here for you, you know that. If you need anything, just pick up the phone and call me. Even if it's to pawn your kids off on their awesome aunt for a few hours so you can have a break."

She leaned over, resting her head on my shoulder. "Thanks, hon. But enough about me and the sad state of my marriage. What brought you by tonight?"

"I had that cooking class tonight and just thought I'd swing by on my way home."

She perked up, sitting up straight so she could twist to face me. "That singles cooking class? How'd it go?"

"Well, the meal I made came out semi-edible, so I'd consider it a win."

Tali narrowed her eyes, staring shrewdly. "Why do I get the feeling you're leaving something out?"

I chewed on the corner of my bottom lip, contemplating my wine like it was the most interesting thing in the room before admitting, "Pierce Walton was also in the class."

Her mouth dropped open and her eyes bugged out like it was 1997 and I'd just told her all the members of the Backstreet Boys had been taking a cooking class for singles. "No *way*! Hotty Pants McDouchnozzle was in the class?"

My brows pinched together. "I thought we agreed his name was going to be Lord Stickuphisass Shithead, Duke of Assholedonia."

"Oh, that's right," Tali said. "I forgot we changed it after binge watching *Bridgerton*. So, what did you say to the dickish Duke?"

"Nothing," I answered on a scoff. "I didn't say a damn word. I high-tailed it out of there before he saw me."

"What? Why?" My sister widened her eyes, letting the disappointment shine through.

I swallowed some more wine as my brain flipped over to images of him from earlier that night. That stupid, silky-looking hair, those strong arms, the impeccably tailored clothes that highlighted his gross, sexy muscles perfectly. *God, what a jerk!*

"Because I have nothing to say to him," I answered, hoping the blush I felt beneath my cheeks wasn't making itself known on my skin. "It's not like we really know each other. We hardly ever talked the whole time Frank and I were dating. I don't even know if he's aware we broke up."

Tali's face crumbled into a sever scowl. "You think he

knows his brother is an abusive son of a bitch who deserves to burn in hell?"

To say my sister had been pissed off when she found out I'd been keeping the fact that my ex had a habit of leaving his marks on me whenever he got pissed—and he got pissed *a lot*, considering he was a miserable bastard—a secret from her would have been a serious understatement.

At first she'd cried hysterically, carrying the weight of what had happened to me on her own shoulders and blaming herself for having failed to protect me. Once I finally got her to realize that there was nothing she could have done, she got ragey. Like, *seriously* ragey. Imagine the baby from those *Incredibles* movies. You know, the one who just catches fire spontaneously and looks like a miniature devil? Yeah, that was Tali. I'd actually had to jump on her back and wrestle her to the floor as she tried to get out the door so she could hunt Frank down and run him over with her car.

After that, she cried again, but this time, her sadness was due to the fact she thought I hadn't told her I was suffering because I didn't trust her. The fact I'd made my sister cry had hurt worse than any blow Frank had ever landed.

Between the two of us, I was pretty sure there'd been enough tears to fill several buckets that night. By the end of it, we'd aired all our dirty laundry, confessing things to each other we'd been holding onto for years and years. I admitted that I was the one who'd accidentally ripped the side view mirror off her car while backing out of the driveway. I told her that I'd taken the keys without permission so some of my friends and I could go see *Twilight* in the theater, but I hit the mirror on the fence, freaked the hell out, re-parked the car, and returned the keys to where I'd stolen them from like it had never happened.

After she frogged me good and hard on the arm, she forgave me and confessed that it had actually been *her* joint our mother found in my underwear drawer, which resulted in me being grounded for an entire month and having to suffer through nightly lectures on the evils of drugs.

It helped to ease her frayed nerves when I told her my friend Charlotte shattered Frank's kneecap when he came storming in while she was helping me pack and move out of that piece of shit's house for good. He was *still* walking with a noticeable limp. And as an added bonus, she had also been carrying a stun gun on her at the time, so I got in a few good zaps before it was all said and done.

In the end, Tali and I had come out of that conversation even closer than before, the bonds of sisterhood rock solid.

I finished my wine and reached for the bottle to pour myself another. "I have no clue if he knows about his brother. From how Frank acted and the things he said, I don't think they were very close."

Bombshell

In fact, the way my ex used to talk about his brother, it was obvious he held an unhealthy amount of contempt for the man who was his own flesh and blood, something I never quite understood, given how tight Tali and I were.

"Yeah, well, screw that family, right? You're done with them and there's no point in looking back."

I clinked my glass with hers. "To being done with losers."

"Amen to that." She took a large gulp.

I hung around a while longer to make sure she was okay and to let her vent about her husband a bit more. There was a gnawing in my gut, a nagging worry as I headed home. I hated that she was struggling, and it was obvious she was putting on a brave face for the sake of me and the kids, pretending things were better than they actually were.

All I could do was hope that Nick got his head out of his ass. And if he didn't get his shit together on his own, I had no problem with helping speed that process along by making sure my moron of a brother-in-law saw the light before everything blew up in his face.

Chapter 3
Pierce

"I don't want meatloaf for dinner. Your meatloaf smells like dog poop."

I looked down at my six-year-old son and arched my brow. He stood next to the cart with his little arms crossed over his chest and scowled murderously.

"My meatloaf doesn't smell like dog poop."

He scrunched his nose up like he'd gotten a whiff of shit just then. "Yeah it does."

"It does not, and you're being rude, Eli."

"It smells just like Titan's farts."

I had to bite the inside of my cheek to keep from laughing at that particular declaration, even though it was funny as hell—and maybe slightly true. I wasn't the best cook in the world. If I were being honest, I was pretty damn bad at it, and a lot of what I cooked ended up making the house smell an awful lot like it did every time our gassy dog got into the garbage—a weekly occurrence no matter how hard I'd tried to break him of the habit.

"All right. What about spaghetti?"

I couldn't really blame him when his lips scrunched up and his face pinched like he'd just sucked on a lemon. That was one of the only meals, other than meatloaf, that I could cook. Sadly, I couldn't make either of them well, which was why I'd taken that stupid cooking class last week.

My son's head fell back dramatically, the groan emanating from his chest sounding like it belonged to a wounded animal. "I'm gonna starve!"

Oh, for Christ's sake.

I wanted to turn to all the people giving me the side-eye in the grocery store aisle and tell them I did *not* starve my kid, but from the looks on their faces, they wouldn't have believed me anyway, so I figured why bother?

Reaching up, I pinched the bridge of my nose, feeling an all too familiar dull throb start behind my left eye. It was the beginning of a regularly occurring tension headache that came with the realization that I was failing as a father. If Constance were still here, she'd know what to do. She was the best mother. She'd been born for it, so the fact she was no longer here was the worst kind of cosmic joke. The second she learned she was pregnant with our son, some instinct deep inside of her clicked on. She knew exactly what to do. I still didn't have a clue. I tried, God knows I tried constantly, but it seemed like I just couldn't stop fucking up.

I feared that if she were able to see me now, she'd be disappointed in the man she'd been married to. Each night I went to bed, I asked the higher powers for only one thing: Please don't let me screw my son up. Please don't let me ruin him for life.

"Fine," I said on an agitated huff as I tried to pull in a calming breath so I didn't lose it in the middle of the grocery store. "Then what do you want to eat?"

"Mac and cheese with hot dogs," he answered automatically.

"We've already had that for dinner twice this week. Pick something else."

He got that hard look of determination on his face that always sent a sharp pang through my chest. He looked so much like his mother when he made that face. When Constance was in the mood to dig her heels in and stand her ground, she always looked so goddamn adorable, I'd feel myself melt right before caving and giving her what she wanted.

Eli had the same effect. "All right. Let's go," I relented, feeling just a bit more of my power burn away. I couldn't help myself when I saw my wife in my boy's eyes. I was utterly helpless. Christ, I was bad at this parenting gig.

My son's little hand latched onto the cart, walking alongside of it as I pushed us toward the aisle that contained the boxes of the powdered mac and cheese he loved so damn much.

I guided us around the corner and jerked to an immediate stop when I caught sight of the woman standing halfway down the aisle.

Marin Grey. One of the most beautiful women I'd ever laid eyes on, and the bane of my existence.

My chest tightened at just the sight of her. It was panic, brought on by my body's incomprehensible reaction to her. It was the exact same thing I felt the very first time I laid eyes on her and every time after that.

I could still remember like it was yesterday, walking into my mother's kitchen and seeing her standing there. At the time, it had been three years since I'd lost Constance. I was no longer buried under the grief of that excruciating loss, but I still missed her every goddamn day, and the last thing on my mind was putting myself back on the market. I didn't want or need another woman, and I wasn't sure I ever would. Eli was all I cared or thought about. I had to take care of him, protect him from the harsh, ugly world he'd been born into. It was just me and him, and I was more than okay with that.

Then my eyes locked with this sexy goddess across the room, and it felt like someone had taken a sledge hammer to my chest.

I couldn't make myself look away. I didn't know who she was or what she was doing there, but I couldn't seem to bring myself to care. A basic instinct reared up inside me, one word bouncing around in my brain as I stared at the bombshell of a woman.

Want.

It was all I could think, all I could feel. Something about her brought out the caveman in me, and that scared the hell out of me, filling me with dread.

Then my mother introduced her as my little brother's girlfriend and it was as if a bucket of ice water had been dumped on the fire burning wild and out of control in my gut.

Frank was my blood, but that didn't mean I couldn't see him for exactly what he was. The man was a worthless waste of space, a goddamn leech that sucked as much as he could from those around him, be it money, time, or patience. Hell, the self-centered asshole would take the marrow from your bones if he could. He was an entitled little prick who expected shit to be handed to him for no other reason than he simply existed, and he went into a rage any time things didn't go his way.

In just the handful of seconds I'd been staring at that woman, it had been obvious she was too good for my little brother. It was a fact I knew down to my bones. She deserved better.

However, knowing that didn't matter. With just a handful of words, it became clear that the only woman I'd been drawn to since my wife died was off limits in a profound and very permanent way. I might not have liked Frank all that much, but there were still lines even I wouldn't cross, and fawning over your brother's woman was a huge, glaring NO.

The way my body responded to her just then as she danced around the aisle to whatever was playing in the earbuds she had stuffed into her ears was so intense, so visceral, that I felt my muscles tighten and my jaw clench. I shouldn't feel this way, and the fact that I couldn't make myself stop, that I had all the self-control of a hormonal teenager being led around by his dick, pissed me the hell off.

As irrational as it was, I found myself in a bad mood whenever she was around. The tempest of emotions I was forced to tamp down in her presence caused physical pain. I didn't *want* to want any woman, not when I needed to focus solely on Eli, and certainly not *this* woman. It was a headache I didn't have the time or inclination to deal with. That was why, over the past few years, I'd done my best to keep my distance, and on the few occasions it couldn't be helped, I'd found myself taking that bad mood out on her.

It had been a while since the last time I saw her. It wasn't just that I was trying to avoid seeing her but also because I did my best not to spend too much time in Frank's company. He had a nasty habit of getting under my skin and trying to pick a fight whenever we were together. When I got word a few months back that they'd broken up,

I knew I had to stay the hell away for the sake of my own sanity. Then last week I spotted her near the front of that damn cooking class, and all those feelings I'd tried to ignore for the past couple of years, the ones I'd managed to push to the back of my mind, reared up and refused to be ignored any longer.

I'd been failing epically at the first dish that pain-in-the-ass instructor was attempting to teach us to make when I caught a wave of familiar golden honey out of the corner of my eye that made my heartrate kick up. My pulse began to thrum beneath my skin when I saw her in profile, chewing on her lip as she squinted down at the sheet of printed instructions. Tunnel vision had kicked in, and she was all I could see.

Her hips moved ever so slightly like she was swaying to a beat only she could hear as she chopped and stirred, while I was rooted in place with a kitchen knife gripped in my hand.

I'd noticed a while ago that she always seemed to be in motion, even when it wasn't required. It was as if there was always a song in her head she had to dance to. It was mesmerizing to watch, and made my dick strain behind the fly of my slacks.

With Marin as a constant distraction, I moved through the rest of that class in a fog of lust for her and annoyance at my lack of restraint. I'd ruined the meal I was trying to make, and made such a mess that it took me longer than everyone else to clean my station. Hell, it was a wonder I hadn't chopped off a finger at some point.

By the time I finished getting everything back to rights, she was gone. I never thought of myself as a masochist, but I signed up for the next class simply because I liked the idea that I might see her again.

"Daddy, look! It's Ms. Marin," Eli exclaimed, ripping me from my thoughts and back into the present.

It might have made me pathetic—okay, it *absolutely* made me pathetic—but I felt a bit more capable of handling a run-in with her as long as I had my son as a buffer.

"Eli, don't run—" I started, but of course he didn't listen. Letting go of the cart, he sprinted down the aisle shouting, "Ms. Marin! Ms. Marin!" loud enough for the whole store to hear.

Her head whipped around at the sound of my boy shrieking her name. Her eyes were a shade of amber that always reminded me of the heat that followed that first sip of whiskey on a cold night and how it could warm you from the inside out. They landed on me first, growing wide with what looked a hell of a lot like panic just before she schooled her features and shifted her attention to my son.

Her lips curved up into the most spectacular smile just before my kid crashed into her waist, wrapping his arms as far around her as he could. She hugged him back, her giggle tinkling like bells.

"Well, if it isn't Eli, Eli, the coolest guy." She reached up to ruffle his dark hair, and I felt an annoying sense of jealousy that I wasn't the one receiving that innocent touch, that I couldn't hug her without giving it any thought like my boy could. For Christ's sake, I was even jealous of the little moniker she'd given him the very first time they'd met. "How's it going, buddy?"

"Good! We're havin' mac and cheese with hotdogs for dinner!" Eli informed her just as I closed the rest of the distance between us.

"Mmm, that's one of my favorites."

"Mine too!" my boy crowed, his little chest poking out like he was thrilled to have something in common with her. It had been like that every time they saw each other, to the point I was pretty sure Eli was just as enamored with the woman as I was. And I honestly couldn't blame him one damn bit. He was like me in many ways, and being inexplicably drawn to Marin Grey was only one of the similarities we shared.

Her attention shifted to me, humor glinting in those tawny eyes of hers. "Guess that cooking class went about as well for you as it did for me, huh?"

Staring into those smiling eyes was like looking at the sun. Needing something else to focus on, I glanced into her cart, and the corners of my lips began to tremble at what I saw inside. There were several boxes of that very same macaroni and cheese I was just about to buy, as well as cans of instant soup, and packets of Ramen.

It took an insane amount of effort to bite back the grin that wanted to split my lips apart, but I somehow managed. "Guess so," I said, my voice coming out much gruffer and more clipped than I'd intended.

Her smile faded, the humor in her eyes snuffed out, and she began to fidget. I felt like an asshole, knowing it was my harsh tone that instigated the change in her. I just couldn't get my head straight whenever she was around.

"Who knows," she continued, trying her hardest to be polite in light of my awkward behavior, "maybe the next class will be a little better."

"Maybe."

For Christ's sake, Pierce. Use your goddamn words, I scolded silently.

She gave her head a shake, the small chuckle she let out dripping with disdain just before she said, "Well, I guess I'll see you guys around." That tightening in my chest returned. Only this time the panic came at the thought of her walking away.

She reached down to ruffle Eli's hair again, giving him a much warmer goodbye, and started to push her cart when the words slipped past my lips before I could give them a thought.

"I heard you and Frank broke up." She froze in place, jerking to a stop like her feet were suddenly encased in cement. "I'm sorry to hear it didn't work out," I offered when she looked back over her shoulder.

There was something in her gaze, something hard and frigidly cold. "Don't be," she said flatly. "Because I'm certainly not."

And on that note, she disappeared, leaving me wondering what the hell had happened between her and my younger brother.

Chapter 4
Marin

"I THINK you should try one of those dating apps."

Covering my face with the washcloth I'd been using to clean off all the layers of stage makeup I'd been wearing, I let out a frustrated and somewhat dramatic groan.

Three nights a week I performed at *the* premier burlesque club in the state of Virginia. People came from all over and stood in a line that usually wrapped around the building nearly every night for a chance to get into Whiskey Dolls. The food and drinks were top-notch, the atmosphere was cool and classy, but it was the entertainment everyone came for.

The Whiskey Dolls put on a hell of a show night after night, keeping the patrons in their seats until our security team had to start ushering everyone out at closing time.

I *loved* my job, and normally I loved the girls I worked with. But lately they'd been getting on my damn nerves.

They'd all been in support of me tossing Frank to the curb, the majority of them turning slightly murderous when they'd found out what an abusive prick he actually was, but now that months had passed, they were all way too eager to see me get back on the horse—so to speak. They wouldn't let up on how I needed to put myself back out there, find a *nice* guy, or—in my friend Alma's opinion—have lots and *lots* or torrid, gymnastics-style sex with whatever guy floated my boat.

Cutting my eyes to Sloane, I gave her the fiercest scowl I could summon up. "No dating apps."

"Oh come on!" she argued. "I'll even set your profile up for you. You won't have to do anything but go on the dates."

Dropping the washcloth, I spun around on my cushy little velvet stool. "You aren't making the case you think you are, babe. Knowing you, the headline above my profile pic would be 'DTF' or 'Up for Anything'."

"Nothing wrong with either of those statements," Alma said from her makeup station a few chairs down from mine, shooting me a wink as she touched up her glossy red lips. "At least then you could clean the cobwebs out of your . . ." She circled her finger in the general direction of my crotch and gave a little whistle.

"I don't have cobwebs, you asshole!" I decreed on a laugh, throwing my damp cloth at her head while the rest of the girls in the backstage dressing room joined in on the teasing. "I've barely had a chance to be single after a three-year relationship from hell. There's nothing wrong with taking a little break from men for the time being."

I looked to my friend Charlotte, hoping she'd agree with me, especially considering she was the one who'd taught Frank the majority of his lesson and graced him with a permanent limp. "Tell them, would you? There's nothing wrong with staying single for a while."

She pulled her lips into a wince, hesitating for several seconds before answering. "Well . . ."

"Oh come on!" I smacked my hand on the table, making the mirror and all my cosmetics rattle around. "Not you too."

"It's all that domestic bliss," Sloane said with a giggle.

"And all that D she's getting from that fine-as-hell man of hers," Alma added, making everyone burst into laughter again, me included.

"I've officially turned into one of those women I never thought I'd be," Charlotte lamented. "I'm so stupidly happy that I want all my friends to be as well. But if you aren't ready to put yourself out there just yet, there's nothing wrong with waiting." She reached over to place her hand on top of mine, giving it a comforting squeeze. "What you went through would make any woman hesitate."

"It's not that," I admitted. "I'm not holding on to any trauma. At least I don't think I am."

"Then what's the hold up?" Sloane asked.

I gave her question a bit of thought before answering. "I'm just not in the mood to suffer through a string of bad dates in an effort to find that one good one."

"Hate to break it to you, babe, but there isn't a crystal ball that'll tell you which dates will be bad and which ones will be good," Alma insisted. "It's the not knowing, the anticipation, that makes it fun. When's the last time you went out on a real date?"

"A long time," I answered flatly. I'd been with Frank for three years, and even before we got serious, he hadn't been the type of man to wine and dine. I hadn't really thought anything of it back then. Sure, I sometimes wished he'd make more of an effort, but I'd loved him—or at least that was what I'd convinced myself of. Hindsight really was a bitch. Looking back on that relationship now, I cringed at all the stupid choices I'd made, all the red flags I'd ignored and bad behavior I'd let slide or made excuses for.

Never again.

"Then you don't really know what you're missing out on." Sloane chided. "And you won't know until you try."

"I've never been a fan of meeting up with a total stranger," I continued to argue, even though I could feel myself losing.

My other friend, Layla, jumped in just then. "All right, then no dating app. But what if we set you up with someone? At least that way we can vouch for the guy beforehand."

My top lip curled up, my face pinching like I'd just smelled something funky. "You mean like a blind date?"

"It's better than some dude none of us have met, right?" Charlotte pointed out.

I let out a defeated sigh and dropped my head back. "You guys aren't going to let this go until I agree, are you?"

The room filled with resounding noes from all directions.

I spun around in my chair to face my so-called friends. "Fine," I relented, rather gracelessly. "I'll go on *one* blind date. That's it. But if it turns out awful, I'm blaming all of you, and you have to promise to let it go. Deal?"

"Works for me," Layla said cheerfully. "And I have just the guy. You're gonna love him!"

* * *

"Ugh! I hate this." Standing in my bathroom, I shimmied this way and that, trying to get the dress up over my ass. Finally, I got the stupid thing in place and turned to look in mirror. "I *hate this*!" I repeated on a pathetic cry. "I look like I just stuffed myself into a sausage casing!"

"Will you stop being so damn dramatic?" my sister's voice rang out from the other side of the door. "I swear to God, you're acting worse than Erika."

"I'm not being dramatic!" I shouted. "When I asked you to bring me a few dress options, I didn't think you'd raid my niece's closet. This thing is indecent!"

"Stop being a baby and come out already. I'm sure it's not as bad as you're making it out to be."

With a disgruntled huff, I flung the bathroom door open and stomped out. Tali was stretched out on my bed, lying on her stomach and flipping through one of the romance novels I kept stacked on my bedside table. She lifted her gaze off the page, her eyes growing so wide I thought they'd fall right out of her skull as soon as they landed on me.

Her stifled laugh came out as a loud snort just before she curled her lips between her teeth.

"I told you it was bad," I decreed, throwing my arms wide.

"I stand corrected." Then the cow burst into laughter.

"All right, it's not *that* funny," I grumbled.

"Oh my God," she laughed hysterically. "You look like a tin of biscuits that's just been popped open."

I pinched the material at my belly, trying to pull it away from my body, only to have it suction to my skin like a freaking wetsuit. "What the hell is this made of?"

"Lycra, I think."

I wrinkled my nose. "When did you ever fit into something this small, Tal? 1993?"

My big sister scrunched her lips to the side in thought.

"I'm pretty sure I bought that dress when I was pregnant with Erika. It was supposed to be inspiration to get back to my pre-baby body. That was back when the emaciated runway model look was all the rage."

Slamming my hands down on my hips, I shot her a killing look. "You stopped being small enough to wear something like this as soon as you hit puberty." We both favored our mom's genes, meaning we'd developed curves all the way back in middle school.

She shrugged, slapping the book closed and pushing up to sitting. "I had pregnancy brain when I bought it. I wasn't thinking rationally back then. You remember what I was like."

"Yes, I remember," I replied flatly. "We *all* remember. You broke down crying in the middle of the ice cream shop when your cone started to melt."

"Hey! I wasn't crying because it was melting. I was crying because they'd run out of toffee crunch. I had to get caramel swirl instead and it did *not* taste the same. No matter what that stupid kid behind the counter claimed," she finished on a grumble.

"You're ridiculous. You know that, right?"

"Meh." She shrugged like it was no big deal before narrowing her eyes and tilting her head to the side in concentration. "You know what? Now that I'm thinking about it, there's a strong possibility I might have gotten that dress from the junior section."

"*Argh!*" I began clawing at the material around my ribs, feeling like I was slowly being squeezed to death by an anaconda. "Just help me get this thing off. I'm starting to lose feeling in my fingers and toes."

It took the two of us, an act of God, and a pair of scissors, but five minutes later, I was free and filling my lungs with some much-needed oxygen.

"Thank you," I breathed, shaking out my arms so blood would start flowing back to them. "You didn't happen to bring any *grownup* clothes, did you?"

She hummed pensively and started flipping through hangers, assessing and discarding dresses before she finally held one up with a triumphant, "Aha! Here. Try this on. I think it'll work."

I slipped the spaghetti straps off the hanger and pulled the dress on. The silk was the color of red clay, the neckline dipping into a V that showed a hint of cleavage, but not so much that I'd be uncomfortable. The bodice was loose, cinching high on my waist with a faux knot, and the wrap skirt hit just below my knees, with a split in front that made it flow as I walked, giving a nice peek at my legs.

The zipper in the back went up without any trouble, and the best part, I could actually breathe in this one.

"Why the hell didn't you just start with this one?" I chastised as I moved back to my bathroom so I could get a better look. I had to admit, I kind of loved the dress. It fit perfectly, was demure but still sexy, and the color looked great with my lightly tanned skin and long blonde hair. Plus, it made my light brown eyes pop. Tali didn't know it yet, but I wasn't giving it back. The dress was mine forever and ever.

"I just grabbed a bunch of stuff out of my closet when you called. I didn't even know what all I brought," she called back.

I gave my hair one last fluff, combing my fingers through the beachy curls, before flipping off the bathroom light and stepping back out into my room to find Tali on her knees with her top half buried deep in my closet.

"What are you doing?"

"Finding you some shoes," she answered. There was more shuffling around. I had to duck to avoid being hit in the head by a Chuck Taylor. Then finally, she announced, "Got 'em!" She crawled backward until she was free of the dark confines of my crammed closet.

Resting back on her haunches, she held up a pair of strappy bronze stilettos with a smile. "These'll look *killer* with that dress."

I took them from her hands and slid them on my feet. Sure enough, they looked great. Grabbing her hands, I pulled her off my bedroom floor and, together, we moved to my dresser to rummage through my jewelry drawer.

"I miss dating," she lamented wistfully as she clasped a long, delicate gold chain around my neck.

"Yeah, well, I'd gladly trade places with you if I could,

but stupid Layla already texted my picture to the guy I'm supposed to meet tonight."

My girls hadn't hesitated to put their plan to get me back on the dating wagon into action once I'd given them the go-ahead. The day after that fateful conversation in the dressing room, I'd gotten a call from Layla informing me she'd talked to Clark, my blind date, and everything had been set without me having to lift a finger—without my knowledge.

"Who is this guy again?" Tali asked as she pulled out a chunky ring I'd gotten on a whim because it looked like the one Cersei Lannister wore all the time on *Game of Thrones* and held it up for inspection before passing it to me.

I slid it into place on my middle finger while answering, "I think he's an accountant or something? She said he does her taxes. I don't have high hopes for tonight."

"Hey, accountants can be good-looking."

I turned back to her with a quirked brow. "Yeah? Name one hot accountant."

She looked up and to the side as the seconds ticked by. "Oh! I have one. What about that guy from Nick's firm? The one I introduced you to at the Christmas party we hosted a couple years back? He was cute."

"Wasn't he fired for embezzling?"

She looked at me with befuddlement. "So?"

My mouth gaped open. "He's in jail right now, Tali!"

"He was still cute," she stated firmly, pointing her

finger like that just won her the argument. "And anyway, cute or not, at least you're getting out and spending time with adults. I'd *kill* to have a conversation with someone over the age of twelve."

My issues and unhappiness with my blind date instantly moved to the back burner when I turned to look at my sister, concern flooding my chest. I knew her almost as well as I knew myself. She was doing her best to hide it, but I could see the pain and sadness beneath the mask she'd superglued into place.

"You and Nick could go on a date. I'll watch the kids so you two can have a nice night." I offered up a smile. "We can have a sleepover at Aunt Marin's house. They'd love that."

Tali let out a snort and plopped down on the edge of my bed, clasping her hands between her knees. "Please. Like he'd take enough time off work to come home and take me on a date." She laughed derisively and shook her head. "The only reason I was able to come over here was because Erika's at the movies with some friends and Matty's staying the night at his friend's house."

"Oh, Tali," I said softly as I moved to the bed to sit next to her. "Maybe you should try talking to him. Let him know you and the kids are feeling neglected."

She blew a puff of air past her lips and gave her head a shake. "There's no point, Mar. It's like talking to a brick wall."

I wanted so badly to make things better for my big sister, but before I could say another word, she'd slid that mask right back into place, clapping her hands together and declaring, "Enough with this sad sack stuff. You have a date you need to get to. Stand up so I can do one last check."

I pushed to my feet and moved to stand in front of her, holding my arms out as I did a little spin.

"Mm-hmm. Mm-hmm. Good. No deodorant streaks, no panty lines, no double boob from your strapless bra sliding out of place. I think you're good to go, sweetie."

I rolled my eyes and laughed. "Thanks for the inspection."

She pushed off the bed and reached for her purse, hooking it on her shoulder. "Go into this with an open mind, would you? Try having a little fun. One of us should, and if it can't be me, then it's your job to allow me to live vicariously through you."

"Wow," I deadpanned. "No pressure or anything."

"Go on now, get. You look hot. Knock this accountant guy on his ass." With that, she smacked me on the butt so I'd get moving toward the door. "Oh," she called out. "And see if you can finagle a discount out of him come tax time. I'm looking for someone else to do our taxes."

God, I loved my crazy-ass sister!

Chapter 5
Marin

M y friends were dead to me. Every single damn one of them, but *especially* Layla for setting me up on this freaking date.

The drive into the city had been a bit of a deterrent, but when my date, Clark, had informed me he'd gotten us reservations at a fancy restaurant I'd been wanting to try for a while, I'd decided to look at that as a silver lining. It didn't take long for me to realize that was going to be the *only* upside to this evening.

Things had started out well enough. He'd been waiting for me near the hostess stand when I first arrived. At first glance, I'd been pleasantly surprised. He wasn't big and brawny like Charlotte's man, Dalton—or half the male population of Hope Valley for that matter—but it was clear he took care of himself. He was cute in a clean-cut, guy-next-door kind of way.

He'd been polite and complimentary as we'd gone through introductions before heading to our table, telling me how excited he was to meet me. I'd even found it a bit endearing when he admitted he'd changed his shirt three times in anticipation. It was nice to hear he'd been nervous, and I'd actually thought maybe the night wouldn't be too bad.

Then between getting our drinks and putting in our dinner order, the vibe began to shift.

"So, tell me, Marin, what's your ten-year plan?"

It was a question more geared toward a job interview than a blind date so, needless to say, I was a little thrown.

"Um . . ." I cleared my throat. "I'm not really sure. I guess I haven't given it much thought."

He arched his brows in bemusement. "You haven't? But aren't you already in your thirties?"

My chin jerked back in shock, my hackles rising at the question and his tone. "I just turned thirty a few months ago."

"That's still in your thirties. So in ten years, you'll be forty. And you're a burlesque dancer, right?"

I wasn't certain where he was going with his line of questioning, but I had a feeling I wasn't going to like it. "Yes," I answered, dragging that one word out cautiously.

"You have what, maybe another five or six years left in a job like that? You know, before gravity comes into play?"

The jackass actually held his hands out in front of his

chest before dropping them like my boobs were only a matter of years away from needing to be tucked into the waistband of my pants.

I choked on my drink, hacking to get up the swallow of gin and tonic that had gone down the wrong way. "It's not like I'm going to wither into dust in the next ten years." I exclaimed on a croak once I was able to breathe again.

"No, no. Of course not," he attempted to backpedal quickly. "Sorry. I didn't mean to imply anything."

He wasn't really implying so much as coming right out and saying I was a hop, skip, and a jump to being past my prime.

"What about marriage and kids? Do you want a family?"

Oh, for the love of . . . "Yeah. One day. But there's still time."

He lifted his glass of wine and gave a thoughtful hum before sipping. When he was done he stated, "Well, not really. I mean, isn't there an age limit on getting pregnant? Like, the plumbing's only good for a certain number of years, right?"

Lifting my drink to my lips, I sucked back the last of it and scanned the area for our waiter. Raising my empty glass to him, I gave it a little wave and mouthed, "*Double.*" He nodded briskly before scurrying toward the bar, and I made a mental note to add to whatever my *date* planned on tipping him.

In only a matter of minutes, this dude made me feel like I was close to retirement, with cobweb-riddled ovaries.

I took a fortifying gulp of my fresh drink the instant the waiter set it down in front of me. I cut Clark off as he rattled on about my dusty old lady parts and the importance of having my eggs frozen . . . just in case. "I'm sorry. I should have asked this at the start of the date, but just how well do you know Layla?"

For the life of me, I couldn't imagine she'd set me up with this guy if she knew him well. Either that, or this was a prank, giving her a massive laugh at my expense.

"Oh, not very well. I've been her accountant for a couple years now, but we only really talk around tax season."

I was going to kill her so dead.

Our entrees arrived after that, and I breathed a sigh of relief, thinking I'd get a reprieve from the weird and outrageously invasive questioning while we enjoyed our meals, but I was so very wrong.

"So what's your retirement plan look like?"

My fork paused halfway to my mouth. "Sorry?"

"It's important to have a plan in place for when you get too old to . . . you know, do what you do."

Tossing my napkin onto the table, I pushed my chair back and shot him a stiff smile. "Excuse me. I need to use the restroom."

I didn't bother looking back as I grabbed my purse and

headed toward the restrooms at the back of the restaurant. I pushed through the door and bent to peek beneath the stalls to make sure I was alone before pulling my phone from my cute little clutch and dialing Layla's number.

"Hey," she answered, surprise laced through her words. "What are you doing calling me? Aren't you supposed to be on a date right now?"

I let out a caustic laugh while leaning my ass against the vanity. "Yeah, I'm on my date. It's still happening. I had to sneak off to the restroom so I could call and tell you that I'm going to get you back for this. I don't know how and I don't know when, but I *will* make you pay."

I could hear the smile in her voice as she asked, "I take it the date isn't going well?" If I could have reached through the phone to strangle her, I would have.

"Uh, no. No, it's not," I hissed through the line. "You barely know this guy, Layla! What were you thinking, setting me up with him?"

"I thought he was nice," she defended. "He's always been polite whenever I've taken my tax docs to him."

"That's because you're *paying* him to be nice! The guy's a weirdo, Lay. In the time I've been here he's already suggested that I'll be too saggy to keep up with my job much longer, and if I don't freeze my eggs, having a baby at my advanced age might be difficult."

She snorted through the phone. "He actually said that?"

"Well, he alluded to the saggy thing, but that stuff about my eggs was practically word for word."

Instead of sharing in my outrage, she burst into laughter, leaving me to have to stand and listen as she cackled for a good two minutes.

"For the love of God, will you stop laughing already? This is serious!" I whisper-yelled. "I feel like I need an AARP membership or one of those cellphones for old people with the ginormous buttons."

"I'm sure it's not that bad," she attempted to be positive. "I mean, he's cute, right? Maybe he's just awkward on first dates."

"You better hope that's the case or, so help me, I'll find a way to give you head lice *and* pink eye all at the same time."

"Okay, crazy. Just relax. I'm sorry I didn't vet the guy better. I promise to do my due diligence next time."

"Oh, there isn't going to be a next time," I informed her. "This was a one-time gig. I don't want to hear another word from you about me putting myself back out there. You got it? And I expect you to tell the other girls the same thing."

"Deal. I can do that. Just no pink eye or lice, all right?"

I let out a sigh of defeat, knowing I'd stalled for as long as I possibly could. "I guess I better get back out there before he gets it in his head I have IBS or something and starts going on about me needing to see a doctor."

Bombshell

I hung up when she began to laugh hysterically again. Depositing my phone back in my purse, I stared at the door for a good thirty seconds while trying to will my feet to move so I could go back out there and finish my date.

"You can do this," I said to myself. "The sooner you get your ass out there, the sooner you can finish your dinner, go home and stare at Henry Cavill's ass while re-watching *The Witcher* for the fiftieth time."

That sounded like a solid plan to me. Shaking out my arms and squaring my shoulders, I walked to the door and yanked it open like I was prepared to go into battle. I'd made the mistake of glancing down, checking the front of my dress for wrinkles as I stepped out into the hallway, and slammed into a solid brick wall that was curiously wrapped in soft cotton and smelled absolutely divine, like clean laundry and the outdoors.

Before I had a chance to stumble back and fall flat on my ass, two large hands shot out, gripping my arms and holding me in place.

"Whoa. You all right?"

That voice—gravelly, yet somehow still as smooth as velvet at the same time—danced along my spine and made me shiver from top to toe. My eyes traveled up. Up over a strong, broad chest encased in a bespoke suit, up past the thick column of his throat and past a jaw square and sharp enough to cut glass, right up into blue eyes the color of ice.

"Pierce," I breathed, the synapses in my brain misfiring

at the unexpected sight of him. Damn, his name was fitting, because every time he looked at me, I felt that gaze pierce right through me.

His dark brows winged up in surprise. "Marin? What are you doing here?"

"I'm on a date," I answered a tad harshly, my tone growing defensive out of sheer instinct.

Those fingers still gripping my arms clenched, pressing deeper into my flesh as his masculine brow slashed downward. "With Frank?"

I could have sworn those two words were accompanied by a growl, but I couldn't be sure over the noises filtering in from the dining area. "What? No! God no. It's just some guy my friend set me up with. What are *you* doing here?"

"Client dinner," he said, those two clipped words slamming into me with the signature Pierce Walton Freeze I felt every time I was in his presence as his chilly gaze scanned every inch of my face.

"Okay, well . . . enjoy the rest of your evening then. I should get back to my date." I moved to take a step back only to have his grip grow even tighter, making it possible for me to escape.

"Um . . ." I looked down at his hands, expecting him to release me now that I'd drawn attention to his hold, but he didn't. When I lifted my head, my forehead creased in confusion. "You can let me go now," I said quietly, feeling my cheeks heat as I grew more flustered with each passing second.

It was almost as if he was in a daze. "Pierce?" I called out, trying again to get his attention.

He blinked, giving his head an infinitesimal shake. "Sorry, what?"

"Can you let me go, please?" I'd expected him to release me quickly, but instead, he dragged his palms down my arms, his touch featherlight before disappearing completely once he reached my wrists.

"Of course," he murmured once his hands were down by his sides. "My apologies. Enjoy your . . . date."

"Thanks, I will," I lied. There was no way in hell I was going to let him in on the fact that it was already a failure, especially not with how he'd all but sneered while saying the word *date*.

Without a backward glance, I sidestepped him and started back toward my table.

"Everything okay?" Clark asked once I returned to my seat. "You were in there a while."

My smile was brittle and forced as I placed my napkin back in my lap. "Yeah, everything's fine. I just ran into someone I knew. Sorry for the hold up."

"No problem at all. You know, I got to thinking about something else while you were back there."

"Oh?" I feigned interest as I cut into my salmon and took a bite. "And what was that?"

"Your life insurance policy." For the second time in one meal, I started to choke and, of course, Clark carried on like it was nothing. "Being a single woman and all, if something were to happen to you, your family would have to cover the costs of a funeral and any unforeseen medical expenses if it happened to be a car accident or something like that. If you haven't already, you really should look into getting something. Just in case."

I suddenly had the eerie feeling that I was sitting in the middle of a *Dateline* episode. There was a woman in my apartment building, Ms. Weatherby, who was obsessed with that show. She was always warning me about the risks of being a single woman this day and age. The woman was constantly worrying that I'd one day be abducted and stashed away in some maniac's basement. Thanks to her, I now knew how to break free of my restraints if my potential kidnapper bound my wrists with duct tape. She was going to have a field day when I told her about Clark.

"That's kind of deep for first date talk, don't you think?"

He lifted his napkin, dabbing at his mouth before speaking again. "Not particularly. We're both of an age where we need to be serious about settling down, don't you think? If I'm going to consider something long term with a woman, I'd like to know what I'm getting into."

My brows shot up toward my hairline. "And what you need to know is how much I'm worth if I die?"

He cleared his throat and tugged at his collar, chuckling nervously. "Well, when you put it like that it sounds kind of harsh."

And mildly psychotic, I thought to myself.

"Do you have a basement, Clark?" I blurted, all of Ms. Weatherby's warnings now floating around, front and center, in my head.

He gave me a quizzical look. "That's an odd question."

I slurped back half of my drink. "Yeah, well, you're already batting a thousand with that so I figured I'd join in. So? Do you?"

"Well . . . yeah."

"Sorry, Clark, but this isn't going to work out."

Chapter 6
Pierce

THE CONVERSATION at my table flowed all around me while I sat there in silence, tuned out as I stared across the expanse of the restaurant. How I hadn't seen her when she'd walked in was beyond me, but now that I knew she was here I couldn't make myself pull my eyes off of her.

She had the power to steal my breath on any given day, but seeing her now, all that sunshine hair of hers hanging down her back, her bee stung lips slicked with a tantalizing rosy color, and that goddamn *dress*, my brain had short-circuited.

Even from this distance I could see the pink hew on the apples of her cheeks and couldn't help but wonder if it was her makeup or a flush from something the jackass sitting across from her had said.

There was a part of me that wanted to be the one to

make her blush like that, but more specifically, to be the one to inspect just how far down that kiss of pink went.

Running into her in the hallway earlier had been a happy coincidence. The moment she crashed into me, I was overcome by the intoxicating fragrance of something that smelled floral and a bit sweet, something so uniquely Marin. The scent was faint, not overwhelming in the slightest, and I'd found myself breathing deeper with her standing so close, trying to pull as much of her smell into my lungs as possible.

When she'd said the word *date*, my muscles had gone tense and a red film had coated my vision. At first it was the thought of her with Frank, knowing she could do so much better, that had tipped me toward my boiling point, but when she confirmed it was with another man, the anger bubbling up inside of me hadn't lessened in the slightest.

I hadn't meant to sound so cold, I just couldn't control my fucking emotions whenever she was around. It was getting ridiculous. I was thirty-seven, for Christ's sake. I should have learned some goddamn self-control by now.

I was grateful when the dinner ended a short while later. I managed to get through several handshakes and back slaps, but while everyone else headed out of the restaurant, I made my way over to the bar, taking up residence on a stool that gave me a perfect line of sight to Marin's table.

Ordering a double scotch, I rested my elbows on the bar top and leaned in, sipping casually at my drink as I tried to discern how Marin's date was going by watching their—most specifically, *her*—body language.

Damn, I would kill to be able to read lips at a time like this, I thought to myself while another part of my brain yelled at me to get the hell out of there. I shouldn't stay, I knew that. It was like walking a tightrope over a flaming pit. For some reason, this woman was my kryptonite. I should stay as far away as possible, but something about her kept pulling me in. So I stayed where I was, like a creeper, watching a woman I barely knew in a way that would surely get any man out there slapped with a restraining order.

Being a lawyer, I had an affinity when it came to reading people, and judging by the way Marin was holding herself and the look on her face, it didn't take a genius to realize the date wasn't going all that well.

Words were exchanged, then whatever she said made the guy across from her turn tomato-red. He replied with something I couldn't make out, but the head shake she gave him in response was firm, no nonsense. Seconds later, he shoved back from the table and shot to his feet. Marin looked almost bored as she sipped her cocktail while he stormed out of the restaurant.

I wasn't sure what it was that made me act, but before the door of the restaurant could close on her date's ass, I was waving the bartender over, asking him to make a gin and tonic. It was just a guess, but that was what the drink she'd just finished sucking back looked like.

As soon as he slid it across the bar, I was on my feet, moving across the room without a single thought as to whether or not what I was doing was a terrible idea.

She dropped her face into her hands when I was only a few feet away, so I was able to hear her frustrated groan loud and clear by the time I reached her table.

"I take it the date didn't go well?"

Marin's head shot up, her gorgeous amber eyes narrowing into unhappy slits. "No," she replied flatly. "It *really* didn't."

Holding out the glass, I gave it a little shake so the ice inside would rattle. "Gin and tonic, right? I took a shot and guessed."

The annoyance melted from her delicate features, replaced with surprise and a large dose of curiosity. "Yeah. Um, thank you."

"No problem." I pointed to the chair her date had abandoned, asking, "Is it alright if I sit?"

She blinked slowly, the long fan of her lashes kissing the tops of her cheekbones. "What about your client dinner?"

"Ended already. I was at the bar when I saw your date leave."

She looked to the empty chair and back to me with

trepidation before giving me a nod. "Oh. Okay. Yeah, sure." She didn't sound all that comfortable with the idea of me joining her, but I wasn't going to let that stop me.

Before she had a chance to change her mind, I pulled out the chair and sat, lifting my scotch to my lips and taking a fortifying drink. "You want to talk about it? Or would you rather just sit here in silence and finish your dinner?"

She let out a small laugh and gave her head a shake. "There's really not much to talk about. Just the tragic tale of a blind date gone bad."

I felt one corner of my mouth curl up ever so slightly. "So, not a love connection, I take it?"

The megawatt grin that tugged at her plump lips hit me like a fist to the gut, making my dick start to swell behind my fly. "Definitely not. I was holding out hope, but I just couldn't get past the creepy, this-dude's-gonna-tape-me-up-in-his-basement vibe he was putting off."

I snorted mid-sip, causing scotch to go right up my nose and burn like hell. My eyes began to water and I coughed violently.

"Oh, God!" She lifted her hands to cover her mouth as she began to giggle hysterically. "I'm so sorry. Are you okay?"

"Jesus," I croaked once I was able to speak against the fire in my sinuses. "I wasn't expecting that."

Her giggles had tapered off, but it was still one of the

best sounds I'd ever heard now that I could actually focus on it. "I'm really sorry."

"It's fine," I said, clearing my throat just as the waiter stopped at our table.

He looked over at me and did a double take before his gaze bounced to Marin. "Is there anything else I can get you? Maybe the dessert menu?"

Her shoulders sank as she glanced over at me. It was most likely wishful thinking on my part, but I wondered if maybe she didn't want the evening to end just yet. If that was the case, the feeling was absolutely mutual. She finally sighed and turned her focus back to the waiter. "Actually, I think I'll just take the check."

The guy pulled a small black folio from his apron pocket and placed it on the table with a smile before taking off.

"I've got this," I said, quickly reaching across the table to grab the check before she could.

"Oh, no. You don't have to do that," she insisted as I leaned to the side to grab my wallet from my back pocket. "Really. I can—"

"I insist," I said as I flipped through my wallet and pulled out my credit card. "Even if the date was a complete shitshow, that asshole still should have paid for dinner. On the behalf of all men, let me make it right."

Marin's sharp inhale pulled my attention back to her just in time to see her eyes drift down to my lips, and I realized the smile I was giving her just then didn't feel forced or plastic.

Eli was the only person in my world who could get a genuine smile out of me, and all he had do to earn one was simply breathe. My boy was the only bit of light I'd had over the past several years, so over time my smiles had grown brittle and forced around everyone but him. However, in the past few minutes, I'd had more fun with someone who wasn't my son than I'd probably had in the past six years combined, and that realization was a punch of guilt straight to my chest.

Marin's eyelids hooded. Her chest rose on an inhale as she stared at my mouth, and hand to God, just having her look at my mouth like that made my dick twitch.

That feeling was accompanied by a voice in the back of my head screaming that this was a huge fucking mistake. A frigid chill worked its way down my spine like a bucket of ice had been dumped right over my head.

It took everything I had to keep from shooting to my feet and bolting for the door. However, before I had a chance to react in any way, Marin's eyes bugged out and for some inexplicable reason, she threw herself out of her chair.

"*Shit*," she hissed as she crawled behind the table on her hands and knees. "Shit, shit, shit!"

"Uh . . . something wrong?" I asked as my gaze darted around the restaurant to see that she'd garnered the attention of several other diners as well. Apparently I wasn't the only one wondering what in the hell this beautiful woman was doing crawling around on the floor.

"*Yes*," she whispered emphatically while tossing her head back to look at me and blowing wayward strands of golden hair out of her face. "You see that guy who just walked in? The one over by the bar?"

I forced my mind off the fact that her face was now dangerously close to my crotch, and my gaze shot in that direction. But I couldn't possibly distinguish the guy she was talking about from all the other men gathered around the bar. It was bordering on 8:00, so that area was filling up steadily with people coming in from work. "Which guy?"

Her head peeked out over the top of the table so she could scan the area. "Blue button-down, sleeves rolled up, dirty blond hair. The one sitting next to the woman in the tight red dress."

I definitely saw the red dress. It was impossible to miss in a way that the woman wearing it had more than likely intended. Low cut, skin tight, and short enough to reveal a large expanse of smooth thigh when she sat on the barstool and crossed her legs. It was the kind of dress that screamed for attention.

"Okay, yeah. I see him. So what's the big deal? You know him or something?"

She snorted indelicately, and damn if it wasn't

adorable as hell. "Yeah, I know him. He's my brother-in-law."

I looked down at her with an arched brow. "Then why are you hiding instead of going over to say hi?"

She looked up at me with an expression that read like I was the stupidest kid in school. "Because that woman he's with is *not* my sister."

Oh. "*Oh.*"

"Yeah, *oh*." She continued to whisper-yell. "My sister is currently at home, taking care of their two kids and their household all by herself because her husband is supposedly always too busy at work to come home at a reasonable hour to spend time with his family."

My head whipped back around to study the couple. The woman in red leaned in close, twisted in his direction as they spoke, but the man stayed straight on his stool, his body facing the bar. "Maybe it's not what you're thinking," I suggested, but it sounded weak, even to my own ears. His body language might not have been giving anything away, but hers most certainly was.

"What are they doing now?"

I looked down at her with a bewildered expression. "You want me to spy on them for you?"

Her pretty features twisted up in a *duh*. "Well, I can't do it! If he sees me, the jig is up."

I had to swallow back my laugh and bite the corner of my mouth to keep from smiling again. Fuck me, but she was cute as hell. I *really* should have gone home as soon as my own dinner ended. When the hell would I learn?

"Um, excuse me." At the sound of the newcomer's voice, Marin and I both looked over to see the waiter standing there, shifting from foot to foot with uncertainty. "Is everything okay?"

"Yep," Marin answered brightly. "Just lost a contact is all."

"Do you need some help?"

"Oh, no. I'll find it. But thank you."

To help push the guy along, I handed him the folio with my credit card in it, and he quickly retreated, probably in a hurry to close out the table so he could get rid of us.

"Okay, what's happening now?" Marin asked, pulling my focus back to her.

Knowing I wasn't getting out of this without playing spy for her, I turned back to the bar to watch. "Nothing's really happening. They're just talking."

"But how do they *seem*?" she pressed, still crouched down, hidden behind the table.

"They seem . . ." I trailed off, unsure how to answer when I saw the woman reach over and place her hand on the man's thigh.

"You got quiet all the sudden. Why'd you get quiet? What's going on?" Her head darted back up, and she sucked in an affronted gasp. "That little hussy!"

Placing my palm on top of her head, I shoved her back down. "Will you keep it down? You're going to get us caught." I was in this now, no going back, so I figured I might as well see it through. Truth be told, I was kind of curious how it was going to play out.

"But she's *touching* his *thigh*!"

"Yeah, but he just pulled away," I told her, fully immersed in this little spy operation. "And now he's fiddling with his wedding ring like he's trying to draw attention to it."

"Okay, so maybe he's not a complete ass," she grumbled almost resentfully, like having to relent that he wasn't totally in the wrong left a sour taste in her mouth.

"Do you not like him or something?"

"Of course I like him," she said with no small amount of defense. "He's family. He's just screwing up with my sister and their kids over and over again, and it's really starting to piss me off."

The sound of a throat clearing broke through the strange conversation. "Here you go," the waiter said, dropping the folio back on the table. "Hope you enjoyed your meal."

To save face, Marin smiled brightly up at him. "Oh here it is," she chirped, pretending to find her imaginary contact. "Found it."

She let out an embarrassed giggle and began to push up off the floor. Before I could think better of it, I stood tall and reached out to help her up, taking her hand in mine. Just like when we'd collided back in the hallway, the touch of her skin against mine sent a jolt of electricity through my entire body.

From the way she gasped, I sensed that she'd felt it too. That voice in my head was yelling at me to retreat, but before I had a chance, her heel caught on the carpet and she stumbled, right into my chest. My hands instinctively wrapped around the curve of her waist to keep her on her feet.

Her plump lips parted on a breath as she stared up at me, the amber in her eyes growing a touch darker, and I swear to Christ, I felt her lean in even closer.

The realization that she fit me perfectly was too goddamn strong to ignore as I held on to her. Her mouth was *right there*, just a few inches away. All I had to do was lean in, just a bit, and I'd be able to taste her. As it was, she was all I could see and smell.

Reality came slamming back into focus when someone dropped a dish somewhere in the restaurant, the loud clatter snapping me right out of the daze she'd just put me in.

Clearing my throat, I dropped my arms and took a step back. "I have to go. I need to get back to Eli." *Eli.* My son I should have been on my way home to at that very moment. Instead, I'd left him with my mother longer than I should have, all because I'd been sidetracked by a woman who made me lose myself. A woman who was so off limits it wasn't even funny.

"Oh. Yeah. Of course." I detected a hint of disappointment in her tone, but I refused to let myself dwell on it.

"See you around." I grunted, unable to meet her gaze as I pushed past her.

I could hear the befuddlement in her voice as she murmured, "Yeah, see you." I felt like an asshole as I bailed out of the restaurant, but I couldn't allow myself to look back.

Chapter 7
Marin

IT HAD BEEN three days since I'd run into Pierce—literally—during my disastrous blind date, and I hadn't been able to get that damn interaction out of my head. There was a point where I could have sworn he was about to kiss me. He'd shown me a side of him, a warmth, that I hadn't thought he was capable of. He'd smiled, and it stole every bit of air from my lungs. Then, from one heartbeat to the next, that warmth disappeared and that icy cold came rushing back.

He'd been so desperate to escape that he ran out of the restaurant like his ass was on fire, leaving his credit card behind. A credit card I'd been carrying around for days. For reasons I could not and absolutely *would not* dissect, I'd caught myself pulling that damn card out of my purse at least once a day and staring at it.

Odds were, he'd canceled it already, and I could probably just cut it up and throw it away, but I couldn't seem to make myself do it. I kept telling myself that I'd find the time to return it to him, *that* was why I still had it.

I was lying to myself because the truth was, I'd felt . . . *something* that night. For a moment in time, I'd completely forgotten I hated the man, and, more importantly, that he hated me for some ungodly reason. How could he? I was a freaking *delight*!

I didn't know why I hadn't been able to pull that brief, very faint flutter of attraction out of my mind, but it had been nagging at me for days to the point I felt like I was going crazy.

As if that wasn't bad enough, if I wasn't thinking about that stupid jerk, Pierce Walton, I was in a constant state of worry over my sister and what I'd seen at the restaurant.

I'd wavered back and forth for days trying to decide what to do. Should I tell her or should I keep it to myself just in case Pierce was right about reading too much into it? The last thing I wanted to do was hurt my sister in any way, but I also didn't want her to be blindsided.

"Hello? Earth to Marin."

The sound of Ms. Weatherby's voice jolted me out of my melancholy and back into the present, where I was sitting in her living room, surrounded by her outrageous collection of Precious Moments figurines that gave me the creeps, having our weekly tea.

I'd taken a shine to my elderly neighbor back when I'd

first moved into the building. She and Charlotte had lived across the hall from each other at the time and had grown close during their time as neighbors. That was how I'd met the eccentric, hilarious, and extremely wise old woman.

Now Charlotte was living with her hunk of a man, Dalton, in his beautiful house, but she still made time to come visit Ms. Weatherby. However, she and I had started our own tradition, which consisted of me making finger sandwiches once a week—because Ms. Weatherby might be wise as hell but she was arguably even worse in the kitchen than I was—and she'd set out a full tea service.

She also tended to put salt in her lemonade instead of sugar because the poor woman was blind as a bat, even with her coke-bottle thick glasses. But I'd nipped that little issue in the bud by labeling her canisters for her in thick, black, three-inch tall bubble letters that she could read clearly.

You'd think that a thirty-year-old and a woman well into her eighties wouldn't have much to talk about, but you'd be very, *very* wrong.

"You know, it's rude to come to someone's home and ignore them when they're in the middle of talking," she admonished.

"Sorry," I said with a small cringe. "I didn't mean to zone out. I've just had a lot on my mind the past few days."

She studied me behind those crazy thick lenses that made her eyeballs look like tiny beads as she lifted her teacup to her lips and sipped. "Well, you can't drop a little nugget like that and not expand on it, so you might as well tell me what's goin' on inside that pretty head of yours."

Honestly, one of the reasons I enjoyed coming down here every week was because Ms. Weatherby's advice was unparalleled, so I didn't hesitate to dive right in.

"Let's say that you were out to dinner, and you saw something that could possibly have been something bad, but it also could have been innocent and you just read the situation wrong. You aren't certain exactly what it was you witnessed, but it has the potential to ruin a person's marriage. Do you tell that person what you think you may have seen, or do you keep it to yourself?"

She rolled her beady eyes and let out a frustrated huff. "Young people these days. Will you stop tap dancin' around your story and just spell it out for me already? I'm not as young as I once was, and I don't have the time or inclination to try and figure out what you're askin'."

"I was out last week on a blind date—which is something I'll get into with you another time," I quickly added when her white eyebrows shot up. "But while I was at the restaurant, I saw my brother-in-law, Nick, there with a woman who wasn't my sister. The woman's behavior was questionable, but I couldn't tell if Nick was reciprocating or not."

"And you want to know whether or not you should tell your sister."

"Yes! Exactly." I placed my teacup and saucer down on her coffee table and leaned over, bracing my elbows on my knees. "What should I do, Ms. W?"

She went silent for several seconds, as if she were giving it some serious thought. "That's quite the pickle you got yourself in, there."

"Tell me something I don't know," I replied flatly, lifting an egg salad finger sandwich to my lips and biting down.

"You can't go to your sister with this if you aren't sure of what you saw," she stated.

"So you think I should just keep it to myself?"

Ms. Weatherby snorted loudly and waved me off like what I'd just asked was completely ridiculous. "Of course not! If he's a cheatin' scumbag, your sister needs to know so she can get her revenge. Plain and simple. What I'm tellin' you to do is get yourself some proof. Confront your brother-in-law. Once you do that, *then* you can tell your sister . . . if there's somethin' to tell, that is."

Like I said, wisest woman I knew.

"How'd you get to be so smart, Ms. W?"

"Age, darlin' child. Age and a whole hell of a lot of mistakes." She pointed a gnarled, arthritic finger in my direction. "So you'd do well to listen to me."

I smiled at her, lifting my teacup and taking a sip of the overly bitter tea she'd made, schooling my features to hide my wince as I forced it down my throat. "I always listen to you. You know that."

"Mm-hmm," she hummed, unconvinced. "Then what were you doin' going on a blind date with a man you don't even know?"

"It was set up by a friend, Ms. W," I assured her. "He wasn't a *total* stranger."

She harrumphed, giving her head a shake. "Yes, well, I saw this *Dateline* special the other night where—"

And that was how I got stuck listening to Ms. W prattle on about how I could have ended up in some strange man's trunk, on the way to the Mexican border without anyone the wiser until it was too late.

Man, I loved my crazy-ass neighbor.

* * *

"This is so boring! Do we have anymore cheese puffs?"

Without looking away from the binoculars I had pressed against my eyes, I grabbed the last bag of cheese puffs from the center console and threw them at Layla, hoping it would shut her up.

After tea, I'd decided to take Ms. Weatherby's advice about getting proof. Well . . . sort of. Instead of confronting Nick outright, I'd opted to go a different route. Which was why I was currently sitting in my car outside his office building at 8:30 at night, with everything I assumed I'd need for a stakeout—a ton of junk food, bottles of Gatorade (for the electrolytes), water, binoculars, a tape recorder so I could document what I saw without having to take my eyes off the building long enough to write anything down, and a thermos of coffee to keep me awake and alert.

I may have gone a little overboard.

"I told you this was going to be a long, tedious process," I said in a scolding tone, pulling my gaze from the building just long enough to shoot her a scowl. "It's not my fault you didn't bring a book to read like I suggested."

"Well, I *could* watch Netflix on my phone, but you won't let me."

I rolled my eyes to the ceiling before turning back to her. "Because we need your phone just in case we see something that needs to be recorded. I can't have you draining the battery just so you can binge on *Schitt's Creek*." I let my eyes travel down her frame and felt my face pinch up in a scowl. "And what the hell are you wearing?"

She gave me an affronted look before lowering her head and tugging at the hem of her T-shirt. "What's wrong with what I'm wearing?"

"I told you to wear something dark. This is a stakeout, Lay." Her bright white shirt and cut-off jean shorts weren't even close to appropriate. Meanwhile, I'd nailed the whole look, dressed in all black: black jeans, a black long-sleeved shirt, and I had even tucked my long blonde hair into a black wool beanie to hide it. Sure, I was sweating buckets, what was happening beneath my disguise was so *not* okay. But if that was the cost of getting answers for my sister, then so be it.

"What if we need to pursue him on foot, huh? You'll stand out like a sore thumb."

"There will be no foot pursuit," she declared vehemently. "I know I set you up on a shitty date, and slowly being bored to death in this car next to your stinky ass is my punishment for that. But I draw the line at a felony. And dressed in all black, skulking in the shadows while stalking an unsuspecting man will *definitely* get us arrested! Also, just a side note, for the love of God, turn on the A/C already! Your Secret deodorant gave up the secret a long freaking time ago."

"I can't turn the car on," I argued. "A running car just sitting here will look suspicious."

Layla bugged her eyes out. "And you sitting here with military grade binoculars, casing a joint, and looking like you're seconds away from robbing it *isn't*?"

I was just about to explain all my reason as to why what I was doing was the smartest, wisest decision, following all that up with "Ms. Weatherby told me to," if necessary, when Nick stepped out of the building I was staking out.

"There he is!" I whisper-yelled, for some reason thinking we needed to be quiet, like he could hear us from across the street and down the block. "Quick! Take pictures," I exclaimed, reaching over to smack at Layla to make sure I had her attention.

"Pictures of what?" she demanded, her tone flustered as she smacked me back. "He's just standing there!"

"Will you just take the damn pictures like I asked?" With a roll of her eyes, she lifted her phone, and I could hear the shutter begin to click as she snapped photos. "And make sure to zoom in." I ignored the insults she started hurling under her breath and grabbed my tape recorder, promptly pressing play. "The time is approximately 8:36. Scratch that, 8:37," I corrected just as the digital numbers on my dashboard changed. "The unsub has just stepped out of the building at 1100 Lamar, and is—"

"For Christ's sake, Marin, he's not an unsub. You *know* him. He's your brother-in-law, for crying out loud."

"Will you be quiet and let me do this?" I hissed, giving her a killing look. "I know what I'm doing."

"That's debatable," she snarked. "Just because you've watched *Criminal Minds* doesn't mean you know what you're doing."

"It's not *just* because I watch *Criminal Minds*. I've also watched *Law & Order: SVU, Bones,* and *Luther*. Oh, and a documentary on Ted Bundy. Now shut the hell up already. The tape's been running this whole time, so I'm going to have to cut all this out. Thanks a lot."

"This is the stupidest thing ever," Layla grumbled as

she turned back and started clicking away. However, her mumbled curses quickly cut off a second later. "Uh-oh."

"Uh-oh? What uh-oh?" I lifted the binoculars just in time to see the woman in the red dress from the other night follow Nick out of the building.

"Is that the woman you saw him with at dinner?"

"Yes," I gritted out. "Time is 8:40, and unsub has just been joined on the sidewalk by a female companion," I said into the tape recorder. "We'll call her . . . Slutzilla."

"Nice," Layla said with a nod.

Slutzilla reached Nick's side a moment later, and through the binoculars, I watched her tip her head back and smile up at him seductively as she placed a palm on his chest. If I got the chance, which I sure as hell hoped I did, I was going to rip all that long, glossy black hair from her scalp by the handful.

"This doesn't look good—wait," Layla said. "He just stepped back. Did you see that?"

I sure did. "Slutzilla attempted to caress unsub's chest, but he stepped out of her reach and is now offering his hand for a companionable shake," I told the recorder.

Layla and I watched in rapt fascination as the woman took Nick's offered hand, but instead of leaving it at a shake, she stepped closer and lifted up on the tip-toes of her pencil-thin stiletto heels to press a kiss on his cheek . . . *dangerously* close to his mouth. The instant she did that,

Nick disengaged and took a step back. Moments later, they both turned in opposite directions and took off.

"Well this whole damn thing has been one giant waste of time," I groused, dropping the binoculars back into my lap with an unhappy frown.

"I told you it would be," Layla chided, popping a cheese puff in her mouth and crunching down. "I said this was a stupid idea, and I was right."

I kept my eyes pointed at the windshield, to the spot where my brother-in-law had just been. "I *still* don't have any clue what the hell is going on."

"And you probably won't until you pull up your big girl panties and just *go talk to him already*." She smiled sweetly when I threw her a nasty look. "Can we go home now?"

With a defeated sigh, I turned the car on and put it in gear.

"Do you think there's a drive-thru around here somewhere? I'm starving, and I've got a craving for tacos."

She might have been the worst stakeout partner ever, but her suggestion of tacos was brilliant, so I decided to forgive her.

Chapter 8
Marin

I WASN'T sure what the hell it was that brought me back to the seven circles of hell, also known as that stupid singles cooking class, but it *wasn't* because I wanted to see Pierce again. It wasn't! And I absolutely did not feel a pang of disappointment in my chest when the class got underway and he still wasn't there.

Nope. Not even a little bit. I didn't care if I ever saw him again. I was living my life, doing my thing, and I was going to conquer the shit out of the little taco cup thingies Chef Jodi was having us make.

I had all my ingredients lined up on my work station and was rereading the prep and cooking instructions for the fourth time when Chef Jodi let out a happy little chirp at the front of the classroom.

"Looks like we have a latecomer, class," she said,

pulling everyone's attention to the person who'd just entered the room.

My heart lodged in my throat when I turned and saw Pierce walk into the room. "There aren't any empty stations, but I'm sure Marin wouldn't mind sharing." She glanced over at me with a smile. "You don't mind, do you? As a matter of fact, maybe it would be good for the both of you to have a little bit of help."

I wasn't sure if that was a slight on my cooking skills—okay, that was a lie, I totally knew it was a slight—but it wasn't like I could refuse to share a workspace after she'd called me out in front of the whole class. Chef Jodi was a pain in the ass, but I'd always been somewhat of a teacher's pet, and I found myself nodding in agreement just before the woodsy scent of Pierce's cologne invaded my senses when he stepped up to the table beside me.

"Sorry I'm late," he mumbled slightly under his breath.

"No worries," the instructor waved him off. "Marin can help you catch up." And with that, she flitted away, leaving him in the hands of the worst cook in the whole class.

Yay.

I watched surreptitiously from the corner of my eye as he slid an apron over his slacks and button-down, looping the strings around his waist and tying them in place. An apron shouldn't look sexy, but the way it highlighted the trimness of his waist against the wide expanse of his chest and broad shoulders made my mouth feel dry all of a sudden, my tongue like sandpaper.

My cheeks heated, and I had no doubt they were stained with a pink blush when I looked over and saw him watching me intently. "Hi," I muttered. *Real lame, Marin.*

"Hey," he returned, one corner of his mouth lifting infinitesimally.

"I didn't think you were coming tonight." I wanted to reach into the ether and rip the words back so they'd never happened. I hadn't meant to say that out loud. Hell, I hadn't even meant to think it. My lips had parted and the words just came spilling out before I could stop them.

"Wasn't sure I was going to be able to," Pierce confessed, keeping his eyes to the worktop as he reorganized all the ingredients.

I should have left it at that. A tiny voice inside my head screamed at me to let the subject drop right then and there, but it was becoming clear that my brain and my mouth weren't on the same page this evening. "Everything okay?"

He sighed, reaching up to drag a hand through his dark hair. Even slightly disheveled, he still looked like an Adonis. The way his forearm flexed beneath the rolled cuffs of his sleeves was way more tantalizing than it should have been.

Damn it. Maybe my friends were right, maybe I did need to start dating again, or at least get laid so I'd stop looking at a man I hated like he was a Grade A steak and I hadn't eaten in a month.

"It's nothing, really. The sitter fell through. My mother agreed to watch him for me, but not before giving me a lecture about it first."

My brows dipped into a V as I studied his profile, mainly the five-o'clock shadow that was sprinkled across his extremely tense jaw. "Why would your mom need to lecture you on anything?" I asked in bewilderment as he began to chop the vegetables on our table.

The laugh he let out was caustic, riddled with contempt. "She doesn't need a reason to do it, trust me. But the one tonight was because she feels I'm not there enough for Eli."

"I'm sure that's not true," I offered. I didn't know him well, but the times I'd seen Pierce with his son back when I was dating Frank, he seemed like a very hands-on dad.

He let out a noncommittal grunt before changing the subject altogether. "Anyway, what are we making tonight?"

"Um, well, we're supposed to be attempting taco cups."

He shot me a narrow-eyed look. "What the hell are *taco cups*?"

My attempt to hold in my laughter resulted in me snorting, which in turn, made him smile in a way that I felt deep in my belly and between my thighs. *Damn it all to hell.*

"I haven't quite figured that out yet. Apparently we

shove tortillas into a little cupcake tin, fill them up, and finish everything off in the oven, but I'm kind of skeptical."

His full lips pursed together as he blew out a breath and rested his hands on his trim hips. "Well, I guess we better get started."

I gave him a small, self-deprecating grin. "I have to be honest with you, I'm kind of the worst student in the class. I'm not sure you want any help from me."

His chuckle definitely didn't send a shiver up my back and across my shoulders. Nope. Not at all.

"You can't possibly be any worse than I am. Trust me. Eli went through a phase as a toddler where he ate playground sand, but when it comes to my cooking, he straight up refuses to eat it. Hence why I'm taking this class to begin with."

"I don't know," I said on a giggle. "My last meal here was the consistency of rubber."

He turned to me, giving me those crystal-clear blue eyes. "At least yours was edible. I think mine might have poisoned anyone who attempted to eat it."

I gave him another smile before looking back to my prep station and sliding him the notes I'd taken, along with the cooking instructions. "Guess we'll see how we do this time around."

We lapsed into a silence that was surprisingly companionable as we attempted to cook something that wouldn't come out looking, smelling, and more than likely tasting like shoe leather. I was attempting to brown hamburger meat in a skillet, worrying about the amount sticking to the bottom of the pan, when he spoke a few minutes later.

"So, how are things between your sister and her husband?"

I let out a sigh of frustration, feeling my shoulders slump as I scraped at the burnt bits on the bottom of the skillet. "Pretty much the same. I tried staking him out at his office the other night to see if there was really something going on with that woman he was with, but I still left there without any answers."

I felt his penetrating gaze on the side of my face and slowly turned to look at him. He was staring at me with a flummoxed expression, the corners of his mouth trembling with suppressed laughter. "You staked him out?"

My cheeks flushed as I pulled my bottom lip between my teeth and bit down. "Yeah. When I say it out loud it sounds pretty ridiculous. I dragged my friend Layla with me, and she said I was being an idiot. But it seemed like a good idea at the time," I defended. My face drooped into a frown. "I just wish I hadn't spent so damn much on those binoculars and those stupid black clothes."

He did something just then that I'd never seen him do in all the years I'd known him. Pierce's head fell back on a bark of laughter that was so unexpected I jolted before I let the sound wash over me. He had a *really* great laugh. And damn, but he looked good while he was doing it. His throat bobbed, the cords on the side of his neck tensed and flexed, the corners of his eyes creased with laugh lines I hadn't known existed, and all those straight white teeth were on perfect display.

There hadn't been a single instance where the man hadn't looked handsome as sin, but there was just something downright sexy about him when he laughed. I didn't know what the hell was going on with me, but my lady parts stood up and took notice. This wasn't a man I was supposed to feel any kind of draw to. For any tiny bit of warmth he might give, there was a wall of ice just around the corner.

Yet, there I was, staring up at him, with what I could only assume was a goofy, lust-struck look you'd expect to see on a school girl if the captain of the football team suddenly came out of nowhere to talk to her.

"Sorry your stakeout didn't result in any answers." He chuckled once he was able to speak through the hilarity. "But I have to admit, I'd have liked to have seen that."

I gave him a sly grin. "Well, if I plan another stakeout, I'll be sure to call you."

"How's it going over here?" Chef Jodi popped up just then like a demented Jack-in-a-Box, scaring the hell out of Pierce and me. I flung my spatula wide while the knife in his hand clattered to the floor

"Jeez, Chef Jodi," I gasped, placing a hand on my

chest. "Maybe don't scare the hell out of us while we're wielding dangerous kitchen implements?"

Instead of acknowledging that she'd nearly lost an eye for her carelessness, she looked at our work station with a displeased frown. "Pierce, these knife cuts are . . ." I glanced down and had to stifle a laugh when I saw that he'd basically massacred a whole head of lettuce and a couple of tomatoes. It looked like a crime scene.

Before I had a chance to make fun of him, she pointed to my skillet. "What do you have going on here?"

"Uh . . . I'm browning hamburger meat?"

Her face went pale and she slowly started to back away. "All right, well . . . keep up the good work."

She turned on her heels and scurried off, leaving me to believe Pierce and I were, in fact, *not* doing good work.

We stopped chatting after that so we could both concentrate, each of us putting our all into the dish in the hopes of making something palatable. I'd been hopeful by the time I slid my cups into the oven, thinking I might have actually pulled it off, but when the timer dinged and I pulled the tray out, what should have been six perfectly proportioned taco cups looked like black lumps of coal that seemed to have baked themselves into the tins in a way that they were *never* coming out.

"Oh no," I whispered, feeling disheartened as I picked up the instruction sheet and scanned down the bullet points. "I don't know what I did wrong. I followed the instructions perfectly."

"I think maybe the directions were wrong."

I turned to look at Pierce's handiwork and let out a bubble of laughter. While my meal had turned into carbon bricks, his was a soupy, congealed blob of something that didn't even resemble food.

Our instructor popped up once again, looking down at our meals in total bewilderment. "You know, I think this class might be a bit too advanced for both of you," she said, taking the cupcakes in with a sorrowful frown. Something told me it wasn't sadness that she hadn't been able to teach us so much as she wasn't looking forward to shelling out the cash to replace the cookware we'd ruined. "Maybe you should look into something for beginners."

My jaw dropped and I gaped at Chef Jodi as I wrapped my brain around what she'd just said. "Are you . . . kicking us out of your class?"

That teacher's pet in me shriveled. I'd never failed in a class before, and I'd certainly never been *kicked out*.

"You can't kick us out," Pierce objected. "We paid for these classes."

"And I'll be issuing you a full refund. I'm so sorry," she said with a shake of her head. "But you two are just unteachable."

We got pitying looks from the other people in the class as we cleaned our station and prepared to leave.

"I can't believe that just happened," I lamented once the room started to clear out.

"I wish I could say I was sad about it, but . . ." Pierce looked around the room before he finished his thought to make sure no one was close enough to hear. "Chef Jodi's kind of a pain in the ass."

I snorted as I nodded in agreement.

"Come on. I'll walk you out since this is our last class together."

A flurry of butterflies took flight in my belly as he placed his hand on the small of my back and began leading me out of the building. Once we were halfway to my car, I remembered the credit card that had been burning a hole in my purse for the past several days.

"Oh, I almost forgot." Stopping on a dime, I spun around to face him and began rifling through my handbag. Once I had the card in hand, I pulled it out and looked up at him. Damn it, even standing beneath the glow of the unforgiving lights in the parking lot, he looked hot as sin. Clearing my throat and pushing that thought to the back of my mind, I thrust the credit card in his direction. "You left that in your hurry to get out of the restaurant last week. I took it thinking I might run into you so I could return it."

He looked at my hand, slowly reaching out to take the piece of plastic. A fission of electricity shot through my fingers when he grazed them, skating up my arms and spreading through my whole body like a crack spidering out in a million different directions on a windshield.

"Thank you," he said, those two words coming out thicker and raspier than normal. When his gaze lifted to mine, I thought I saw a flash of heat in those icy depths, but I told myself it had to have been a trick of lighting, that there was nothing to see. We barely even liked each other. "Look, about that night. I'm sorry I—"

I quickly waved him off. "Nothing to apologize for. Really." *It's not as if you ran out of there like my mere presence offended you or anything*, I thought to myself. But instead of saying that, I gave him an out. "You had to get back to Eli, after all."

He nodded slowly, never taking his eyes off mine. "Right."

I wasn't sure what the hell came over me just then. It was another case of my mouth getting too far ahead of my brain, but I found my lips parting and the words just came spilling out. "And speaking of, if you ever find yourself in need of a sitter again, I'd be happy to watch him for you."

His chin jerked back in shock. "Really?"

"Yeah." I shrugged my shoulder. "I always liked the little dude. I mean, I work nights, but only three times a week, so I have more down time than most people. If you're ever in a pinch, I'm your girl."

Jesus, where the hell had that come from? Yeah, I liked

Eli. I liked him a lot, but the last thing I'd expected to do tonight was offer babysitting services.

The grin he gave me wasn't a full-blown smile, but that didn't mean it didn't pack a serious punch, because it absolutely did. "I may have to take you up on that, if you really mean it."

"I do."

"I have a case that's heating up at work, and it's going to require a bit more of my time. This would actually be a huge help."

I went back into my purse, coming out with a pen and a crumpled receipt from a gas station. I quickly scrawled my number on the back of it and passed it to him. "Well, now you have my number, so feel free to call and I'm sure we could set something up."

His gaze darted down to my smiling lips, and that trick of light happened again, making the icy depths look like liquid pools. "Thanks, Marin. I really appreciate this."

"Not a problem," I offered as I started moving backward. "See you around, Pierce."

"Yeah. See you."

I spun on my heel and headed the rest of the way to my car alone, but I could have sworn I felt his gaze on me the entire way.

Chapter 9
Pierce

THE HEADACHE I'd been trying my best to ignore had gotten so fucking bad it felt like my eyeballs had a pulse. This case was going to be the death of me.

Eli's regular sitter decided to pack up her life and follow her boyfriend to the West Coast so he could pursue his dreams of being a musician. I'd heard the guy play. He was in for some serious disappointments. And I didn't feel like getting a lecture from my mother every time I asked for her help.

While my loser brother Frank could do no wrong in her eyes, she never failed to make me feel like I was a shitty dad for, in her words, "pawning my boy off whenever I felt like it." Not having anyone to help meant I was working my ass off during the day at the office, then again at home after I got Eli fed, bathed, and tucked into bed.

I was functioning on little to no sleep, and I wasn't sure how much longer I could handle it.

Meanwhile, Marin's number had been burning a hole in my pocket for the past week, yet I hadn't managed to find the courage to call her and take her up on her offer. I'd lost count of how many times I'd pulled that damn receipt out and re-read the numbers. It was so often that I'd had to program it into my phone because the ink was starting to fade, not that it mattered, seeing as I'd already memorized it.

I knew she'd be a huge help, and not calling her was getting harder and harder, but I knew that much close contact with her would make it too goddamned hard to ignore the burn I felt in my gut every time I laid eyes on her.

There hadn't been another woman since Constance, and there was a part of me that was pissed as hell the first woman I'd been drawn to since my wife's passing was my own bother's ex.

I'd poured all my time and energy and love into Eli. We were all each other had, and I refused to take time away from my boy for a woman. Especially when I had no intention of ever letting it get beyond something physical. I'd gone down the marriage and family road once already, and I had absolutely no desire to ever travel that path again. I'd given everything I had to Constance and Eli.

When Constance died, a part of me had died with her. All that was left was what I had for my son.

I couldn't afford to let my attraction to Marin Grey lead me around by my dick.

The intercom on my desk buzzed, followed a second later by my assistant's voice. "Mr. Walton, you have a call on line one."

I hit the button and spoke back, "Please take a message, Abigale."

"I tried," she returned reluctantly. "It's your brother, sir. He's very insistent."

Of course he was. That pulsing in my eyes grew worse. "All right, thanks. Go ahead and put him through." This was the last fucking thing I needed. Frank and I hardly talked, so the fact that he was reaching out now sent a chill down my spine. I couldn't imagine he'd have anything to say that I wanted to hear.

I snatched up the receiver from the cradle and brought it to my ear. "Frank, I really don't have time for whatever you're calling about," I said in place of hello. "I'm in the middle of an important case."

My brother snorted through the line. "Of course you are. Because you're so fuckin' important, aren't you?"

"All right, I'm hanging up now."

"Wait," he called out before I could slam the phone back down. "Pierce, just wait, for Christ's sake."

"What do you want, Frank? Just spit it out so this conversation can be done."

"Jesus, dude. Can't a man ever just call his brother?"

"If it were anyone else, I'd say yes. But not you. The only time you ever reach out is when you need something." As much as I hated that fact, it was the truth, plain and simple. I'd tried with Frank. Hell, our entire childhood into our early adult years, I'd tried to be a brother to him, tried to be there, tried to build some sort of relationship. But our mother had spoiled his ass rotten, looking at him as the baby of the family, and when our father passed when I was in law school, she'd gotten even worse without him there to temper her coddling, even though it had never really helped. Frank had been treated differently from the very beginning.

But even with having everything handed to him on a silver platter, he resented me. I'd always had the best grades in school, which led to an academic scholarship to the college of my choosing while Frank had been lucky to have graduated. I'd been a natural athlete, whereas Frank didn't have an athletic bone in his body, causing him to be dropped in the first round of tryouts for the varsity football team. I was popular, named prom king my senior year, but Frank didn't have many friends because he was an asshole to pretty much everyone who crossed his path.

I'd worked my ass off to get everything I'd had back then, and Frank didn't have any of it because he was a lazy fuck who refused to do more than the bare minimum. But he didn't see it like that. He was a miserable, bitter asshole.

Frank was coddled every time he failed, and that failure was *always* due to lack of trying. It eventually reached the point in our household where excellence was expected of me while our mom praised him for his mediocrity.

Once I'd graduated from law school and got a job at a prestigious firm in Richmond, Frank looked at me and saw dollar signs. It didn't matter that I was only a junior associate. He'd bounced around from one manual labor job after another, usually getting his ass fired after missing too many days or being a no-show all together. He never hesitated to put his hand out to me between jobs, like it was just expected that I'd bail his ass out.

It had driven Constance crazy. To say she wasn't a big fan of my brother would have been putting it mildly. She'd even grown to resent my mother for enabling him to become the man he was. But being the soft-hearted, kind woman she was, she never let that resentment show. Those were conversations we'd had in the privacy of our own home. She never wanted to be the cause of my already contentious relationship with my mom getting any worse. Family meant everything to her, and she never stopped holding out hope that my mother would come around and see the error of her ways.

The final pin in my relationship with my brother came

the day of my wife's funeral. He'd shown up drunk off his ass and it had taken four men to pull me off him. I was grieving while still having to keep my shit together for my infant son when all I wanted to do was fall apart. The love of my life was gone, and that son of a bitch had spent the night before her funeral, all the way past sun-up, partying his ass off until he arrived at the funeral home.

I was done after that. And surprisingly, after witnessing his behavior that day, my mom didn't say a word when I washed my hands of him.

He blew out a beleaguered sigh, like he had any business feeling that way. "You think this is easy for me? Callin' my perfect Golden Boy brother for help? Newsflash, it's not. So how about you cut me a little slack, huh?"

"For fuck's sake," I clipped, losing the tenuous hold on my temper I was always so careful to maintain while at work. "Say what you want or I'm hanging up."

"I need you to front me some cash. Not a lot, just a couple grand."

"No."

"All I'm askin' for is a loan. That's it. I'll pay you back."

"Words I've heard a thousand times, Frank. What the hell have you gotten yourself into now?"

If I listened close enough, I was sure I could have heard the sound of his teeth grinding through the line. "I fucked up, okay? I've been seein' this chick, and she just came to me, telling me she's pregnant, but she doesn't have the money to ... take care of it."

A bark of incredulous laughter exploded from my chest. "Are you fucking kidding me?" I bit out. "This is not a problem, Frank. You're both adults, not pathetic teenagers sneaking around behind your parents' backs. Grow the fuck up and handle your business like a man."

"Neither of us wants a kid right now, okay? She's only twenty, for fuck's sake. She's got college classes and shit, and I don't have the time—"

"Jesus Christ," I seethed, feeling my blood pressure reach an all new high at the same time that pulsing behind my eyes grew into a stabbing pain. "You've been fucking a *twenty-year-old*? You're thirty-five! What the hell is wrong with you?" I shouted.

"Hey, get off my back. She's legal, asshole."

"You're pathetic," I seethed. "I don't know what the hell you did to fuck it up with Marin, but this is just proof of what a loser you are. You had a woman like that, and now you're banging someone fifteen years younger than you. She's not even legal to drink!"

"Fuck you, man," he hissed. "That bitch was psychotic. I'm glad I got shot of her ass."

"Why don't I believe for a second that you were the one to pull the plug on that relationship?"

"You know what? I really don't give a shit what you

think. Marin Grey was a whack job. I'm lucky to be out of that. Now, are you gonna help me or not?"

"Not a chance in hell," I gritted. "You made your bed . . . with a barely-legal *girl*, I might add. Now you have to lie in it. For the sake of this kid, I hope you get your shit straight before it gets here, and I *really* fucking hope this chick has a better head on her shoulders than you do."

"Fuck you, Pierce," Frank seethed into the phone. "*Fuck you!*"

I didn't bother saying another word before I dropped the phone back into the cradle on my desk, ending the call with my piece-of-shit brother.

Before I had a chance to second guess myself, I snatched my cellphone off the desk and scrolled through my contacts, right to Marin's name.

Two rings later, her melodic voice filled my ear. "Hello?"

"Marin? It's Pierce."

"Oh. Hi." The surprise was evident in her voice. It had been a week since she'd given me her number, so I was sure she'd figured she wouldn't be hearing from me. "Uh . . . how are you?"

She seemed a little winded, which added a husky sentualness to her words. "You sound out of breath. Did I call at a bad time?"

"Oh, no. It's good. I just finished rehearsal, is all."

I knew the burlesque club where she worked was a

pretty big deal. It had been featured in all the local papers as well as a few big magazines as one of the hottest spots on the East Coast. From what I read, a majority of that hype was due to the girls who performed night after night, but in my efforts to avoid Marin, I'd made the conscious decision a long time ago not to set foot in that club, no matter how alluring the thought was.

"So what's up? I'm guessing that since you're so busy you aren't calling just to chat."

I could actually hear the smile in her teasing words, and suddenly, the throbbing in my head began to lessen, and I found myself grinning at the phone like an idiot. "I'm sorry it's taken me so long to reach out. Things have been a little crazy." As far as excuses went, it was pretty damn lame, but it wasn't like I could admit that I'd been letting my attraction to her fuck with my head and twist me up inside.

"That's okay. I get it."

She was so damn easy to talk to, which was just one of the many reasons why I knew my brother was full of shit in what he'd said about her. "I was wondering if your offer the watch Eli still stands. I could really use your help."

"Of course," she answered brightly. "I told you before, I'm happy to help."

"Great. I don't know if you're working tonight—"

"I'm off," she replied, sounding almost eager.

"Oh. All right. Great. Um, if it's not too last minute,

how about you come over to my place? That way you and Eli can hang with each other for a bit. I can take care of dinner and we can work out some sort of schedule."

"Sounds good. But when you say you'll handle dinner..."

She trailed off, and I knew instantly what she was getting at, which was why I burst into laughter. "I mean I'll order pizza or something."

"Good," she giggled. "How's seven sound?"

"Perfect. I'll text you my address."

"Great," she chirped. "I guess I'll see you then."

That voice in the back of my head started shouting again, but I slapped a piece of duct tape over its mouth to silence it. This was just one person doing another a favor. That was it. "Yeah. We'll see you then."

We ended the call, and I set my phone back down on my desk and threw myself back into my work, all the while telling myself that I was smiling because this was going to lift a serious weight off my shoulders, not because I'd be seeing Marin tonight.

Chapter 10
Marin

DROPPING my cell back into my gym bag, I dabbed at my sweat-slick chest with a towel, noticing the rehearsal studio in the very back of Whiskey Dolls had grown eerily quiet. When I slowly turned to face the wall of mirrors at the front of the room, I discovered that it was because every single one of the girls was staring at me, each one wearing a version of a shit-eating grin.

"Who was that?" McKenna, known to all us girls as Mac, asked in a sing-song voice. She and her husband, Bruce, had opened Whiskey Dolls a few years back. Theirs was a true fairytale story that we all swooned at hearing. While she didn't perform all that often—too busy trying to run a successful, thriving business—she still attended every rehearsal and choreographed at least half of our numbers.

"Yeah, Mar," Alma jumped in, her tone full-on teasing. "Was that a *man* who put that smile on your face?"

I rolled my eyes as the girls let out *ooh*s and catcalls. "That was absolutely nothing, you freaks. And since when do you eavesdrop on my conversations?"

Sloane sat on the floor, stretching out her limbs after our rigorous rehearsal. "Since your voice got all seductive and breathy while you talked to him."

"My voice wasn't seductive and breathy!" I insisted. "I'm just *out of breath*. That was a hard rehearsal."

Mac rolled her eyes and sucked back the rest of the water in her bottle. "Oh, please. Everyone here knows your stamina is better than that. You could leave practice and go on a three-mile run without getting winded."

A telling heat burned at my cheeks, flooding them with color that my friends didn't hesitate to call me out on.

"*Oooooh*, Layla ribbed. "Someone's blushing."

"I hate you," I grunted, snatching up my own water bottle and sucking back a few healthy gulps.

"But seriously," Charlotte asked with a wicked, sly grin, "we all know what a disaster Layla's set-up was, so who was on the phone?"

"It was no one," I insisted. "It was just Pierce."

"Who's—" Mac's words died off as her forehead pinched in confusing. "Pierce, like your ex's brother, Pierce?"

"Wait." Sloane's head shot up, the curtain of her long, glossy hair swinging around her face. "Didn't you say he's like, a raging asshole or something?"

"Obviously not as big an asshole as his piece-of-shit brother," Alma muttered unhappily. "But you have told us he's a dick."

Layla lifted her hand in the air to draw everyone's attention. "I believe her exact words were 'Satan in a bespoke suit with a square jaw and sex hair.'"

Alma pointed at her in confirmation. "Yeah, that. Hot as sin but a bastard, so why'd he call you?" She suddenly sucked in a gasp and bugged her eyes out. "*Please* tell me you're having lots and lots of hate sex with that loser scumbag's older, hotter brother. That's seriously the kind of revenge I can get behind."

"Oh my God, no!" I cried. "You guys are being ridiculous. He just called to ask if I would watch his son off and on for a bit. He's having issues with his sitter, and I offered to help. That's all it is."

"You know, I think I've read this story before," Charlotte chimed in. "The one with the nanny and the hot single dad she's working for?"

"I've read that one too." Sloane giggled. "Didn't it end up with them humping like bunnies?"

"I'm not going to be his *nanny*," I said snidely. "I'm just an occasional sitter."

"Uh huh. And his soon-to-be occasional bed warmer," Layla said with a lascivious grin.

"I hate you guys," I said in a monotone voice as I bent to retrieve my gym bag, hooking the strap over my shoulder. I turned and started toward the back exit on the sound of their laughter while trying my best to keep my own smile at bay.

Because despite what they were saying, I wasn't excited about seeing Pierce tonight.

I really wasn't!

* * *

My knock was met by what sounded like distant barking. It grew steadily louder as the dog on the other side of the door drew closer, then it ended on a loud *bang* and sharp whine when the rambunctious canine apparently plowed right into the door.

"Jesus, Titan," I heard a low masculine voice say from the other side of the thick wood. "You're gonna give yourself a freaking concussion."

I'd just managed to curl my teeth between my lips to hide my smile when Pierce pulled the front door open. "Sorry about all the noise. He sounds more ferocious than he is, believe me."

The laugh I tried to swallow came out as a snort when I looked at the Bernese Mountain dog making a valiant effort to get to me. "That's okay," I giggled. "I just hope he doesn't have brain damage. Is he all right?"

Pierce rolled his eyes good-naturedly as he held onto the dog's collar, and still, the pup panted and fought to the point I was afraid the poor thing was going to inadvertently choke himself. His tail swished back and forth so frantically his whole body vibrated with excited energy.

"He's fine. He's just a disaster."

Somehow the dog wriggled out of his collar and bolted right for me, taking a running leap that dropped me to my ass on the front stoop.

"Jesus, Titan! No! Bad dog!" Pierce scolded. He struggled to pull the mutt off me while Titan did his best to try and happily slurp my face off. "I'm so sorry, Marin. Are you okay?"

"I'm fine," I laughed. I got my arms around the big animal's neck and held him in a hug as I tried to sit up fully. "He's just not aware of his size." I looked at the lovable pup and couldn't help but smile. He was so damn cute. "Are you, boy? No, you're not."

With my attention now focused on him, Titan seemed to calm a touch as I dragged my fingers through his long, silky fur. "You're a good boy, huh? You just have a lot of energy. Yeah."

He slobbered on my face one last time before turning tail and trotting back into the house like nothing happened.

Pierce held out a hand to help me off the ground, and the second his fingers closed around mine, I felt an electric shock that shot all the way up my arm.

With a wobbly smile, I tried to push the skin-trembling

sensation to the back of my mind as I dusted off my rear end.

"I'm sorry about that. He gets kind of excitable around new people. He looked me up and down, taking stock, and I was suddenly very aware I was still in my clothes from rehearsal. It wasn't any more risqué than most women's athleisure wear, but it was tight. It had to be for dance practice, and for some reason, as his glacial gaze took me in from head to toe, the plain clothes suddenly felt extremely revealing.

He cleared his throat before lifting his gaze to my face, his expression making my stomach feel like a can of soda that had just been shaken. That fizz in my belly overflowed, and I silently berated myself for imagining something that most certainly wasn't there. "He didn't hurt you, did he?"

"No, I'm good. I promise," I told him with a genuine smile. "I'm used to big dogs. We had pets all the time when I was growing up."

His head tilted to the side, those icy blues lighting with curiosity. "But not now?"

I shrugged. "My small studio apartment wouldn't really work for a dog."

Something in his head caused his features to pinch, that familiar coldness returning, and I'd have paid a million dollars to know what he was thinking just then, but instead of giving anything away, he schooled his expression and stepped aside to allow me entrance.

Just as I crossed into the entryway, another ball of energy came rushing down from the top of the stairs, heading straight for me. "Ms. Marin!"

I let out a little laugh as Eli jerked to a stop right in front of me, looking up at me with an adorable little boy smile. "Hey there, Cool Guy Eli."

"Dad said you're gonna be my babysitter sometimes!"

"And your dad was right." Unable to help myself, I reached forward and ruffled his overly long dark hair. *Man*, Eli was such a cute kid. I didn't have a clue what his mother looked like, but it always struck me as uncanny just how much he looked like his father. Stick him in a tiny little button-down and slacks, and he'd have been a perfect mini-clone of Pierce.

He had the same dark hair, the same golden tanned complexion, and the same pale, polar blue eyes, only his were constantly suffused with so much warmth and light that it was impossible not to want to scoop him up and squeeze his adorable chubby little cheeks.

"It's gonna be so fun!" he exclaimed, punching his tiny fist into the air. "Carey was nice, but after she tucked me in, her boyfriend would come over and they'd wrestle on the couch."

"*What?*" Pierce barked, his eyes looking like they were going to pop right out of his head.

"I saw them a couple times when they thought I was sleeping," he continued, oblivious to the crackle of electricity suddenly sparking in the air. "He always won." He looked up at his father with a curious expression. "Dad, why do girls gotta wrestle with their shirts off?"

I snorted loudly, slapping my hands over my mouth to keep my laughter from bursting out as I waited to see how Pierce would handle this line of questioning.

He looked like he was about to be physically ill, which only made the situation that much funnier.

"I'll explain it to you when you're older," he grunted. "Go wash up. We're about to have dinner."

Eli skipped off, no worse for the wear . . . unlike his dad.

"Oh my God," I whispered, unable to keep from giggling. "I'm so sorry. I didn't mean to laugh, but . . ." Another snort burst free. God, I *really* hated that I couldn't laugh without snorting!

"She's just lucky she's already in L.A. or I'd have to track them both down and wring their necks," he grumbled.

"Maybe when you finally find someone full time, you should invest in a nanny cam."

Pierce looked at me just then. "I think he'd be safer if I just padded all his walls and ceiling and locked him in this room for the rest of his life. Christ." He reached up to massage the back of his neck. "I can't believe I didn't have a clue. What's that say about me?"

"Hey." I placed my hand on his forearm and gave it a reassuring squeeze. "Stop beating yourself up. Seriously. You're doing just fine."

He blew out a frustrated sigh. "Sure as hell doesn't feel like it."

"You can't protect your kids from everything. If you knew half the stuff my older sister, Tali, and I used to get into . . ." I shook my head good-naturedly. "Our parents were great, and we still ended up with broken bones and scrapes and were caught in a number of compromising positions." I arched a single teasing brow. "Tali rocks as a mom, and my niece and nephew can still be little monsters from time to time. You can't protect him from the world, and you can't be perfect. You're going to screw up from time to time, and so is he. That doesn't make you a failure. It just makes you human."

One corner of his mouth hooked up in a devilish smirk. "I think I might need to know some of those compromising positions you were caught in when you were younger."

I threw my head back on a short laugh. "Not on your life. I'm taking that stuff to the grave. But if you feed me, I may let some of my sister's secrets slip."

"Well then, I guess I better serve up the pizza, huh?"

Chapter 11
Pierce

As inappropriate and burdensome as it was, I fought with my erection all goddamn evening.

I wasn't sure what I expected when I opened my front door earlier, but the sight of that bombshell managed to lodge the air in my lungs and nearly made my tongue fall out.

It was clear Marin was still wearing the same getup she'd worn to her rehearsal earlier that day, and if that was what she walked around in regularly, I was going to be in *big* trouble.

The deep violet leggings were designed to roll at her waist and fit to her body like a second skin, showcasing those long, toned legs of hers, and when she'd turned around and I got a peek at her ass, my traitorous dick instantly sprang to life. I could see she was wearing a sports bra in the same color as her pants beneath a tight, thin, white camisole. The hem of the top didn't quite reach the waist of those leggings, revealing an inch or two of smooth, lightly tanned skin that my fingers itched to touch. I'd lost count of how many times I'd wondered if it felt as soft as it looked.

Her long golden hair was pulled up into a knot on the crown of her head with tendrils escaping from every which way. With it up like that, it exposed the long, delicate column of her neck, and the few times I hadn't managed to stop my mind from going there, I'd imagined what she'd look like with my fingers wrapped gently around that throat as I hovered above her, driving myself into her tight, wet heat. Would her eyes be glassy as I fucked her to orgasm? Would those tawny depths catch fire as she came, screaming my name until her voice went hoarse?

Fuck. She'd been in my house for less than two hours, and already I was imagining a million things I could never have.

I made it through dinner just fine, but of course I'd had my son as a buffer. It was only once he'd headed up to his room to play for a bit before his bath and bedtime—after Marin had helped me clear the table of the dirty dishes and empty pizza box from Momma Gianna's, and I'd poured her a glass of wine before we moved to the kitchen island to look over our schedules—that my mind fell straight into the gutter. And I'd been fighting tooth and nail for the past twenty minutes to pull it back out.

"I think this will work," she said, leaning closer so she could look at the calendar app I had pulled up on my phone. That sugary floral scent of hers invaded my senses and sent a shot of warmth through my chest. "Eli will still be in school while I'm at rehearsals, so that won't be an issue. I'll get out in plenty of time to pick him up. And on the nights I don't work at the club, I can stay with him a bit later if you need to put in some extra hours."

"Are you sure this isn't too much?" I asked, already feeling like I was taking advantage.

"It's only a few days a week, Pierce." Why the hell did I love hearing her say my name so damn much? "It's totally fine. Just as long as you don't start working late all the time." She'd said it in a teasing manner, but I knew what her sister was dealing with, so I caught the underlying warning in her words. She wouldn't put up with me taking advantage or neglecting my son by staying at the office until all hours of the night, and I had absolutely no intention of becoming that dad.

"You have my word; I won't abuse your kindness." She looked over at me with a smile that I felt in my gut, and the first thought that entered my head was that Frank really was the world's biggest fucking idiot.

"Oh! And also as long as you don't expect me to cook." She pulled a face that had me releasing a full-blown laugh. It sounded harsh and gravelly to my ears, like I'd been out of practice when it came to laughing. I hadn't realized until very recently that I had.

"I'd beg you not to. I kind of like my son happy and heathy, and I'd like to keep him that way."

She narrowed her eyes in a playful glare. "Oh, like you're any better."

"I'm not, which is why I'll always leave cash on the island for you guys to order something if it looks like you'll be here through dinner."

"Perfect. Then it looks like we're set."

She hopped off the stool with the kind of grace I could only assume came from her being a dancer. I wondered what she looked like when she performed. I had no doubt she left the audience in awe.

Pushing the crestfallen feeling at the thought of her leaving to the very back of my mind, I shoved it beneath the steel trap door and locked it away as I walked her to the front door. She bent, giving me another view of that lush round ass of hers as she petted Titan's big head.

When she stood back up, she looked to the stairs and called out, "Good night, Eli! I'll see you tomorrow!"

"Bye, Ms. Marin!" my son returned at a decibel much louder than necessary.

I chuckled and gave my head a shake; her smiling eyes returned to me as she bounced on the balls of her feet, always moving or dancing, never standing still. I was quickly starting to really enjoy that about her. "Well, I guess I'll see you tomorrow then."

"Yes, you will. Have a good night, Marin."

"You too, Pierce. And do me a favor, will you?"

I crossed my arms and leaned my shoulder against the doorframe as she started to back away onto my front porch. "What's that?"

"Try to cut yourself some slack, yeah? From where I'm standing, you're doing pretty damn good at this parenting gig."

I was momentarily frozen in surprise, but even if I had been able to muster up a thank you for those words, it wouldn't have mattered. Before I could get anything out, she was spinning around and skipping down my front walk, throwing a wave over her shoulder.

I waited until she was safely in her car and backing out of my driveway before turning and heading up the stairs to hustle my son into the shower. I lay propped against his headboard with my laptop resting on my lap, reading through some documents while I waited for him to finish up, and promptly closed it when I heard the water shut off.

He came back into his room dressed in his little PJs. Like he did every night, he grabbed a book off of his shelf and climbed up to join me on the bed, his knees and elbows slamming into my gut as he threw himself over me to the other side.

"God, you're getting big, kiddo," I groaned, rubbing

dramatically at my stomach. "Before I know it, you're going to be bigger than me."

He beamed up at me proudly, and I was hit in the chest with a warmth that spread out, radiating through my limbs down into my toes and fingers. It was the warmth that came with the complete and utter contentment I only ever felt with my son.

I read through the book he chose twice, lowering my voice as his eyes became heavy with sleep. When I thought he was out, I slowly closed the book and carefully extracted myself from his hold so I could ease out of the bed without disturbing him.

"Daddy?" he called in a sleepy voice as I bent to place a kiss on his forehead. "I really like Ms. Marin. She's funny."

I brushed his hair back away from his face, silently wishing that he'd stay little forever while knowing I'd never be that lucky. "Yeah, bud. She is."

"And she's real pretty."

I chuckled, thinking my son had pretty damn good taste. "Yeah, she is. Now go to sleep."

His eyelids fluttered open, a tell that he was fighting sleep to get out what he wanted to say. "Do you think, if I'm real good and mind my manners, that maybe she'd wanna be my mom?"

At that questions, it felt like someone had just reached into my chest and squeezed my lungs, ringing all the oxygen right out of them. I couldn't seem to pull in enough air. Collapsing on the edge of his bed, I turned my body to face him better, my words coming out in a croak as I asked, "What brought that question on, bud?"

"Randy Griffin has a mom who brought cupcakes for our class when we had that Valentine's party. And Gracie Pearson's mom comes in for story time. All my friends have moms and I think I kinda want one too. And if I had a mom, maybe she'd be able to take care of you too."

"Eli, you have a mom," I said quietly, taking his hand in mine. "Remember? We talked about this. She might not be here, but she's always watching out for you."

"I know my mom's up in heaven, but do you think I can have one that's down here with me and you one day?"

I didn't know what the hell I was supposed to say to that. There was no right answer. He wanted a mom, but the only way to give him a version of that was for me to do something I had no intention of ever doing again. I'd never get serious with another woman after Constance. Not ever.

"I don't know, son. Maybe one day." It was weak, and I wished I could have given him something better, but those were the only words I could make myself force out.

"Okay. Night, Daddy. I love you."

I leaned in and pressed another kiss to his forehead, pulling his smell deep into my lungs. "I love you too, buddy. All the way to the farthest darkest star in the galaxy and back."

That was something Constance used to say as she caressed her belly while she was pregnant with Eli, and again for the few short months she'd been alive after he was born.

I waited until his breathing evened out and his limbs grew heavy with sleep before standing from the bed and heading out of his room.

As I climbed into bed later that night, Marin's words played over in my head.

"Try to cut yourself some slack, yeah? From where I'm standing, you're doing pretty damn good at this parenting gig."

I might not be able to give him another mom, but I could do everything in my power to be the best father I could be.

And as surprising as it was, considering the bomb my son had dropped on me earlier, somehow, when I fell asleep later that night, I did it with a smile.

Chapter 12
Marin

"What do you know about babysitting?" my sister asked into the phone that was cradled between my ear and my shoulder as I worked to make Eli an after-school snack. I might not have been able to cook for shit, but making ants on a log didn't require skill. It was just spreading peanut butter onto a celery stick and sprinkling some raisins on top. If I couldn't pull that off, I'd failed at life.

"Hey, I'll have you know, I'm a great babysitter. Just look at your kids. I've watched them and they weren't any worse for the wear."

"Simply keeping a child alive isn't exactly a ringing endorsement, babe."

"Says who?"

"Says me," Tali threw back through the line. "Yes, my children were alive when you babysat, but when they decided to color a mural on the living room wall, you joined in instead of making them stop!"

"Only because your children showed exceptional promise! Matt's shading and Erika's creativity were things to be nurtured, not stifled."

"So what's your reasoning for drawing a dick then?"

"It was a spaceship!" I scoffed, knowing I was full of shit. I'd said it was a spaceship for the kids' benefit, but I'd totally drawn a dick in peach crayon on her wall. "Also, it was funny."

"You're the worst. You know that?"

"Well, Eli digs me," I snarked. "And that's all that matters. I've been at this gig for three days now, and not a broken bone or dick in sight."

Just then, the little toot came skipping around the corner, shouting, *"Dick! Dick! Dick,"* at the top of his lungs.

Tali cackled in my ear. "Oh, I'd love to be a fly on the wall when you explain that one to Pierce."

"He obviously must have learned that word at school," I grumbled, making a mental note to be more careful with what I said around little ears. "I have to go, I have a child to watch, and I intend to do it brilliantly, thank you very much."

I hung up on her while she was still in the middle of laughing and looked at Eli with a bright, beaming smile. "Hey, I'll make a deal with you. I'll give you a dollar if you promise not to scream that word when your dad's around. Deal?"

Okay, so maybe this wasn't my finest hour, but he was breathing, uninjured, and relatively happy. Cut me some slack.

He looked up at me as pensively as a six-year-old could manage. "Five dollars."

Oh that little terrorist.

I narrowed my eyes at him. "Two."

"Three," he countered. Clearly this wasn't the kid's first time around the block.

"Fine. Three. But for three dollars, I expect you to forget that word even exists."

"Deal."

"Good. Now hop up. I made you a snack."

He climbed up onto the stool excitedly, only for his smile to fall as soon as he saw what I'd made. "Yuck, is that vegetables?"

I made my eyes comically wide as I pulled up the stool next to him. "What do you mean, yuck? Celery is awesome, Cool Guy Eli!"

His entire face scrunched up into itself. "It is not. It tastes like butt."

I gave him a dry look and arched a brow. "How do you know what butt tastes like?" That got him, and he sniggered. "But seriously, celery's like, the best. I eat it every day." *Lie!*

He looked at me with wide eyes. "You do?"

"Oh yeah," I enthused. "You have to eat your veggies if you want to be big and strong. Look at your dad. You think he got like that without vegetables?" I shook my head solemnly. "No way."

I *really* hoped Pierce ate vegetables, or else I was blowing smoke for no damn good reason.

"Plus, this celery has peanut butter slathered *all* over it, so it's even better."

He still looked reluctant as he gazed at the ants on a log. "What are those black things?"

"Raisins. Because you have to eat your fruit to be big and strong too," I added quickly when he looked like he was about to argue. "Come on, bud. I'll eat it with you."

I grabbed one of the stalks and held it up, waiting for him to do the same. Then I counted to three and took a big chomp, and just as I'd hoped, he followed suit with an adorable little giggle.

"So? What do you think? I asked as I chewed. "Not so bad, huh?"

"Nah. Guess not."

It wasn't a ringing endorsement, but I'd gotten vegetables in the kid with only minimal work. I considered that a serious win. Tali could suck it. For good measure, I took a picture of him eating with my phone and texted it to her, just so she'd have proof of how amazing I was.

Snacks had been consumed and Eli and I were sitting

down in front of the television to watch some cartoon that he loved when my cell rang. "You keep watching, sweetie. I'll be back in just a sec."

"Okay, Mar-Mar." I grinned like a fool, loving that I'd gone from Ms. Marin to Mar-Mar in just a matter of days.

Climbing off the couch, I moved into the kitchen where I'd left my phone on the island. I kept one eye on the living room where Eli was as I picked it up, feeling a rush of butterfly wings in my belly at the sight of Pierce's name on the screen.

It was getting harder and harder to keep telling myself I hated the man. Truth was, I was pretty sure I'd developed a bit of a crush. Which was all kinds of awkward, considering he was the older brother to the spawn of Satan himself—aka my ex-boyfriend. It was a messy situation, and the very last thing I wanted or needed was a mess.

"Hey. How's it going?"

His husky, velvety voice came through the line and made me shiver. "It's going. Just preparing for trial next week."

I knew from the few conversations we'd had since I started watching Eli that he practiced corporate law, but I'd have been lying if I said I had the first clue what he was talking about when he told me about the case he was working on so hard. Something about patents on drilling equipment or something. It went right over my head. All I knew was it took a ton of his time, and he'd be happy once the trial was over and done with so his hours could go back to normal.

"Well that's good. The sooner the trial starts, the sooner it can end, right?"

His chuckle rasped through the line, the pleasant sound of it making me smile. "Yeah, something like that. I was just calling to see if you'd have a problem staying late with Eli. I was hoping to get out of here at a reasonable time, but from the looks of it, it'll be at least 9:00 if I'm lucky."

"Yeah, sure. That's no problem. I'm not on at the club, so do what you have to do."

"Thanks, Marin. I was also calling for another reason."

"Oh?"

"Yeah." The one word curiously sounded laced with humor. "I wanted to say thanks for getting Eli to eat vegetables. That particular fight's a serious pain in the ass, so you just did me a solid."

My back shot straight.

"But maybe try to refrain from teaching my kid any more words that'll result in me getting a call from his principal? Oh, and if you let him, he'll negotiate you right out of every bit of cash you have in your wallet, so be mindful of that, yeah?"

"How did you—?" My gaze began to dart all around.

"I'm surprised you'd have to ask." Yep, that was *definitely* humor in his voice. And damn it sounded good on him. "You're the one who suggested I get a nanny cam, after all."

"Yeah, but not to check up on *me*," I cried. He burst into laughter, and I'd have given my left boob to have been able to see that in person. I lowered my voice so Eli couldn't hear, and peeked into the living room to make sure he was still consumed in his cartoon. The coast was still clear. "It's not like I'll be doing any shirtless wrestling any time soon. I'm the *perfect* sitter."

"From the side of the conversation I overheard you having with your sister, I'm not so sure."

I rolled my eyes at his teasing and looked around for that stupid little camera. "Can you see me now?"

"Yep."

I lifted my middle finger in the air and spun in a circle. "Just for not trusting me, you should know I plan on snooping through all your medicine cabinets and your underwear drawer."

"Why am I not surprised?" he asked with a smile in his voice.

"Get back to work, you slacker. And if you're lucky, you won't have a d-i-c-k drawn on your living room wall when you get home."

All of a sudden, his voice got all low and rumbly as he said, "You do that, I'll have to think of a creative way to punish you."

There was something in the way he said it that made

his threat sound more like a deliciously wicked promise. My cheeks grew hot. My nipples pebbled, and I felt pressure coiling low in my belly.

I couldn't form a sentence, the only thing I managed to get out was a shaky exhale before he told me he had to go and ended the call.

As I headed back to the couch—in a pretty intense daze—I only had one thought rolling around inside my head.

Oh my.

Chapter 13
Marin

Eli was dressed in a pair of cute little PJs and snuggled under his covers by the time I stepped into his room later that night.

"I wanna read this one tonight," he declared, holding up a tiny book with thick cardboard pages.

In the days I'd been watching Eli, this was the first time Pierce had had to work late, so it was the first time I'd been responsible for putting the little cutie to bed. I hadn't been in his room before, but I wasn't surprised to find it was what I imagined most little boys' rooms looked like. The décor theme was sports. There were stickers on the wall and those glow-in-the dark stars stuck all over his ceiling.

The comforter on his bed was covered in cartoon drawings of baseball and football players, and the lamp on his nightstand was in the shape of a bat. The room was cute and totally him. But it was the picture frame beside the lamp by his bed that drew my eye and held my attention raptly.

As I moved toward Eli's bed and sat on the edge, I stared at the woman in the photograph.

Eli's mother.

To say she was beautiful would have been the world's biggest understatement. The woman was breathtakingly stunning. She was standing in the middle of a garden, dressed in a white, flowy summer dress that cascaded down to her bare feet, the material blowing in the breeze. Her dark hair hung in a shiny curtain all the way down to the small of her back.

She had a long-stemmed rose in her hand and had lifted it to her nose. She was smiling in a way that I knew the picture wasn't staged. It was a snapshot of her in motion, and her free hand was held out like she was waving off whoever was behind the camera, shyly telling them not to take her picture.

"That's my mommy," Eli said, obviously having caught me staring at the photograph.

"She's beautiful."

"Yeah. She got real sick when she was pregnant with me. She died when I was just a little baby, but Daddy said she loved me more than anything in the whole wide world."

My heart broke into a million pieces. Needing to see that smile on his face, I situated myself so I was stretched out next to him, leaning against his headboard, and bumped his shoulder with mine. "Of course she did. You're just about the most lovable little boy I've ever met."

That got me a wan smile. "Do you have a mom, Mar-Mar?"

Oh man, this kid was killing me. Every word was like a million papercuts to my heart. "Yeah, honey. I do."

"And she loves you a whole lot?"

"She does."

He looked at the book he was caressing in his little hands. "I wish my mommy wasn't in heaven. A lot of my friends at school gots moms that live in their houses with them."

"Hey," I started softly, looping my arm over his shoulders and pulling him into my side. "You can't look at it like that, sweetheart. Some families only have a daddy, like yours. Some families only have a mommy. There are even families out there that have two moms or two dads."

"Like my friend Jordan. He's got two dads."

"Exactly. All families are different, so you can't compare what you have to what your friends have. You may not have realized it yet, but you're super lucky."

He looked up at me with wide-eyed wonder. "I am?"

"Absolutely," I stressed. "Your mom might be in heaven, but that means she's always looking down on you, making sure you're safe. And you have *the* coolest dad in all of Hope Valley. Did you know that?"

His lips parted in surprise as he shook his head.

"Oh, yeah. Everyone talks about it. Pierce Walton's the coolest of the cool. Why do you think I call you Cool Guy Eli?"

"Wow," he breathed, totally in awe. "I really have the coolest dad in Hope Valley?"

"Yep. Everyone thinks so. So you don't need to be sad, because you're already one of the luckiest kids I know."

With that, the shadows that had been in his eyes cleared up, and his light came shining through once again.

After two readings of a story about a baby bear lost in the woods, trying to find his family, Eli finally lost his battle with sleep.

As I made my way back downstairs, my mind was reeling with a million different questions. I knew that Pierce's wife had passed away, but I didn't know the circumstances behind it. And it certainly didn't feel like my place to ask.

Given that Frank was the world's biggest asshole and, for reasons I'd never been able to wrap my head around, hated his older brother, he'd never talked about it.

After the dinner at his mom's house when he'd taken me to meet his family, I'd made the mistake of asking on the drive back to his place. That had led to our first of many epic fights. He'd somehow twisted my curiosity into me having a thing for Pierce, which couldn't have been further from the truth.

That was the first night he'd hit me. We'd been standing in the middle of his living room, and he'd backhanded me across the face. Looking back, I wished that had been the very moment I walked out the door for good. But he'd been so remorseful, and for a while after that, Frank had doted on me, professing his love and swearing it would never happen again. I'd incorrectly assumed that hit had been a one-time thing. And I'd also learned after that to never ask questions about his brother.

I should have ended that relationship right then and there, but I tried hard not to dwell on that thought. It wouldn't get me anywhere. There was no point in looking back with regrets when it was already over and done. I just needed to keep moving forward. Just keep swimming. That Dory really knew her shit.

Shaking off the melancholy that followed that memory, I curled up on Pierce's big, fluffy sofa and flipped the channels on the television until I got to an episode of *Schitt's Creek*.

The last thing I remembered was laughing at David and Alexis before dozing off.

* * *

PIERCE

. . .

I WASN'T sure what in the hell had possessed me to say those things to Marin earlier. I was just thankful I'd managed to swallow down the rest of my sentence before it could tumble out of my mouth, because something told me that if I'd actually said my punishment would consist of me leaving my nice red handprint on her ass, that she'd run screaming in the other direction.

It was completely inappropriate to think, let alone say, but the more time I spent in her presence, the harder it was becoming for me to keep a lid on my more erotic thoughts and feelings.

She made me laugh. She challenged me in a way I'd never been challenged before, not even by Constance. She gave as good as she got, and she never once hesitated to put me in my place if it was warranted. And most of all, Eli adored her.

I actually found myself enjoying the thought of coming home in the evenings and seeing her, because it never failed that she'd say something that would pull me out of my head and into the present, allowing me to enjoy my time with her and Eli instead of being stuck beneath a dark cloud of doubt and misgivings.

Thanks to her, I was able to enjoy . . . being, even for just a short time. I could be a version of myself that only my son was familiar with. A fun, joking version that laughed as easily as he teased.

Marin Grey made life *fun*. Plain and simple.

Bombshell

My street was dark and quiet by the time I pulled into the driveway shortly after ten o'clock; the downstairs lights glowing through the windows were a welcomed sight. I hadn't been greeted by the illuminated porch lights since Constance passed. Those lights made it feel like the house was still awake, waiting to greet me after a long, taxing day.

Pulling up beside Marin's sporty little sedan, I threw my car into park and killed the engine before climbing out and heading up the walkway to the front door. My limbs were heavy with exhaustion, and I was so damn hungry it felt like my stomach was gnawing at my backbone.

Marin had texted earlier that she'd ordered Chinese, and Moo Shu chicken and egg rolls had never sounded so good. I hoped like hell she'd saved me some.

Everything was quiet when I walked in except for the low hum of the TV coming from the living room in the back of the house.

Before heading in that direction, I took the stairs on silent feet and peeked my head into my son's room. He was dead to the world in his bed, sleeping with the covers half thrown off onto the floor and his pajama shirt creeped up to expose his little belly. I smiled at the sight of him. My boy was a tosser-and-turner in his sleep. Keeping his sheets on his bed was a constant struggle.

Moving into the room, I leaned down and placed a kiss on his brow, hovering over him until he shifted before heading back out.

That was a habit that had formed at his birth and still had a tight grasp on me six years later. I'd had an irrational fear that something would happen to him, and he'd be taken away from me as well, so when he slept, I'd lift and drop his arm or give him a little tickle, anything to get him to move or shift in his sleep. Only then did I feel comfortable that he was fine.

Pulling the door partially closed, I headed for my bedroom at the end of the hall and stripped out of the suit I'd been wearing all day, changing into a comfortable pair of sweats and a threadbare tee before padding on bare feet back down the stairs.

"Marin?" I called out as I rounded the staircase banister and started for the living room. I didn't get an answer.

The volume on the television was low, a show I'd never seen before playing across the screen, but my attention was solely focused on the woman lying on the couch, spooning my mangy dog in her sleep.

Titan lifted his head and glanced over the back of the couch, giving his tail a thumping wag at the sight of me.

"Uh-uh. Don't you look at me like that. You know you aren't allowed on the furniture." He thumped his tail again, and I shook my head. "Nope. Down, boy. You know better."

He let out a huff that sounded so disgruntled that I knew, if he had the capability of speech, he'd cuss me out.

He all but threw himself off the couch and collapsed onto his side on the floor right in front of it with a pathetic groan, and I went back to perusing every inch of Marin's face as she slept, like a creeper.

The long fan of her lashes lay on her sharp cheekbones when her eyes were closed, creating dark feathered crescent moons against the soft pink of her smooth skin. Her button nose was crinkled and those full, bee-stung lips were slightly pursed, causing the quietest, most adorable little snore to whistle through.

Even in sleep she managed to be beautiful, curled up on her side with her hands folded in prayer position beneath her cheek and her knees drawn up toward her belly.

The rational part of my brain said I should have woken her so she could head home and sleep in her own bed, but instead, I stayed quiet as I moved into the kitchen, following the smell of Chinese food, and being extra careful not to wake her.

Because as much as the thought scared the hell out of me, I liked the idea of her being here too much to make her go.

Chapter 14
Pierce

I sat at the kitchen island, dividing my attention between the television across the room and the food I was devouring like a man who hadn't eaten in days. I didn't have the first damn clue what the show was that Marin had tuned into, but whatever it was, it was funny as hell, and I'd caught myself several times having to tamp down my laughter so I wouldn't wake the sleeping angel on my couch.

Once I was comfortably full, I cleaned up the rest of the leftovers and moved toward the French doors that led out into the backyard. I hung on the deck, leaning my elbows against the railing as Titan wandered the shadows, looking for a place to do his business.

My curiosity as to why Marin and Frank had broken up had been gnawing at me for days, and I'd finally reached the breaking point.

Pulling me cell out of my pocket, I scrolled through my

contacts until I got to my mother's name. It would have been way too late to call anyone else, but my mother had always been a bit of a night owl, so I didn't hesitate to press Call and lift the phone to my ear.

"Hey, sweetie," she answered after just two rings. "It's kind of late. Everything all right?"

"Hey, Mom. Yeah, it's good. I was just calling to see how you've been. It's been a bit since we've talked." I left out the part where I intended to prod her for information.

"Oh, well aren't you sweet? Everything's good here. Same old, same old."

"So I take it you haven't talked to Frank?"

It was obvious from the carefree tone of her voice that Frank hadn't called her, asking for a handout like he had with me. Knowing my brother, he'd wait to tell our mother about his latest dilemma until he couldn't possibly hide it anymore. That was his usual MO: bury his head in the sand and pretend nothing happened until he couldn't any longer.

The sigh she let out was one I'd grown far too familiar with over the years. It said that she knew he was probably up to no good, but didn't want to hear it. It didn't take a genius to realize Frank got that particularly nasty trait from our mother.

"No, but, I can only assume you're calling me with bad news, and if that's the case, I'll just tell you right now, I don't want to hear it."

Of course she didn't.

"Not my place to tell you, anyway," I grunted. If she wanted to go to her grave thinking her baby boy was perfect, who was I to disabuse her of that notion . . . ridiculous as it was. "But I have been curious about something."

"Oh? And what's that?"

"Do you know why Frank and Marin broke up?" I was met with complete silence. "Mom?"

"I don't want to talk about that. Such a mess. Just be glad your brother's finally free of that wretched woman."

"But I thought you were hoping he'd propose to her one day. You said she was like a daughter to you."

Her tone grew hard, the mother happy to hear from her son all but gone in the wake of her defensiveness. "Yeah, well, things change. Now, I'm done talking about it."

I felt a pressure beginning to form behind my temples, a pre-cursor to a stress-related headache directly related to my family. "But you haven't said a word."

"And I'm not going to. Your brother went through enough with that breakup, and I'm not going to dredge it all up again."

Squeezing my eyes closed, I dropped my head forward and pinched the bridge of my nose in frustration. "Christ, don't you ever get tired of defending him? Of cleaning up his messes?"

"It's what mothers do," she stated with finality.

It wasn't. It so fucking wasn't. Mothers were supposed to teach their kids to make good decisions, not make excuses for them every time they fucked up. They were supposed to push them to be functioning members of society, not coddle them so they never truly cut the apron strings.

"You see how your attitude isn't helping him, right? He needs to start paying for his own goddamn mistakes."

I didn't realize my voice had risen in frustration until Titan came loping back over with his tail tucked and his ears lowered as he watched me tentatively.

"If you're done, I think I've had enough of your attitude for one night," Mom said haughtily, and I knew anything else I had to say would fall on deaf ears. Beating my head against a brick wall would be less painful.

"All right. Goodnight, Mom. Love you."

"And I you." With that, she hung up, and I lowered my phone with a defeated sigh just as the sound of someone clearing their throat from behind me made me whip around.

* * *

Marin

. . .

I woke up in a foggy state of disorientation, confused by my surroundings for a few seconds as the rusty gears in my brain clicked back into action. I remembered I was in Pierce's house, lying on his couch.

I sat up and wiped the sleep from my eyes, looking at the time on the cable box beneath the TV. It was about a quarter to eleven. I'd been asleep for about an hour.

With a yawn, I pushed myself to my feet and stretched my arms high over my head just as I heard a loud voice coming from the direction of the backyard.

With a jolt, I spun to look out the French doors and sucked in a breath. I didn't know how long he'd been home, but it was enough time for him to change into something more relaxing. I wasn't sure I'd ever seen him so casual, in sweats that formed very nicely to his firm ass, and a tee that hugged him from behind, showcasing the broad width of his back and his tapered waist.

From where I stood, I could only see him from behind, and it was a sight that made me all kinds of tingly. Then I heard his voice again, heard the bite in his unhappy tone, and realized he was on the phone and the conversation he was having wasn't a happy one.

I slowly started to back away to give him some privacy, that was until I heard the muffled sound of him saying my name.

Curiosity got the best of me and, without a thought, my feet started carrying me toward the partially closed door. The closer I got, the better I could hear what he was saying, and an unpleasant tingle shot up my back.

I didn't need to be a genius to know who he was talking to. And when he asked if the person on the other end of the call ever got tired of defending *him*, I knew good and well who he was talking about.

I stood there, frozen in place as the phone call wound down to its end, and when he disconnected, I cleared my throat to alert him to my presence.

Pierce spun around, the picture of cool and casual in his sweats. If I thought he wore a suit well—and he absolutely *did*—then he rocked the hell out of sweats.

"Shit, I didn't mean to wake you," he started, surprising me with the concerned frown that marred his brow.

"You didn't. I woke up on my own. Sorry. I didn't mean to fall asleep on Eli duty, but I promise, he was already out like a light before I dozed off."

He graced me with a smile that made my belly flip. He was doing that a lot more lately, but I still felt that zing of surprise and the tickle of pleasure every time I caught a glimpse or heard him laugh.

"It's fine. Once he's out, he's usually out cold."

I arched a brow and crossed my arms over my chest as I stepped out onto the back deck. "Except for the times he witnessed those shirtless wrestling matches, right?"

"Yeah, except for that." The humor that had filled his eyes just a second earlier faded as he let out a weary sigh and turned to face the dark backyard once again. "So how much of that did you overhear?" he asked a minute later.

I could have lied and told him I hadn't heard any of it, but something in my gut was telling me that honesty was the route I needed to take right then.

"I wasn't going to listen at all, but then I heard my name. Didn't take me long to put two and two together and figure out you were talking to your mom."

"I don't know why I even try anymore," he said, defeat heavy in those words.

I leaned down beside him, mirroring his stance, and braced my elbows on the deck railing with a shrug. "Because she's your mom, and no matter how frustrating it is, you love her, and she loves you."

He sighed again, like it was a pain in the ass for him to admit I was right. "Yeah, maybe."

I leaned into him, bumping my shoulder with his. It was the first time I'd purposely initiated any kind of physical contact. "Definitely," I rebutted.

We lapsed into silence for a bit, and I could practically feel the wind coming from the wheels spinning rapidly in his head.

I was content to leave him to his thoughts when he spoke again, and what he asked surprised me and chilled me to the core. "What happened between you and Frank?"

That was a part of my life I wasn't necessarily jazzed to revisit. It was over and done with, and I just wanted to move past it. I worried if I continued to dredge it up that it would somehow end up defining me, and I couldn't allow that to happen.

"If it's all the same, I'd rather not get into it," I said in a quiet voice, looking out into the yard, watching Titan as he skipped and ran through the shadows.

I felt him turn to me, could feel the heat of his concerned gaze drilling into the side of my face. "Marin—"

I didn't want his pity. Spinning my head around quickly to face off with him, I gave him as much of the truth as I was willing to give. "All I'll say is that your brother isn't a good man. I'm sorry if that bothers you, but, from my standpoint, it's the truth, and that's all I'm going to say."

I wasn't sure what kind of reaction I was expecting from him, but it surprised the hell out of me when he nodded and breathed, "I know he's not."

Neither of us said a word for the longest time as we stared into each other's eyes. The only sound that could be heard was the soft chirp of the crickets. The air around us felt like it was sparking to life as I sank deeper into the clear blue of his eyes. It was like swimming in the ocean. My chest compressed with my held breath, then my head breached the surface, and I sucked in air before Pierce's tide could pull me under again.

"You're not like him," I whispered.

His breath whispered across my face as he said, "I

hope to Christ that's a good thing." Until that moment, I hadn't realized we'd inched closer together. There were barely two inches of space between his arm and mine, between our mouths.

"It is." My tongue peeked out to swipe across my bottom lip, the action drawing his darkening gaze to them.

A warning signal went off in my head, bright flashing lights like you'd see at night as you drove, alerting you to the fact that the road ahead had been washed away. It was the red flag waving you back from danger. But I couldn't seem to make my body stop.

The smell of his cologne invaded my senses, like a physical tether pulling me closer and closer to him.

I was trapped under his spell, and I wasn't sure if I'd make it out alive.

"Daddy, I had a nightmare."

And just like that, the spell was broken.

With a startled gasp, I jerked away from Pierce, standing to my full height and spinning around to see Eli standing just inside the threshold, rubbing at his sleepy eyes with his fists.

Pierce jumped into action, moving to his son and picking him up. Seeing this big, strong man lift his little boy into his arms, propping him against his hip and soothing him after a nightmare, would have made any woman's ovaries explode. And I was no exception, which was why I had to get the hell out of there.

"I should go," I said, my voice suddenly as husky as a phone-sex operator who'd been working some serious overtime.

My plan was to bypass the two guys who had quickly started to become an integral part of my life without me even noticing, but that was thwarted when Eli lifted his arms and held them out wide.

Sometimes he seemed so much older than his age, and other times, like just now, I remembered he was still an adorable little boy. I held my breath, not wanting to risk getting another whiff of Pierce's enticing cologne as I leaned in and returned to the little cutie's tight embrace.

"Night, sweetheart."

"Night, Mar-Mar."

I pulled back, unable to meet Pierce's gaze as I backed away.

"Marin." He said my name in a husky voice that sent a pulse through my core. *Damn it.* "If you could just wait a few minutes—"

"It's okay. Really. Go take care of Cool Guy Eli. I'll see you guys tomorrow."

Without a backward glance, I spun around and bolted for the door, placing a hand on my chest the whole way in an effort to keep my wild heart from beating right through it.

* * *

Pierce

The hard-on I'd valiantly managed to get under control while I helped Eli back to bed, staying with him as he drifted back to sleep, came back in full force as I closed my bedroom door after shutting the house down for the night.

Marin's intoxicating fragrance was still in my nose. I could still see her plump pink lips glistening from where she'd licked them. I'd nearly lost control tonight. And the scariest part about it was, I didn't regret it.

I wanted her. *Christ*, did I want her.

It was no longer about whether or not I could ignore my attraction to her. It was now about whether or not I'd survive it.

Moving into the bathroom attached to my room, I braced my hands against the vanity and clenched my jaw, willing my breathing to return to normal.

The ache in my groin was constant, and I knew there was no way in hell I was getting to sleep tonight unless I did something about it.

With my eyes closed, I reached into my sweats and pulled my dick out, hissing at the sensitivity. I'd only just touched myself and I already felt ready to blow.

I stroked my length in a tight fist as I pictured Marin. I imagined it was her delicate, feminine hand wrapped around me, stroking me over and over. I imagined she was beneath me, her pussy clutching me as I slid into her.

A groan worked its way up my throat as I picked up the pace. I could feel my release building and building, the tingle forming in my spine. I was close, but there was a part of my brain that knew it still wouldn't be as good as it would have been if I were with her.

My jaw flexed and the muscles in my arm began to heat as I fucked my fist, wishing it was *her*. Seconds later, I came, releasing my load all over my hand and the bathroom counter, all the while, chanting Marin's name like a goddamn benediction.

Chapter 15
Marin

I WAS A COWARD, I knew that. I just couldn't help it. I'd gone from hating the man, to kind of sort of becoming his friend, to wanting nothing more than to climb him like a tree. I didn't need a shrink to tell me it wasn't necessarily the healthiest option to get involved with the brother of a man I despised with every fiber of my being.

Avoidance: that was the name of the game, and it wasn't easy at all, what with me watching his son nearly every day.

I'd had to work the club tonight, so I used that as an excuse to bail almost the moment Pierce's sleek black Audi pulled up into the driveway. I'd given Eli a hug and kiss and ran like Usain Bolt for my car, spitting frantically, "Sorry, have to go! Running late," when Pierce tried catching my attention.

Now I was sitting at my station in the dressing room at

Whiskey Dolls, done up in a barely-there sailor costume covered in sequins, with my hair and makeup done like a 50s pinup model, complete with vintage pin curls, red lips, and winged black eyeliner.

Usually I loved getting all dolled up for this particular number, but tonight I couldn't concentrate on anything but the text that had come through my phone three hours earlier.

Pierce: *You can't avoid me forever. We need to talk.*

I knew we did, but I couldn't bring myself to reply. Like I said, I was a coward.

"Hey, you good?"

I looked up to find Alma watching me curiously. I gave her a smile I knew didn't reach my eyes. "Yep. All good here."

She lifted one perfectly arched, thick black brow. "You sure? Because you've been staring at your phone for the past five minutes with this deer-in-the-headlights look on your face."

Carefully blanking my expression, I shoved my phone back into my bag under my little makeup table, determined to put the text out of my mind, at least for now.

"Nope. All good." She was dressed in the same exact costume as me, with her hair and makeup done up just like mine. "You ready to go out there?"

She narrowed her eyes skeptically, but eventually gave in and nodded. "Yep. Let's go put on a killer show."

And that was exactly what I intended to do. Out front, the lights on the stage went down, and I took my place with the other girls. As soon as the music kicked on, I wiped my mind clean of everything except what I'd be doing for the next several minutes.

Dancing had always been an escape for me, and I needed it now more than ever.

* * *

I WAS UP and out of bed the next morning much earlier than I normally would be after working at the club, but no matter how hard I'd tried the night before, I hadn't been able to find sleep. Thoughts of the kiss I'd almost shared with Pierce wouldn't stop playing on a loop in my mind. A pulsing ache had formed between my thighs, alerting me to the gnawing emptiness, and it hadn't gone away since I all but ran out of his house that night.

During the rare couple of hours I did manage to doze, my sleep was riddled with dreams of him touching me, kissing me, saying my name in that gravelly velvet voice of his.

There were two more texts on my phone by the time I climbed out of the shower, and each increased in frustration, telling me that Pierce was most certainly *not* happy with me.

Pierce: *I never took you for someone who'd tuck tail and run. Guess I was wrong.*

The first time I read that one, a lump of shame had formed in my throat, making it almost impossible to breathe, but as I read and re-read that message, that shame gave way to anger. He didn't know me. Not really. So who the hell was he to make judgements on my character?

Full of righteous indignation, I'd nearly texted that back to him. Then I read his last message, and the fire in my belly had been snuffed out like someone had just kicked sand on it.

Pierce: *If you want to avoid me, that's fine. But don't even think about disappearing on Eli. He doesn't deserve it.*

Oh hell.

That was a direct shot.

I thought back to that sweet little boy, to the conversation we'd had in his bedroom and the sadness on his face when he talked about wanting a mother. There wasn't a chance in hell I'd consider disappearing on him. I cared about that kid more than I cared about myself.

I couldn't *not* reply to that one.

Me: *I'd never do that.*

I could see that the message had been read, but he never bothered responding. Not that I blamed him.

I was out of my apartment before eight, swinging into Muffin Top, the best coffee shop in all of Hope Valley, and probably the country, loading up on sweet caffeinated drinks and pastries before I pointed my car in the direction of Tali's house.

My sister answered the door, surprised to find me standing on her front porch.

"What are you doing here at eight in the morning? Didn't you work last night?"

"Just felt like visiting with my sister," I said nonchalantly as I shoved past her and into the house, making a beeline for the kitchen. "You already drop the kids at school?"

"Yeah. I have a blissful few hours of silence before the drama starts again." She spotted the logo on the bag and coffee cups I'd just placed on the kitchen island. "Is that Muffin Top coffee?"

"You bet."

"Ugh! I love you so much. I'm going to leave everything to you in my will," she declared as she grabbed the cup I held out to her and took a big swig while I pulled the pastries out of the bag.

"Danika is trying out a new muffin flavor," I stated, waving it beneath her nose. "I lucked out and got there early enough to grab a couple before they sold out."

She sniffed, her eyes going wide. "Is that—"

"Maple bacon? Yep."

"Gimme!" She snatched it out of my hand so fast I was afraid she'd take one of my fingers off. Chomping off a big bite, she closed her eyes and groaned. "I take that back," she said through a full mouth. "I'm leaving everything to Dani in my will," she mumbled through a full mouth, speaking of Danika, the woman who owned the coffee shop and the brilliant mind behind the pastries.

I rolled my eyes at her dramatics as I bit into my own muffin. The saltiness of the bacon combined with the sweetness of the maple syrup created a party in my mouth that I never wanted to end.

"Damn," I sputtered, sending crumbs flying. "I should have ordered more."

"Yeah, well, just be sure to remember next time."

The minutes ticked by as we finished off our muffins and coffee, and the whole time I felt itchy and agitated, that sensation of ants crawling across my skin.

"Will you just spit it out already?" Tali huffed. "It's so obvious you're here because you need to talk about something, so quit stalling."

"Am I that obvious?"

She lifted her brows. "Babe."

I waited for more, but that was all I got. "Is that supposed to be an answer?"

"Everything you're feeling is written all over your face. Always has been. Why do you think you're such a shitty poker player?"

"I'm a great poker player." I harrumphed.

"Oh please! Remember that sister trip we took to Vegas? You couldn't stop giggling every time you had a good hand. You lost every dime you brought with you on the very first night. Had to spend the rest of the trip playing penny slots."

"Only because I went all in on that one hand," I argued, feeling the irrational need to defend myself.

"You went all in on a pair of twos," she declared, her tone screaming *you big dummy*.

I shrugged innocently. "I thought I'd try my hand at bluffing. Everyone else was doing it."

"And the lesson you learned there is that you suck at it. Now stop changing the subject. You didn't come here just to see my beautiful face, so either tell me what's going on, or I'm going to make you help me clean the bathrooms."

"I almost kissed Pierce the other night," I spit out. The thought of having to go anywhere near Matt's bathroom would have been enough to scare anyone into talking. I firmly believed that if the FBI or CIA needed to extract information from terrorists, all they needed to do was bring them over to Tali's house and lock them in my nephew's bathroom for five minutes.

Tali's eyes bugged out comically wide. "You did *what*?"

"Actually, *he* almost kissed *me*. I think. It all happened so fast."

"Well? What stopped you from going all the way, so to speak?"

I gave her a bewildered look. "You mean *other* than the fact I hardly even like the guy?"

She pinched her lips together and to the side, blowing out a loud raspberry. "*Pfft.* Oh, please! You've been talking about the guy for days now. It's clear to anyone around you that you like the guy just fine." She hit me with a cheeky smile and waggled her eyebrows. "Maybe you *more* than like him if you almost kissed him."

"What are you, twelve?" I deadpanned.

Tali responding by singing, "Pierce and Marin, sitting in a tree. K-I-S-S-I-N—ow! Damn it." She glared and rubbed at her arm where I'd just pinched her.

"Will you knock it off? In case you haven't noticed, I'm kind of freaking out right now."

"Oh, I noticed. Everyone in the whole town's probably noticed. So what's the problem? Let's talk this through. Tell me all the reasons this is a bad thing."

"Okay, well, he's kind of cold and distant. I mean, yeah, he's not as bad as he once was, but he's still really, I don't know . . . aloof, I guess. I don't know what he's thinking half the time, and that drives me crazy. Then there's the fact that I babysit his son. I mean, that right there just screams messy. I really care about Eli. I wouldn't want to do anything to mess that up."

"And?" she dragged out, knowing good and well there was more.

"And . . . he's Frank's brother."

At that, all the teasing went right out of her tone. "Are

you worried he'll turn out to be just like Frank?" she asked gently, her voice laced liberally with concern.

"No," I stated vehemently. "He's nothing like Frank. In fact, the two of them are like night and day. Hell, I'm not even sure Pierce *likes* him."

"Then what's the problem?"

"It's all so complicated. I mean, how would it look, starting something with him when I dated his brother for three years. People would talk."

"Fuck 'em, then," she snapped. "If they want to talk, let them talk. You can't put stock in other people's opinions, and you certainly can't make decisions based on what other people may think. It's your life, not theirs."

"Yeah? Well what about the tiny little fact that his mom pretty much hates me and blames me for the whole breakup?"

She sat up straight on her stool. "There's something seriously wrong with that woman."

"Yes, we already know that. But if I start something with Pierce, I'm putting myself right back into that whole screwed up dynamic."

She shrugged casually and sipped her coffee. "Then it's simple. Don't get involved with him."

I felt my forehead pinch, creasing into a frown at the idea of nothing happening between Pierce and me.

"See?" Tali cried, stabbing her finger in my face. "That

right there. You can't hide anything. You *want* to get involved with him."

"Okay, so what if I do?" I relented with frustration. "That still doesn't mean it's a good idea."

Her face was serious as she put her cup down and leaned forward. Taking my hands in hers, she adopted her serious big sister persona. "Babe, good idea or not, you aren't going to be able to ignore your feelings or simply turn them off. You like this guy, and that's not going to go away. The longer you try to bury it, the more miserable you'll be. You came here for my advice, right?" I nodded. "Well, then I say throw out all the reasons you *shouldn't* do this, and just have fun. You deserve it."

Flipping my hands over beneath hers, I laced our fingers together and held tight. "You're the bestest big sister ever. You know that?"

"Well, duh," she said with a snort.

The mood began to lighten, and as I turned to reach for the coffee that had been sitting neglected on the counter, I spotted her laptop and noticed the webpage she had pulled up.

"Are you looking for a job?"

She puffed out a heavy sigh and reached across me to slap the laptop closed. "It's something I've been thinking about lately. I updated my resume last week, not that there was much of anything to add to it. Despite how freaking hard it is, Stay at Home Mom doesn't really catch people's eye."

"Hey. This is a good thing," I said enthusiastically. "Maybe if you have something for yourself, something that'll get you out of the house for a while that doesn't revolve around being a wife or a mom, things will start to get better?"

The look on her face just then didn't fill me with hope. "Actually, the reason I started looking is because . . ." her words broke and her voice cracked as her eyes began to well up. "I think I'm going to leave Nick."

All the air whooshed from my lungs. "What?"

"Yeah." She laughed bitterly, batting at the few tears that had broken free. "I think he's cheating on me."

Oh God.

"I don't have proof or anything, it's just a gut feeling, but . . . yeah. This is the first time I've said it out loud. I feel like I'm going to be sick."

Oh shit. Oh God. Oh no. Shit, shit, *shit*!

"Tali, maybe it's not what you think."

"Not that it really matters if he is or not," she continued like she hadn't heard me. "We're basically just roommates at this point. *God*, Marin. I can't even tell you the last time we had sex. I just . . ." Her throat worked on a thick swallow. "I can't do this anymore."

"Sweetie. What can I do? How can I help?"

"You're doing it, right now. Just being here and

listening to me. That's all I need. Oh, and maybe wine. And definitely more of those maple bacon muffins."

"The wine I can do. And I'll get you more muffins if it means I have to tackle everyone in line ahead of me or hold Dani hostage until she makes a thousand just for you."

I pulled her into a tight hug, and she returned the embrace, laying her cheek on my shoulder and letting out a sigh that sounded like it was carrying the weight of the world.

"Thanks, Mar. I love you."

"Love you too, Tali."

It was official. I was going to kick Nick Allen's *ass*!

Chapter 16
Marin

EVERY SINGLE PART of me was itching to drive all the way to the city just so I could rip my stupid, idiotic, moron of a brother-in-law a new asshole for making my sister cry. Unfortunately, that wasn't in the cards. I'd had rehearsal earlier that day, then picked Eli up from school.

"So what's the plan for today, Cool Guy?" I asked, glancing briefly in the rearview mirror. Eli was sitting in the booster seat I'd gotten from Pierce, swinging his little legs back and forth.

"I think I wanna color."

I scrunched my face up in mock thought. "Hmm. Coloring. That could be fun."

He tapped his chin like a little man considering his busy afternoon schedule. "And then maybe I'll jump on the trampoline."

"If you do that, I could set up the hose and spray you while you jump."

"Yeah!" He punched his little fist into the air. "Let's do that!"

"But you have to eat your snack first. You know what that means."

His tongue peeked out of his mouth like he'd just gotten a whiff of dog poo. Or maybe one of Titan's farts. My God, who knew a dog could be so damn gassy? No matter how many times I yelled at him to stay out of the trash, it felt like each time I turned around, he was back in it again.

"Fruit and vegetables," he grumbled sullenly.

"Yep. Fruit and vegetables."

I was actually pretty pleased that I'd gotten him to choke down the healthier food the past few days. I should have gotten a prize or some kind of medal for that.

My laughter at his grouchy expression lodged in my throat when I turned onto their street and spotted a familiar black sedan sitting in the driveway.

"Dad's home!" Eli cheered from the back seat. It warmed my heart that he'd be so excited, but at the same time, I felt a fizz of anxiety at the thought of seeing him again. Especially after my conversation that morning with Tali.

Just have fun. You deserve it.

Just have fun. You deserve it.

Those words were repeating in my head like a demented parrot that wouldn't shut the hell up.

As soon as the car stopped and I threw it in park, Eli bolted out the door like he hadn't seen his dad in a million years. It was a testament to what a good father Pierce was that his child was so excited to see him after only a few hours. If only he could cut himself some slack.

The front door opened before I reached the porch steps and my heart nearly fell out of my butt. Pierce in a suit made my mouth water. Pierce in sweats made me tingly everywhere. But Pierced in distressed jeans and a faded old concert tee made my lady parts stand up and sing the Hallelujah chorus, because *dayum*!

"Daddy! You're home!"

"Yeah." He smiled warmly at his son, returning his embrace before ruffling his hair. "Figured I'd shake things up a bit today and work from home."

"Look what I made at school!" Eli shouted, jumping up and down with his picture held high above his head and his little backpack bouncing so hard I worried it would smack him in the back of the head.

"Wow, bud. This is awesome. Is that you?" He pointed to the little stick figure wearing a baseball hat, carrying a long sword. "Yep! And that's you." He indicated the figure that was wearing a tie. "And that's Titan."

Pierce's eyes narrowed with curiosity. "What are those little swirls behind Titan?"

I slapped my hands over my mouth to keep my snort in, but it was too late. He looked at me with a quizzical arch to his brow until Eli explained, "Those are his farts!"

Just as I'd done when he explained the picture to me when I'd first picked him up, I fell into a fit of giggles so hard I worried I might pee my pants.

Pierce's mouth quivered before he finally lost his battle and joined me in the hilarity. That laughter promptly stopped when Eli went on to explain the last remaining stick figure.

"And this one here, that's Mar-Mar."

My little figure was standing on the opposite side of the big, boxy house he'd drawn, away from him, his dad, and a farting Titan, but the fact I'd even made it onto that sheet of yellow construction paper had melted my heart into a puddle of goo. I could only hope Pierce didn't have a problem with it. However, with his stony jaw and chilly eyes staring blankly, it was impossible to tell.

Until he spoke. "This is great, son. I love it. I'm going to hang it up right on the front of the fridge."

And cue swoon.

Man, I was in trouble.

"Awesome! I'm gonna go put my swim trunks on!"

With that, he darted inside the house and charged up the stairs, sounding like a herd of elephants.

"Swim trunks?" Pierce queried.

"I told Eli I'd rig the water hose up to spray on him while he jumped on the trampoline. I can do that real quick, then I'll be out of your hair."

My heart actually sank at the thought of leaving. I loved these hours I got to spend with my little cool guy, and I was going to miss him this afternoon.

"Actually, if you don't mind, I'd like you to stay. I really have been working from home, and I still have a few hours of work left to do."

"Oh. Okay. Yeah," I said brightly, feeling a weight lift off my chest. "I can totally do that."

The warmth he'd greeted his son with was long gone as he looked at me. The ice man was back, only this time I really only had myself to blame. I'd pushed him away, bringing that chilliness right back to the surface. "Thanks."

He turned to move deeper into the house when I spoke, hopping quickly up the stairs and following after him almost frantically.

"Pierce, I'm sorry," I blurted as the front door swung closed behind me. He stopped in the middle of the entryway and slowly turned to face me, stuffing his hands into the pockets of his jeans, an action that drew my gaze like a heat seeking missile to his crotch. *Damn it, Marin. Get your shit together*, I silently scolded myself, forcing my eyes up to his, only to find he'd caught me and was smirking in a way I'd never seen before.

"You were saying?" he said in a tone that I could have sworn was almost teasing.

"What? Oh! Right, yes. I was saying I'm sorry. I'm sorry I bolted out of here yesterday when you tried to talk to me and I'm sorry I ignored your messages. It was a shitty thing to do, and . . . well." I lifted my hands at my sides before letting them flop back down. "I'm sorry."

As far as apologies went, it certainly wasn't my best, and the longer we stood there in a silent standoff, the twitchier I got.

"Well?" I finally snapped when I couldn't take it anymore.

"Well what?" He was the picture of casual and I kind of wanted to punch him in his sexy face.

"Am I forgiven?"

"Depends," he replied with a shrug. "If I tell you I want you to stick around this evening so we can talk after Eli goes to bed, are you going to freak the hell out and run away again?"

Maybe. Possibly, I thought, but to him I said, "No."
Just have fun. You deserve it.

He nodded resolutely. "All right then. You're forgiven. I'll order dinner in an hour. What are you in the mood for?"

"Burgers!" Eli shouted as he raced down the stairs, jumping them like an Olympic hurdler, nearly giving me a heart attack in the process.

Bombshell

"Burgers it is. But what have we said about running down the stairs like that," Pierce asked in a very commanding Dad voice.

"Not to, 'cause I'll crack my skull open."

"Right. Don't do it again."

I expected an argument, for Eli to offer a bullet-pointed explanation as to why flying down the stairs in a single jump was better than taking them carefully, one at a time. Over the past several days, I'd discovered the kid could argue like it was his profession. He'd find himself a hill and he was determined to die on top of it. By the time he finished talking circles around me I'd have caved and developed a twitch in my eyelid.

But he didn't give his dad any of that just then. He simply nodded and said, "Okay, Daddy." Then looked at me. "I'm ready, let's go!"

He ran off in nothing but his little swim trunks that were covered in cartoon characters, and I could hear Titan's nails clacking on the hardwood floors as he followed after his person.

"I guess I should . . ." I threw my thumb over my shoulder in the direction Eli had just taken off in.

"You guys have fun."

"Yeah, thanks." I felt awkward as hell all of a sudden. I knew it was because of what Tali had said earlier about me wanting him and my every emotion being written on my face. "You have fun . . . working."

Lame.

I whipped around and started toward the back of the house, doing my best to suppress a delighted shiver as the sound of his chuckle followed after me.

Chapter 17
Pierce

I couldn't focus with them out in the backyard, laughing and yelling and running around. It wasn't that the noise was a distraction so much as I'd have rather been out there with them than stuck in my office, reading over briefs and documents until my vision began to blur.

Whatever they were doing back there, they were having a hell of a time, and envy was sinking its claws into my gut.

I glanced out the window, taking in the beautiful sunny day. Maybe it was all in my head, but the grass looked greener than usual, the sky a brighter blue. And here I was, missing it all.

At the sound of Marin's shriek and, "Eli! You little tooter!" I couldn't take it any longer. Slapping the file shut, I dropped it onto my desk and clicked save on my computer before pushing out of the chair and starting for the back door.

When I stepped outside, I saw Eli bouncing on the trampoline with the hose in his hand, pointing the spray right at Marin as she tried to run and avoid it.

"I'm gonna get you!" he shouted.

She squealed as he hit her with water. "You're going to pay for that." She laughed.

"What's going on?" I barked, infusing my tone with annoyance. The two of them stopped in their tracks and turned to look at me with trepidation.

"I was getting Mar-Mar with the hose, Daddy."

A waterlogged Marin pushed her damp hair out of her face. "Sorry. Were we being too loud? We'll keep it down."

With my face a hard mask, I stomped toward the trampoline and reached my arm through the opening of the safety enclosure net. "Give it to me," I said to Eli.

He hesitated, his face falling as he bounced his way toward me and handed me the hose.

As soon as my fingers wrapped around it, I gave him a secretive smile. "If you want to get her good, you have to do it from out here. Watch."

With that, I took off after Marin, putting my thumb over the stream so it sprayed harder and wider. Her momentary confusion was her downfall. Before she could figure out what was happening, I hit her square in the face with the water, soaking her to the bone.

Bombshell

She sputtered and coughed when I lowered the spray, swiping at her face.

"Get her again, Dad! Get her again!" Eli shrieked from the safety of the trampoline.

Marin narrowed her eyes at me and lifted a finger. "Don't you dare."

A slow, wicked smile stretched across my face. "Or what?"

"Or . . ." She took off running and I chased after her. She went straight for the trampoline, diving through the opening of the safety net and grabbing my boy around the waist, holding him in front of her like a shield as I drenched them both.

They were both a soggy mess by the time I was finished, and we'd laughed so hard the muscles in my stomach were tense and spasming.

"Truce, truce!" Marin shouted. "No more!"

"Say 'Pierce is the best.'"

"Pierce is the best!"

"My dad's the coolest!" Christ, I loved hearing that.

"All right. Truce. I'll go shut off the water."

I dropped the hose and started for the shut-off valve, realizing my mistake almost instantly. But it was too late.

"Eli now!" I heard just before a stream of icy cold water got me right in the back.

* * *

"Today was a lot of fun," Eli said sleepily as he snuggled deeper into his pillow.

"Yeah, bud," I said softly, brushing his hair back and pressing a kiss to his forehead. "It was, wasn't it."

After the impromptu water fight in the backyard, we'd gone inside and dried off. Marin had a change of clothes in the back of her car. The only problem was, they were rehearsal clothes, meaning the shorts were hardly longer than underwear. The only saving grace was the big black hoodie she wore up top. But those mile-long curvy legs were on full display, driving me out of my mind.

Dinner had gone off without a hitch, but when we'd moved into the living room, her legs once again became the only thing I could focus on. We put on one of Eli's favorite movies, but while they stared at the screen, I'd stared at her legs from the corner of my eye. She'd been sitting against the arm of the sofa, curled up in a dainty little ball, and all I could think was: I wonder what she'd feel like if I pulled her against me. Would she feel as soft as I imagine? Would she fit against me as perfectly as I think she would?

Those thoughts were interrupted when it came time to get Eli showered and into bed for the night.

Before we headed upstairs, my son climbed into Marin's lap to give her a hug goodnight.

"Night, Cool Guy. I'll see you Monday, okay?"

I felt a sudden uncomfortable pang in my gut at the realization that I was about to go two days without seeing her. Today was Friday, meaning I'd be home for the weekend, so Eli wouldn't need a sitter.

"Okay, Mar-Mar. Love you."

I saw her eyes go wide for just one second before they squeezed closed and she held him even tighter. "I love you too, sweetheart," she said, her voice taking on a throatiness alluding to the emotion she was feeling just then.

And I wasn't immune. Not. At. Fucking. All.

There was a sensation in my chest, hearing my son tell this woman he loved her, that made it hard to breathe. A crushing weight rested there, creating a pressure I didn't know what the hell to do about.

The only people who'd ever gotten that from him were me and my mother. I wasn't sure how I was *supposed* to feel about this, but I couldn't help but love the fact that my boy had another person in his life to give that gift to.

Now he was lying beside me in his bed after I'd read through two books, sleeping like the dead, and the woman who now had a special place in my boy's heart was downstairs, waiting for me just like she'd promised she would before I'd headed upstairs.

After that night on the deck, everything had changed. I'd come to a decision. I was done trying to ignore my attraction to her or will it away. To hell with Frank, and to hell with my mother's opinion of her. Maybe if I just gave in, I could eventually work her out of my system.

I might not have it in me to give myself to another

woman as completely as I had with my wife, but for as long as it worked for us, for as long as she'd let me, I could at least give Marin what I had left. That was, if she wanted it. And *Christ,* I prayed she wanted it.

As it was, I couldn't get the woman out of my head. The other night was just the first of many times I'd jacked off with Marin's face on the backs of my eyelids, and I was tired of fighting it.

I knew she wanted me just as badly as I wanted her. I'd seen it written on every inch of her face. Hope spread through my chest as I pressed a kiss to my boy's forehead, whispering, "I love you all the way to the farthest darkest star in the galaxy and back," before I headed back down toward the living room.

She was in the same place she'd been when I'd left her twenty minutes earlier, still curled into that ball, but I got the sense that it was now more for protection than comfort like it had been earlier.

At some point, Titan had commandeered my spot and was now stretched out across the other cushions with his head near Marin's lap as she slowly dragged her fingers over his head.

"He asleep?" her voice quivered with nerves, and her tongue darted out to swipe across her bottom lip.

Oh yeah. She definitely wanted me. *Fuck yeah.*

* * *

Bombshell

Marin

"Yep. Like a light," Pierce said as he moved to the kitchen. He grabbed the bottle of wine he had opened for me during dinner, and poured us both a glass before heading to me. I took the glass he offered, then gave a little jolt when, instead of joining me on the couch, he grabbed my hand and pulled me from the sofa, leading me toward the back door.

"Wh-where are we going?"

"Figured we could sit on the deck for this conversation. It's a gorgeous night. Might as well take advantage, don't you think?"

Titan woke up and hopped off the couch, following behind us so he could roam and sniff. Pierce left the door partially open so he could hear in case Eli needed him, then he guided me to a set of loungers off to the side, partially in the shadows.

He was the picture of comfort, his feet extended, crossed at the ankles, one arm behind his head. Meanwhile, I sat with my whole body stiff as a board as I clutched the glass in both hands and stared off into the yard. Silence enveloped us, and I was slowly started to calm down, feeling my shoulders sag, when he spoke, undoing all of that.

"Tell me what you're thinking right now."

Oh man, talk about diving right into the deep end.

Unable to meet his piercing blue gaze, I kept focused on the darkness in front of me and lifted my glass to my lips, sucking back a huge, fortifying gulp. "I'm thinking . . . that I feel overwhelmed right now," I finished on a whisper.

The concern I heard in his voice as he asked, "Because of me?" was finally enough to forced my head around so I could meet his gaze.

His forehead was furrowed, the blue in his eyes glinting like icy fire. "Yes," I breathed.

He placed his wineglass on the ground beside him and threw his legs over the side of the lounger to face me full-on, his elbows braced on his knees. "I'd never make you do anything you don't want to do. You know that, right?"

I closed my eyes and shook my head, trying to force the scattered, jagged thoughts flitting around in my head into something I could understand, something I could explain. It was the world's most complicated jigsaw puzzle inside my skull.

"No, I know. It's not that. I just . . . being *around* you is overwhelming. I feel like you surround me. You invade everything, even the air, and I sometimes forget to breathe."

My eyes darted open and flew to his when I felt his fingertips caress my cheek. His gaze had darkened in the past several seconds, the intensity in his eyes stealing the air from my lungs. "I know the feeling."

"You—" I swallowed thickly. "You do? Because of me?"

He nodded, then he spoke, and his words made the ground fall out from beneath me. "I want you more than I can ever remember wanting anything before. I can't stop thinking about you, even though I know I should."

I nodded, surprisingly relieved to know he was struggling with this whole thing as much as I was. "If anything were . . . to happen . . . between us, it would be messy. I don't know if I'm ready for messy." I sighed and tried to look away, but he refused to let me, taking my chin between his fingers and holding it in place. "Honestly, I don't know what I want. After Frank, I told myself I was going to take a break from men. The only reason I went on that terrible date was because my friends wouldn't let up."

I could see the questions swirling around in his eyes, but was grateful when he didn't ask them. "You know, it doesn't have to be messy." I gave him a look that said, *come on man*, making him laugh. "No expectations, Marin. We take it a day at a time and just enjoy what we have. I want you. I know you want me too. I'm tired of thinking of a million reasons why this is a bad idea."

Before I could form a response, his hands spanned my waist, and he was pulling me off my lounger and onto his lap. My legs widened instinctively, straddling his thighs and sucking in a surprised gasp when I felt his hard length press against my center through our clothes.

"What are you doing?" I asked on an exhale as he took my wineglass and set it on the ground beside his.

"Testing a theory," he replied, then he fisted my hair and slammed his lips against mine.

Chapter 18
Marin

I NEVER KNEW a kiss could be like this. With his lips on mine, his tongue a sweeping invader, he became the sole focus of my universe. The kiss became an all-consuming entity, stealing every thought from my brain except *more* and *this* and *now*. I was lost in the ocean, surrounded by glaciers that reminded me of Pierce's eyes, and I was *absolutely* okay with that.

The sound he made was rough and animalistic, and I felt my panties instantly dampen. "Fucking knew you'd taste this sweet," he growled against my mouth before tightening his grip on my hair and tipping my head to the side so he could get a better angle.

The kiss started out like an explosion of fireworks, but just like that, it turned into a battle. His teeth sank into my bottom lip and my nails raked down his back, fisting at the material of his shirt. He soothed the sting with his tongue and groaned when I pulled at the cotton at his back so I could press my palms against his smooth, hot, bare skin.

His hands came down, his fingers digging into my ass cheeks. He used his hold to rock me against the hard length straining to escape his jeans. I pulled in a stuttered breath at the shock that friction sent through my whole body. "Pierce," I said on a sigh, sinking deeper into him.

"Been waiting to hear you say my name like that."

I hadn't realized just how much control he'd been holding on to until that very moment, because at the sound of me sighing his name, that one word dripping with lust like a wet sponge, he snapped.

Suddenly, I was no longer straddling him, but on my back on the lounger beneath him, my legs wrapped around his thighs as he shifted his hips to rub against my sex while plundering my mouth.

He whispered a word of encouragement when I arched my back to press harder against him. He broke the kiss to drag his lips and teeth along the column of my neck to my ear where he spoke of how long he'd wanted this, how crazy I made him.

The feeling is mutual, buddy, I thought to myself.

His hand skated along my outer thigh, pulling my left leg up higher. "These fucking shorts," he groaned when he reached the leg of my boy shorts. "I think they might be the death of me."

"But what a way to go, right?" I teased before fisting his

Bombshell

hair and bringing his mouth back to mine. "Don't stop kissing me," I panted as his erection rubbed at the seam between my thighs. "Never stop. Do it forever."

"Gladly." His hand traveled farther up, dipping beneath my hoodie. "So soft. Are you this soft everywhere?"

I took his hand beneath my top to be a tit-for-tat scenario and slipped mine beneath his shirt, rubbing my palms along muscles I hadn't known existed beneath all those starched button-downs of his. "Are you this hard everywhere?"

He lifted his head and gave me a smirk that was so hot I thought it might actually kill me before rotating his hips. I felt a coil tighten low in my belly. "You tell me." Oh God, I was about to come. Just from him dry humping me. If I didn't feel so damn good right then, I might have been a little embarrassed that I was pawing and tearing at him like a teenager.

"Mmm." My head fell back as he kissed down my throat, pulling at the neck of my hoodie so he could get it out of his way. "Why don't you find out if I'm this soft everywhere?" I offered, wanting nothing more than for him to strip me naked and take me right then and there. To hell with his neighbors if we happen to get too loud.

"Oh, I intend to," he said against my collarbone. "Just not right now."

Wait . . . the sound of tires screeching to a stop on

cement bounced around inside my skull as I leaned deeper into the lounger cushions so I could see his face. "What?" Before I could stop it, my bottom lip poked out. "Why the hell not?" I pouted.

The stupid jerk smirked at my neediness, and the desire to punch him in the face returned. "Because I plan on taking my time with you. I'll need hours or days, maybe months, and I'm still not sure that'll be enough time to do everything I want to do to you. But the first time I feel you wrapped around me isn't going to be a quiet quickie on my back deck while I have one ear listening out for my son."

"But I'm okay with quiet quickies," I insisted. Honestly, I actually wasn't, but I felt so greedy for this man, I'd take what I could get. "I'm actually really good at them. Let me show you."

He pulled out of the reach of my lips. "You have no goddamn clue how tempting that is. But I want to be able to savor you."

Savoring is good, a voice inside my head screamed. *Savoring means multiple orgasms and more of a chance to find our G-spot. Stop arguing, you stupid cow!*

My head fell back against the cushion on a sigh. Now that the adrenaline had worn off, I felt like I'd just lived through the hardest dance rehearsal of my life, then tacked on a climb up Everest for good measure. The phrase "wrung dry" suddenly seemed extremely appropriate for how I felt.

"Eli's having a sleepover at my mom's house this weekend. Can I see you tomorrow?"

I pulled my bottom lip between my teeth and bit down, feeling a sting from how thoroughly Pierce had just abused them in the very *best* way. "I'm working at the club tomorrow night. And aren't you supposed to be preparing for trial next week?"

"Tomorrow after your shift then. I'll work during the day. You can come back here after you get off." He leaned closer, the smell of the outdoors and clean laundry invading my senses as he spoke against my lips. "Stay the night with me, Marin. My mom is taking Eli to the botanical gardens Sunday, so he won't be home until afternoon. I want you in my bed. I want to have you all to myself for as long as I possibly can."

I wasn't sure I'd ever had a more tempting offer. "All right," I relented, not feeling the need to put up much of a fight. "I'll come over after my shift. I go on early, so I'll only have to work until about ten."

"Perfect. Be sure to pack a bag."

As ridiculous as it was, I felt a sudden wave of sadness as Pierce pushed off the lounger and took my hand to help me to my feet.

My knees felt shaky as he guided me inside, letting out a sharp whistle for Titan to follow after us. He walked me to my car where he planted another earth-shaking kiss on me before holding the door open as I climbed into the driver's seat.

"Tomorrow night," he repeated, like he had to make sure I hadn't forgotten during the walk from the backyard to the front.

"Tomorrow night," I confirmed.

With my reassurance, he closed the door for me like a gentleman and waited in the driveway with his hands in his pockets as I started my car and backed out.

I felt a wave of something I hadn't felt in longer than I could remember as I drove home, and that feeling didn't let up for the rest of the night.

Giddiness. I was straight-up twitterpated at the thought of spending the night with Pierce Walton tomorrow.

As I climbed into bed and fell asleep, I did it feeling like I was floating on a cloud.

* * *

"What's got you all smiley this morning? You get yourself some last night?"

At Ms. Weatherby's question, I choked on the sip of bitter tea I'd just taken. Charlotte had joined us for this week's little get together, and promptly began to beat on my back as tears blurred my vision.

Leave it to my brash old neighbor to say something that

could possibly end up killing me before I had a chance to see everything Pierce was working with. I had a sneaking suspicion he was working with quite a bit, and I'd be pissed as hell if I didn't get to see it before I croaked.

"Jeez, Ms. W." I admonished once I could inhale again. "*No*, I didn't get me some last night."

Did *almost* orgasming from a little dry-hump sesh fall into the category as "some"?

"Well something's put a little spring in your step today. So what is it?"

"It's nothing, really," I lied. I could feel Charlotte's attention of my face, and refused to look in her direction, worried she'd see the truth on my face. Ever since Tali said that, I couldn't help but wonder how much I'd given away over the years. As ridiculous as it seemed, I wanted to keep this thing—whatever it was—with Pierce to myself.

We'd agreed there'd be no expectations and we'd take it a day at a time. I was fine with that, but I worried if people found out, they'd start asking questions, and I wanted to remain in this private little bubble, just the two of us, and keep the rest of the world out for as long as humanly possible.

"I just got a really good night's sleep last night. A solid eight hours would put anyone in a good mood."

Truth was, I'd barely gotten five. That giddiness had stayed with me, making me feel like a kid on Christmas Eve, waiting impatiently for Santa to squeeze his fat ass down my chimney. I was too excited to sleep and found myself tossing and turning until exhaustion finally won out in the wee hours of the morning.

"*Pfft*," Ms. Weatherby lifted her bushy brows and turned her beady eyes to Charlotte. "Well, this one here"—she threw her thumb in my direction— "isn't gonna provide me with any entertainment today, so what do you got? How's that fine man of yours? Man like that, bet he's got the stamina of an angry bull."

It was Charlotte's turn to choke while I busted out laughing.

"Dalton's great, Ms. W," she said. "I'll be sure to let him know you asked about him."

"You do that, and you tell him I'll be expecting a visit soon. He's stayed away too long."

"Yes ma'am." Charlotte said with a Cheshire grin. She got a kick out of throwing her soon-to-be husband into the wily clutches of Ms. Weatherby. She might look like an innocent little old lady, but we knew the truth. She was hilarious most of the time. Wise all the time. But there was occasion when she could be scary as hell, and something told me the big, strong, private security guy who looked like he could bench press a car was terrified of this crouched, five-foot-nothing woman.

I *loved* it.

I wanted to be just like Ms. Weatherby when I grew up.

She shifted her coke-bottle glasses back to me. "So any updates on the situation with your sister's possibly-good-for-nothin' husband? You get that proof like I told you to?"

I spent the next fifteen minutes getting Charlotte caught up on the story of Tali and Nick's marriage before updating them both on the latest.

Ms. Weatherby shook her head and *tsked*. "These damn fool men. I swear, they'll let somethin' good slip right through their fingers, 'cause they're too busy to notice they're losing their grip."

"Well, I have a plan," I announced. "I'm going to confront him Monday. I'm going to storm into his office, and if necessary, help him extract his head from his ass."

Ms. Weatherby lifted her teacup in salute. "And if I had even one good hip, I'd be right there with you."

I had no doubt about it, and something told me Ms. Weatherby was the type of woman who, if she didn't like what you were saying, would shove your head right back up your keaster until you learned your lesson.

I could only hope that when I got to be her age, I could be even half as cool as she was.

Chapter 19
Pierce

I KNEW Whiskey Dolls was a big deal, but I guess I'd never stopped to consider what that meant until now. I'd stood in the growing line outside for half an hour before I finally reached the front and was able to pay my cover charge to get in.

The place definitely wasn't what I'd expected. The deep reds and rich woods, the soft lighting and the uniforms the bartenders and waitresses were wearing felt like stepping back in time to the prohibition era. There was only one way to describe the atmosphere, and that was just plain cool.

I'd avoided the club like the plague, knowing that seeing Marin up on that stage would be too much of a temptation, but I no longer had to worry about that. After tonight, she'd be mine. I didn't have to avoid it any longer.

In fact, the need to see her before she showed up at my house later was like a siren song: too strong to ignore.

Dressed in a pair of black slacks and a white button-down, I weaved my way through the club, surprised at the sheer size of the place, especially the stage that extended across the entire back, with a long platform that came out, leading to another smaller stage area that fell in the middle of a whole section of tables.

Of course, all the seating in that area was taken, so I did my best to find any empty seat available. I finally lucked out, coming across an empty high-top four-seater.

The woman on the stage was dancing to an energetic, sultry number and holding two huge feathered fans in front of her. She was terrific, no doubt about it, and the audience was riveted, but there was only one woman I'd come to see.

A woman dressed in an old-school cigarette girl uniform came up to me. "Can I get you something to drink, darlin'? Kitchen closes in thirty if you're wanting something to eat."

"Just a scotch, thanks. Make it a double." She scribbled it down and began to turn when I called her back. "Can you tell me when Marin Grey is performing?"

For some reason that question made her expression go guarded. "So you're a fan, huh? You're not gonna cause any problems tonight, are you? Because I won't hesitate to call security over."

Bombshell

"No, nothing like that," I assured her, but I could tell she wasn't buying it. "Does that happen a lot here?"

"These girls are the best at what they do. If I had a dime for every man who went falling into lust with one of the Whiskey Dolls, I'd be able to retire tomorrow *and* still afford to put my kid through college, and he's only two. Our security guys are built like brick shithouses and paid *very* well to take care of problems." She arched a brow pointedly.

I did my best to ignore the niggling unpleasantness in my gut at that information. I lifted my hands in surrender. "We're just friends. She babysits my son, and I wanted to see her perform tonight. That's all. You won't get any problems out of me. Promise."

That put her at ease. "So you're the dad of that cutie-pie she's been showing all of us pictures of?"

My chest swelled with pride and warmth to know she'd been doing that, especially considering how smitten my son was with her. "Yeah. Eli's my son."

The waitress smiled then, all hostility gone. "She goes on right after this number. Then again at nine thirty."

"Great. Thanks."

"No problem. I'll be right back with your drink."

She took off and I was left wondering if Marin had ever had any trouble with an overzealous admirer. There wasn't really anything I could do to stop it, so I hoped the security was as good as the waitress had indicated.

I did a slow scan of the club, noticing for the first time that there were men dressed all in black, standing a few yards apart up against the walls. Sure enough, each one was built like a fucking Mack truck, and they were all scanning the area in front of them with eagle-eyed clarity.

Just like that, I relaxed.

The performance on stage came to an end, and the whole building erupted into applause as the woman left the stage dressed in a barely-there bra and panties that looked like it was covered entirely in gemstones.

Seconds later the lights went out. The atmosphere in the place went wired as everyone, including me, waited with bated breath to see what was going to happen next. The song started, a heavy bass beating through the floors, then, just like that, the stage lit up. There were four screens on the stage, two on each side, with a woman behind each. All you could see were their silhouettes as they moved to the song. Then, as soon as the song hit the first chorus, they came stomping out like they were walking down a catwalk, and my jaw nearly hit the floor when I finally got my first look at Marin in all her glory.

She wore a pair of ankle boots with a heel so thin and high, they looked impossible to walk in, let alone dance. But *fuck me*, could she move.

Her long legs were encased in fishnets that disappeared under black underwear that sat high on her waist and cut high up on her ass cheeks, giving just the barest peek at those firm, round globes. Her breasts were pushed high in a black bra that was covered in silver fringe all the way around that hung to her hips, and every time she moved it swayed, giving the audience a glimpse of the toned stomach and tiny waist behind it.

I was transfixed as she danced. She'd bend forward then snap back up, sending all that long, silky hair flying. She was a goddamn vision, and I couldn't rip my eyes away from her.

"She's good, huh?"

I jolted at the sudden reappearance of the waitress. I'd been so busy watching Marin I hadn't even noticed her approach. Hell, for all I knew, the club could have caught fire and completely emptied, and I wouldn't have realized.

"She's more than good."

She gave a little giggle and shook her head. "Drink up, honey. You look like you're about to start drooling."

I didn't even look at the glass as I picked it up and brought it to my lips, savoring that initial burn as the first sip went down.

All too soon, Marin's number ended, and I was left to wait for her next one. Because there was no way in hell I was leaving without seeing her dance again.

* * *

Marin

I WAS RIDING an adrenaline high that had nothing to do with performing and everything to do with the fact I was about to see Pierce as I headed out of the club after my shift ended.

I practically threw myself into my car and started it, eager to get rolling. I fished my phone out of my purse and shot off a quick text.

Me: *Leaving the club now. You still up?*

His reply was almost instant.

Pierce: *Wide awake. Feel free to break some driving laws if it'll get you here sooner.*

I did an excited little shimmy in my seat and started out of the parking lot. The drive from Whiskey Dolls to Pierce's house felt like it took a lifetime yet also seemed to pass by in a flash. A spike of frustration would shoot through me with every red light I hit, and by the time I finally pulled into his driveway and killed the engine, I felt like I was coming out of my skin.

My hands shook as I reached into my backseat to get my overnight bag. It had taken me forever to find the damn thing earlier that day. When I moved into my own apartment months ago, it had gotten lost in the shuffle, and I'd had to dig through the deepest, darkest recesses of my closet to find it.

I climbed out of the car on shaky legs. I'd been here

nearly every day for the past several days, yet, for some reason, Pierce's big, gorgeous house looked different to me now. Moving up the front walk, it even *felt* different.

I'd just lifted my hand to knock when the door swung open. Pierce's large frame nearly took up the entire doorway, and I felt a rush of arousal as I scanned him from head to toe, taking in the slacks and pressed shirt.

He was sans tie, and his sleeves were rolled up in what I liked to call his Pierce After Work Look. It was a damn good look.

"Did you go in to the office tod—" My question cut off on a shocked yelp as his arm shot out. His hand swept around and grasped me by the nape of my neck, and he used his hold to jerk me into the house. The door slammed behind me, and a moment later, my back slammed into it, and I found myself pinned between the unforgiving wood and Pierce's rock-hard body from one blink to the next.

My chest was rising and falling on sharp, startled breaths as I looked up at his face. It was as hard as pure granite. His jaw was ticking, and his eyes looked positively wild. I wasn't sure if I should be scared or incredibly turned on, but for some reason, my body decided to be a little bit of both.

"What's wrong?" I panted, feeling panic and excitement coursing through my veins. "Did something happen?"

"I didn't go to the office," he growled, leaning so close he was all I could see. All I could smell.

"Oh. Okay."

"I went to the club to see you."

That threw me for a second, and I had to give my brain a beat to catch up. "You did?"

"I did. Caught both performances."

I still couldn't read his mood. All I knew was it was dark and overwhelming. But then again, so was everything about him. "Are you . . . are you mad?"

He stayed motionless for ten seconds. I counted each and every one of them, and it felt like it took an eternity. Then he slowly shook his head. "You were a goddamn vision up on that stage," he said softly, closing the distance so his lips brushed against mine as he spoke. "Never seen anything like it before in my life. I couldn't take my eyes off you. I'm not sure I breathed the entire time you were dancing."

Oh. *Oh*. Okay, so he wasn't mad.

Nope, he was *incredibly* turned on. And all of a sudden my panties were uncomfortably damp.

I felt my lips curve up in a triumphant grin. "So I take it you liked the show?"

"Oh yeah, baby. I liked the show. Haven't been able to get my dick to go down since you stepped out from behind that screen."

To make sure I believed him, he pressed harder against

me, letting me feel the evidence of his arousal against my belly.

"And tonight I'm going to fuck you, knowing all that beauty, all that talent, the persona up on that stage that every man in the room wants, is all *mine*," he finished on a growl.

I only had one thought in my head in that moment.

Yes, please!

Chapter 20
Marin

HE PICKED me up like I weighed less than a cloud, leaving me no choice but to wrap my legs around his waist and hold on to his shoulders as his mouth fed from mine and he began carrying me up the stairs.

I'd never been manhandled like that, so . . . perfectly. It was brilliant. I felt like a tiny little doll in his arms, something he could pick up and move around and take complete control over. And I was *down with that*.

When it came to Pierce Walton, I gave as good as I got. I didn't cower under his iciness. I threw that shit right back at him. But when we were like this . . . well, like this, I *wanted* to cede control. I wanted to feel his strength surrounding me completely.

We hit the middle of the staircase when Titan decided he wanted to get in on the action and caused Pierce to trip, nearly dropping me on my ass.

I let out a laugh, looking up at him with a goofy grin. "Maybe I should walk the rest of the way to prevent any potential bodily harm."

The look on his face just then, sheer determination mixed with frustration that his dog had ruined the moment, was so freaking adorable I laughed again. I couldn't help it. He looked so cute when he was petulant.

"Titan, go lie down," he commanded his pet, and the poor dog looked positively crestfallen as he lowered his head and sulked down the stairs toward his big bed in the living room.

"Aw, poor—" My words were cut off when Pierce took my hand and hauled me up, all but dragging me the rest of the way up the stairs and down the hall to his room.

I'd never been in there before, but upon first glance it was very obviously *him*. Dark rich wood furniture, cream sheets beneath a dark blue bedspread. The walls were painted a lovely neutral gray. And that was all I was able to take in before he was all over me.

"You have no idea how badly I want you," he growled against my lips as he reached for the hem of my T-shirt, breaking the kiss only long enough to whip it over my head and leave me in nothing but my bra and yoga pants. Thank *God* I remembered to wear my pretty underwear.

"Watching you tonight . . . Christ, Marin. You were the only thing I could see, the only person who existed in that entire club."

A whimper of need worked its way up my throat. I was quickly losing my mind as his mouth traveled down my neck. He reached my collarbone and bit, the sharp sting causing a delicious clench between my thighs. "Pierce."

His head came up, those icy blue eyes now black thanks to his blown pupils. "Let me make you feel good, baby."

"Okay."

I felt his lips smile against the top swell of my breast, then he wrenched the cup down and sucked the stiff peak of my nipple into his mouth, drawing deep. It felt like there was a line inside of me, leading from my nipple right to my clit, and the electric shock between my legs made me gasp. Reaching up, I slid my fingers into his hair, fisting it tight so I could hold him against me as I arched my back to get closer.

"Most perfect tits I've ever seen," he grunted as he moved to pay equal attention to the other one. By the time he released it with a loud pop, they both felt swollen and incredibly sensitive, and I'd have melted into a puddle of lust on his bedroom floor had he not been holding me up with an arm banded around my waist.

His hands shifted, sliding around so they could rest at the small dip in my waist. He stared down at them in fascination, and I couldn't help but look. His wide, tanned hands looked so good spanned across my lighter skin. "You fit me perfectly," I said, giving voice to my thoughts.

His expression was positively wicked as he promised, "I'll fit you just as perfectly everywhere."

"Show me."

A primal growl worked its way up his throat, and a second later, my bra joined my shirt on his bedroom floor, and I couldn't help but think that was exactly where it belonged.

I could feel each puff of his breath against my skin. It made my entire body feel like a live wire. Then, before I knew what was happening, his hand pressed into the center of my chest, and I was falling. The soft fluff of his mattress stopped my descent, and Pierce's big hands came up, wrenching my leggings and panties down my thighs so fast I thought I might get a friction burn, but damn if I cared.

"Why are you still dressed?" I panted, propping myself up on my elbows to give his offensive clothes a nasty glare.

"Apologies," he chuckled. "Let me do something about that."

The bastard proceeded to tease me, slipping one button of his shirt open at a time, moving so slowly it was as though he was wading through molasses.

With a frustrated growl, I sat upright and grabbed his shirt on either side, tearing it open so fast that buttons went skittering all over the place.

My mouth went dry at the sight of his chest. It was the

first time I'd ever seen it, and there was only one word I could think to describe it. *Perfection.*

His muscles were stacked, one on top of the other, starting at his pecs, which were the biggest, and tapering down over his abdomen. A thin smattering of hair covered his chest before narrowing into a line that traveled down the center, past his belly button like an arrow on a treasure map before dipping into the waistband of his slacks where that treasure was hidden.

"I take it you like," he said smugly in response to the needy sound that rumbled from my chest. Oh, that arrogant man. He *knew* he looked good, and he had every intention of teasing me until I lost my mind, damn him.

Two could play that game. "I want to feel you all over me." I raked my nails across his chest, through the small bit of hair. "I want to feel this scratching my nipples while you're inside me."

I almost crowed in victory as he made a noise and ripped at his belt, quickly unbuckling it and stripping out of his pants at record speed. Then all the triumph I felt just a moment earlier disappeared when I finally, *finally* saw his cock.

I sucked in a huge lungful of air at the sight of it. I never thought the word *pretty* could be used to describe a man's dick, but I'd been so very wrong. Because that's exactly what Pierce's was. Pretty. Perfectly shaped, long, with a blunt mushroomed head . . . and *huge*! Oh my God. There was no way that was fitting inside of me!

As if reading my thoughts—or my face—he put his knee to the bed and pushed up, crawling over me until I was forced to lie back, my head on the soft downy pillows as he hovered over me.

His length hung heavy between us, that crown bumping against me and leaving little beads of precum on my belly with every ragged breath I pulled in.

"I'll fit. Don't worry," he promised, but I wasn't convinced.

"Pierce—"

He silenced my concern with another bone-melting kiss, and I felt all the tension leave my body as I relaxed into the mattress. "I'll fit, baby. I promise."

I spread my legs wide so his hips would fit between them, and he lowered into place. "I'm clean," he said as the underside of his erection dragged through my slit before notching into place. "Are you on the pill?"

I knew what he was asking, what he was wanting, and I felt the heaviness of the silent request hanging in the air. It felt big, *huge*, so much more than the no expectations arrangement we'd agreed to.

Once again, he read me like a book. Lowering his mouth to mine in a featherlight kiss, he spoke. "Let me have you like this, Marin. Nothing between us. I want to feel you completely."

I nodded jerkily, my words clipped and stuttered as I replied, "I-I'm on the pill."

With a masculine groan, he fed the first few inches of his cock inside me, causing me to inhale sharply and slam my eyes closed against the invasion. He paused just long enough to allow my body to stretch so it could accommodate him better.

"Marin, baby," he said in a voice I'd never heard from him before; it was so gentle, so tender, that my eyes began to sting. He waited until I lifted my lids and looked up at him before speaking again. "You okay?"

I nodded, rounding him with my legs in an effort to get him deeper. Now that I'd opened up, I wanted to feel all of him inside of me.

"Tell me you're mine," he said in a soft command.

"Pierce," I pleaded, my hips beginning to writhe beneath him. "Please move. I need more."

"Then say it, and I'll give it to you."

He wanted me to be his, but what did that even mean? His for now? His for as long as we were sleeping together? Or . . . I decided to put those questions out of my head.

"I'm yours," I told him, willing to say anything at that point if it meant he'd move and put me out of my misery.

On my answer, he pumped his hips, fucking himself inside of me until he was as deep as he could possibly go.

I cried out at the exquisite feeling of being filled fuller than I ever had in my life. It. Was. *Sublime*!

"Oh God, Pierce. You feel so good."

"Told you we'd fit," he gritted, drawing nearly all the way out before pounding back in. "Ah, fuck! You feel so good around me."

I could feel my walls squeezing him, could feel how impossibly hard he was as he drove in and out. He grabbed behind my right knee, lifting my leg higher, and the new position made him bottom out with every thrust. "Pierce!" I shouted as the head of his cock rubbed against my G-spot over and over again.

I was going to die. Death by orgasm. This man was quite literally going to fuck me to death, and I couldn't possibly think of a better way to go. I'd had a good life. I was ready.

"Breathe," he coaxed when he saw I was holding my breath. I exhaled a large gust of air and refilled my lungs as the pressure deep inside me began to grow.

I grabbed onto his back, digging my nails in deep like I was holding on for dear life. I worried for all of one second that I could possibly be hurting him, but then he pressed my knee up so high my thigh was flush with my chest, and he began to pound into me like a man possessed. He liked that little bite of pain. He got off on that, and that got *me* off.

"I feel you, Marin. You're so close." Grabbing one of my hands, he wove his fingers through mine and pressed it into the pillows above my head, holding me captive. He'd given me exactly what I'd asked for. I could feel him *everywhere*. His chest hair abraded my sensitive nipples. His erection rubbed against a place deep inside me no man had ever reached before. He was all I could see, all I could smell. The only sounds in the room were our labored breathes and needy moans.

Once again, he'd overtaken everything, and I loved it.

"Stop holding back," he gritted.

"I'm not," I whimpered, biting my lower lip. I was lying, but I didn't want this to end. I wanted to stay like this forever and ever, amen.

"I can feel you, baby. Stop fighting it and let go."

I felt the sudden humiliating urge to cry. I didn't understand why. All I could figure was I was just feeling too much of everything.

"I don't want you to stop," I admitted. "I never want you to stop, Pierce."

"This is just the beginning," he assured me. "We'll do this again." Thrust. "And again." Snap. "And again." Rotate. "I knew all it would take was one time for me to be addicted to your pussy."

I lost the tenuous grip I had on my control. Something inside me snapped, and I went off. Every muscle in my body locked tight, my sex clamped down around Pierce like a vise, and I peppered his name among unintelligible ramblings until my throat began to burn.

I came until I saw stars dance behind my eyelids, and

when I felt the hot spurts of his release shoot inside me, I spiraled down into the abyss again.

It was, hands down, the best orgasm I'd ever had. It was the best sex anyone in the history of time ever had. No one could have done better or would ever do better than Pierce just had. I was certain of it.

"Holy shit," he panted, releasing my leg so he could collapse on top of me in a pile of sated, liquefied limbs. "I knew you'd feel amazing, but I never could have imagined it would be this good."

His hand still held mine pinned to the bed. He was still everywhere, and I was feeling smug as hell. "I think you may have just killed me. I'm dead right now. I hope you're okay with fucking a ghost from here on out."

His whole body shook against me as he laughed, and while I would have loved to see it, it was just as nice to feel it against my skin as he buried his face in my neck.

"I'll let you get some rest while I rehydrate, but just a heads-up, that was only the starter. There's still so much I plan to do to you before the night's over."

That giddiness came back in full force as I lifted my free hand high above my head and squeaked, "Yay."

That time, I got to see his laugh, and it was as gorgeous as always.

Chapter 21
Pierce

THE FEELING in my chest wouldn't go away. It was a tightness, a pressure that had formed the moment I slid into Marin's hot, wet sheath, and it hadn't disappeared or even lightened since then.

The clock on my bedside table read three in the morning. I'd had her two more times after our first, and still, I felt a clawing need deep in my gut for more. More of her taste, more of her smell, more of the feel of her soft skin against mine and the sound of her throaty, sexy voice.

More, more, more, more.

I couldn't get enough of *anything* when it came to her. I couldn't stop touching her. When she climbed out of the bed and moved into the bathroom to clean up, I found myself following after her simply so I could press my chest against her back and loop my arms around her from behind as she stood at the sink. I wanted to hold on to her and stare at the reflection of us in the mirror as she washed her hands. I wanted the visual confirmation that we really did fit together as perfectly as I expected.

When we were in bed together, I couldn't stop my hands from roaming, my lips and tongue from tasting. Only one night and I'd managed to memorize every single inch of her. I knew now, without a shadow of a doubt, that everything about her was now burned into my brain for the rest of my life.

That first initial fix was all it took for me to become a junkie. But as I lay in my bed on my back, one arm propped behind my head while the other held her tightly against my side, the realization that scared me the most was that it wasn't just the physical part that had sucked me into her orbit. It was *everything* about her.

Yes, I'd been hoping I'd eventually be able to work this attraction from under my skin if I just gave in to my physical desire for her. But now I wasn't so sure that would work. I feared that the more I had her, the deeper she'd burrow inside me.

She stirred against me, pulling me from the melancholy fog that had drifted over me. I twisted my neck just as her eyes fluttered open, that whiskey color warming me from the inside out like I'd just downed a shot.

"You're still awake," she noted groggily. "Everything okay?"

Was it? I didn't know for sure, but I decided that

tonight wasn't going to be the night to delve into all that shit. "You're naked beside me. I've come three times tonight, you six." My lips curled up in a satisfied smirk. "I think it's safe to say everything's pretty fucking great at the moment."

She smiled lazily and lifted her arms, stretching her long, lithe limbs out like a cat basking in the sunshine. "Well then you're welcome," she teased, that light of hers effectively blasting away the last of the shadows that had been clouding my thoughts only seconds earlier.

I rolled until she was tucked beneath me. My dick stirred to life, but in a half-assed sort of way, like a man who'd just gotten the shit beat out of him, but still insisted on getting up and facing his opponent instead of staying down. I'd given him quite the workout tonight, and I wasn't as young as I used to be. I'd maxed myself out, at least until the sun came up. But I wasn't dead, and Marin was . . . well, Marin. So any sort of reaction was a given.

"Oh God," she said in a pathetic pout. "Pierce, I can't. Not again. I need a break. As it is, I'm not sure I'll be able to walk tomorrow."

Good Lord she had a gift for making a man feel like a king. "Relax, babe. I'm not going to attack you again. I'm good, but I'm not a machine. I don't think there's any fluid left in my body."

The relief that flitted across her face was ridiculously adorable.

I reached up to brush the hair away from her face, enjoying the way she sighed and pressed her cheek against my palm. "I just wanted to look at you for a bit."

Her eyes widened with surprise before going half-mast. She liked that, and a bolt of male pride shot through my chest that I'd been the man to put that look on her face.

"Man, you can be sweet. Who would have guessed?"

I jerked my chin back and scowled in mock offense. "What are you talking about? I'm always sweet."

She snorted, rolling her eyes playfully. "Uh-huh. I'm not buying it. You've basically hated me from the moment you met me."

This time, the jerk and scowl weren't fake at all. "What are you talking about?"

"Oh, come on. Like you don't know. You didn't exactly keep it a secret you didn't like me."

"Marin, I never hated you. Not for a second."

The surprise registered over every inch of her face. "But . . . any time I was around, you were always frowning and giving me dirty looks. If I entered a room you were in, you'd storm out. You did your best not to be anywhere near me."

Ah hell. This was a conversation I knew would be inevitable, but I'd hoped I'd have a little more time to warm her up to me before we had to get into the whole ugly truth.

"Sweetheart, I never hated you. I avoided you because,

from the moment I first laid eyes on you in my mother's kitchen, I wanted you. And when I found out you were with Frank, it pissed me off. I couldn't be around you because I knew I wouldn't be able to control myself for long. You were my brother's, and I knew before I even talked to you that you were too good for him. But I told myself it didn't matter, nothing could ever happen between us, because he'd had you first. That meant you were off limits to me."

Her sweet, minty breath fanned against my face as she exhaled a gust of air. "Really?"

"You were the first woman who made me feel anything after my wife died," I confessed on a whisper, the pressure in my chest building and squeezing even tighter. "I didn't *want* to want you, but I couldn't help myself."

The sadness she felt for me couldn't have been more obvious if she'd taken a Sharpie and written the words out on her cheeks. She'd make a terrible poker player.

"What—I mean, are you—can I ask what happened to her? Your wife? I don't know the story there, but if you don't want to talk about it, I totally get it. You don't have to. I don't want you to feel like I'm pressuring you into—"

I silenced her rambling by placing a thumb over her lips as my brows pinched in confusion. "You don't know? Frank never told you?"

She let out a frustrated huff and wrapped her fingers around my wrist, pulling my hand away so she could speak. "I think we both know what an asshole your brother is. I asked him once, and let's just say, my curiosity about you didn't sit well with him. I never asked again after that." She said it in a way that made my skin prickle and the tiny hairs on the back of my neck stand on end, but I knew not to ask as I watched in fascination as those shutters I'd only seen when my brother was mentioned slammed down over her eyes.

This wasn't a conversation I could have lying on top of her so I moved, propping myself up against the headboard as I blew out a breath and raked my hands through my hair.

Marin eyed me warily as she sat up, holding the sheet across her naked breasts. She didn't scoot close, somehow sensing that I needed space to get out what I had to say.

"Constance was six weeks pregnant with Eli when we found out she had breast cancer." Just saying those words made it feel like all the air had been sucked out of the room. "We'd been trying to conceive for a few years by that time, but weren't having any luck doing it on our own, so we'd started seeing a fertility specialist. It was still early enough in the pregnancy that she could have terminated it and begun treatment, but she'd wanted a baby so badly. We both did. Eli was our little miracle, so it wasn't even a decision for her. Ending it was absolutely out of the question."

Her eyes had gone glassy with tears as she lifted a hand and pressed it against her mouth. "Oh God."

"I fought with her at first. I told her we could try again once she was in remission, but she refused. It took me a while to see her point, but I'm glad I did, because I can't imagine a world without my son in it.

"The cancer had progressed too far by the time she had Eli. There was nothing we could do about it by then. Eli was three months old when she passed away." I looked over to see Marin had tears streaming down her cheeks. "She might have been sick, but those were still the best three months of her life, because she got to spend them with our son. I'm thankful every day for that."

"Can I—" She swallowed down a croak. "Can I come to you?"

I answered by reaching out and grabbing her by the waist. I spread my legs and twisted her around so she was resting pressed up against me from shoulder to groin, her back pressed into my chest. I wrapped my arms around her tight, one along her collarbone, the other at her waist, and burrowed my face in her sweet-smelling hair.

Her hands came down on my arms, squeezing tight, trying to pour all her comfort into me. "Pierce, I'm so, so sorry."

"It was a long time ago."

She twisted her head around and looked up at me. "That doesn't mean it doesn't still hurt."

She was right. It still hurt every goddamn day, but it was much more manageable than it used to be.

"Thanks, baby."

"Am I—am I the first woman? Since . . ."

"Yeah," I answered in a gravelly voice.

She broke out of my hold then, turning around so she could straddle my thighs and take my face in the palms of her hands. "Then I want you to know how much that means to me, that I get to be that for you."

For as long as this lasts, I thought, but for some reason, those words lodged themselves in my throat, and I couldn't get them out.

For as long as this lasts was all she and I would ever have, all I'd be able to give her. But I couldn't deny that there as a part of me that hoped it lasted for a good, long while. Even if this was all it would ever be.

Chapter 22
Marin

I was doing my best to concentrate, but it was getting harder and harder to focus, because Pierce was doing his best to distract me.

He came up behind me, his hands landing on my hips as he used his chin to nudge my hair to the side and pressed his lips to my neck.

"Will you stop?" I giggled and squirmed, trying to get away from him.

"Can't help it," he grunted against my skin. "I can't stop touching you."

I wasn't sure there was a woman alive who wouldn't melt on the spot at hearing that. "I'm trying not to burn this, and you're making it impossible."

"Give it up, babe," he said on a chuckle as the eggs in the frying pan began to put off a smell that couldn't have possibly been right. "You and I aren't built for the kitchen.

Whatever you're trying to make is going to come out ruined. It's inevitable."

"It's eggs over easy, and you're wrong. I can do this!" I declared, trying to will it to be true. Unfortunately, when I slid the spatula under the egg and flipped it, the underside was completely black. "This is your fault," I accused, spinning around and stabbing my finger into his chest. "If you hadn't been distracting me with your big hands and soft lips and good looks, I wouldn't have messed that up."

He grinned patronizingly. "Hate to break it to you, but I could smell that burning five minutes ago."

I knew he was right, I'd smelled it too, but I wasn't willing to let him off the hook that easily yet. "Yeah, well maybe if you weren't making my head all fuzzy, I would have noticed before it was too late."

The expression on his face screamed *arrogant, satisfied male*. "I make your head all fuzzy?"

I rolled my eyes, trying to play it off that I wasn't freaking out that I'd possibly just given too much away. "Don't pretend you didn't already know that."

Flipping the burner off, I carried the pan to the sink and dumped the ruined contents down the drain, flipping on the disposal. Steam rose up with a hiss as cold water slid across the scalding pan.

Grabbing the sponge, I squirted soap onto it and began scrubbing at the charred bits that had burnt on when Pierce came up behind me and pressed against my back.

His hands slipped around the front of me. One traveled up, cupping my breast while the other slipped beneath the waistband of my shorts.

"Wh-what are you doing?" I asked, my question coming out breathy as arousal flooded my veins.

"Helping you learn to multi-task better," he answered against my neck. "Maybe if I keep touching you, you'll eventually get used to it and your head won't get so fuzzy."

"I-I don't think . . ." I swallowed past the tightness suddenly squeezing my throat as his fingertips breached my panties and slipped between my thighs. "I don't think it works that way."

His teeth scraped along the cord at the side of my neck. "Guess we'll just have to see. Keep washing, baby."

I blinked against the heaviness in my eyelids and looked down at the sink to where I was squeezing the sudsy sponge in a death grip. With a stuttered breath, I went back to scrubbing the pan, only to lose focus once again when Pierce's finger glided through my slit and the wet that he'd built there.

A needy moan burst past my lips when he reached my clit and pressed down, circling it with just the right amount of pressure. "*Pierce.*"

"Christ," he grunted, his tongue snaking out to pull my earlobe into his mouth so he could nip down on it. "Don't think I'll ever get used to hearing you say my name like that. Say it again, Marin."

"Mmm. Pierce," I hummed as my hips began to move with his hand. As good as what he was doing to me felt, it wasn't enough. My walls were spasming, achingly empty. "I need more. Please."

"Keep scrubbing and I'll give it to you."

That sadistic jerk. I was just about to spin around to punch him in his sexy face when he drove two fingers into my channel, giving me exactly what I'd just asked for.

My head fell back against his shoulder and my hips snapped to meet his fingers as he began plunging them in and out of me. "Yes, baby. Just like that."

He hummed against my ear, the sound like lust and sin and everything utterly decadent. "So fucking tight and wet for me. Jesus, I love your pussy."

Giving up on my task all together, I dropped the sponge in order to grip the edge of the sink with both hands as he began to fuck me even harder with those skilled fingers. I rocked my hips back into him, feeling his straining erection against my ass as I rode his hand, desperately chasing that feeling building deep in my core, twisting tighter and tighter.

"Oh, God. Don't stop," I panted. "I'm almost there." I let out a cry when Pierce yanked his hand from between my thighs. "No! What are you—?" Before I could finish that sentence, he wrenched my shorts and panties down my thighs. A second later, I felt the blunt head of his cock slip into place between my thighs, then he slammed in, bottoming out on the very first thrust.

I went off like a rocket, my walls clamping down around him as I screamed his name and white-knuckled the edge of the sink.

"Fuck yes," he hissed, holding onto my hips in a bruising grip. "Give it to me, baby," he grunted as he powered in and out, dragging my release out until I feared I might lose consciousness.

Just as I collapsed forward, he circled my throat, using his hold to pull me back up so we were pressed together, back to chest.

"You like it when I fuck you, Marin?"

"Yes," I moaned, that pressure in my core building to a new height. "Don't ever stop, please."

"Fuck, your greedy pussy's going to be the death of me."

My chuckle was husky and wanton as I turned my head to smile up at him. "You're welcome."

He slammed is lips down on mine, driving his tongue into my mouth at the same time he swiveled his hips in such a way that I fell over the edge into another orgasm even stronger than the last.

I swallowed down his grunts as he drove in once, twice, a third time, before burying himself deep and releasing into me, coming so hard I could feel his whole body shake.

Both of us struggled to pull in much-needed air as we came down from the most incredible high.

Once we were able to move again, he pulled out, grabbing a hand towel off the counter and cleaning himself from my sensitive skin before pulling my clothes back into place.

He chuckled as he looked into the sink while tucking himself back into his pants. "Looks like we'll have to keep working on your multi-tasking."

"Screw the pan," I giggled as I turned on wobbly knees to face him. "I'll just buy you a new one."

He leaned in, giving me the most tender kiss. "Just so you know, you make my head fuzzy too," he rumbled just as my stomach let out a growl. After our strenuous activity, my resources were depleted, and I needed food in my belly before it started eating itself.

Hearing the loud, garbled noise, he chuckled and gave his head a good-natured shake. "Come on." He grabbed my hand and started leading me out of the kitchen.

"Where are we going?"

"While I commend your effort at trying to make breakfast, we're both starving, so I'm taking you to Evergreen diner before you expire in front of my very eyes."

A whole swarm of butterflies took off in my belly at that, and the biggest, goofiest smile stretched across my face. What transpired between us last night and just now didn't feel like *no expectations*, and a breakfast date out in public where the whole town could see us together *certainly* didn't feel like *no expectations*. It felt like something real, and in spite of what I thought I wanted or needed, I was suddenly excited at the prospect of having more with this man.

"Okay, just let me grab my purse and shoes really quick."

He let go of my hand so I could dart up the stairs where I'd left my overnight bag and purse after getting dressed earlier. I slid my feet into a pair of pink flip-flops that matched the T-shirt and looked cute with my frayed denim shorts.

I grabbed my purse and was starting down the stairs when my cell began to ring. Stopping three steps from the bottom, I fished it out, smiling at Tali's name, and swiped to answer.

"Hey, babe."

"Marin," she sniffled. My back went straight at the tears in her voice, concern flooding my veins.

"What's wrong?"

"I-I did it," she said brokenly. "I kicked Nick out this morning." Her sentence ended on a sob, then, "Can you come over, please?"

"Of course, honey. I'll be right there."

"Would—would you stop and get more of those muffins on your way?"

"Absolutely." My heart splintered into a million pieces

for my strong big sister. "Are you going to be okay until I get there?"

"No . . . but also yes."

"Okay. I'm on my way. I'll be there as soon as I can."

I disconnected and dropped my phone back into my bag before hurrying down the rest of the stairs. "Pierce, I'm so sorry, but I have to go."

He stopped me with a palm to the side of my neck, worry etched into his masculine features. "Is everything all right?"

"No," I said on a sigh, giving my head a shake. "That was Tali. She's a wreck. She kicked Nick out."

Understanding washed through his eyes. "Okay. Go, take care of her, babe."

I leaned into him already addicted to the heat he provided. I didn't want to leave him, but I had to be there for Tali. That wasn't an option. "I'm sorry," I said quietly. "I know this was supposed to be our time—"

"Don't apologize," he interrupted. "She's your sister, and she needs you. I totally understand. Call or text me later whenever you can. Let me know if there's anything I can do."

Lifting up on my tiptoes, I pressed a kiss to his lips, already missing him before I'd even left. "You're kind of incredible, you know that?"

"I do, but feel free to say it as often as you want."

I lowered back down, feeling my lips pull into a pout as

I stepped back, preparing to leave. Why did it suddenly feel so damn hard?

Once again, my stupid face gave me away. "I don't want you to leave either," he said, flooding my chest with warmth. "But your sister comes first." He looped his finger in one of my belt loops and pulled me to him. "Besides, we'll have plenty of time for us."

"I'm going to hold you to that," I said with one last kiss before finally forcing myself to the door. "I'll talk to you soon. Don't get into any trouble while I'm gone."

"I'll try not to, baby."

I gave myself until I reached Muffin Top to wipe the elated smile off my face. I needed to be there for Tali, and there was no way I was walking into that house with a just-banged-to-within-an-inch-of-my-life glow while her marriage was falling apart.

* * *

I BARELY RECOGNIZED the woman who answered my sister's front door. Her eyes were bloodshot, her cheeks were red, and her nose was swollen from a serious crying jag. Her hair was piled in a ratty mess on top of her head, and it looked like she was still in the clothes she'd worn the day before.

"Kitchen or living room?" I asked.

"Kitchen. If I sit in the living room I'm going to wallow right into the furniture."

I followed her into the immaculately clean kitchen, taking the stool next to hers, and began unloading everything I brought from Muffin Top. Six maple bacon muffins, all for her, and the largest coffee they sold.

"All right," I started once I had her all set. "Start from the beginning, but first, are the kids home?"

She shook her head. "I called Mom super late last night and asked her if she and Dad could come get them early this morning. They showed up just before eight to take them to the lake for the day."

I nodded and braced for what was to come. "Okay, then hit me with it. Let it all out, that's what I'm here for."

"Okay." She sucked in a fortifying breath and jumped right in. "He got home late last night, *like always*," she added sarcastically, "and *like always*, he took a shower and passed right out. So I went through his phone."

"Oh God. Tali—"

"I know! I know, okay? Anyway, he had all these emails and texts from this woman named Eve. Apparently she's an intern at his office." I imagined Slutzilla. The home-wrecking shrew had a name now, and for some reason, that made me hate her even more. "All her messages were really flirty, bordering on inappropriate, you know? Like, as a woman, I was able to read between the lines to the subtext."

Bombshell

"Were his responses the same?"

"Well . . ." She bit down on her bottom lip and hesitated. "No. But that doesn't matter! Not once did he tell her to stop or that she was being inappropriate. He just ignored the flirty banter, which is just as bad!"

I nodded solemnly.

"It was seeing those messages that finally pushed me over the edge. I called Mom, like I told you, and then I started packing up all his shit."

Leaning over, I placed a hand on her arm. "Honey, have you even slept?"

"I can't. I can't sleep, I can't eat—" She stopped to chomp into one of the muffins. "Well, I can't eat anything but *these*. Anyway, he was still asleep by the time the kids left with Mom and Dad, so I dragged his suitcases down the stairs, making sure to be as loud as humanly possible. He woke up and came out of the room in time to see me heaving them into the front yard." She washed the muffin down with a gulp of coffee.

"What happened next?"

"I ripped into him. I told him I'd seen the messages and everything. He swore up and down that nothing had happened and was never going to happen, that he didn't look at her that way, but when I pointed out that he never once said in any of his replies that he was a married man or asked her to stop, he didn't get it. It was like I was talking to a freaking wall, Mar. I got so angry that it all started pouring out of me. I yelled about him never being home, about missing important milestones in our kids' lives because he's always at work. I got in his face and accused him of being a shitty, absentee father. I said he'd basically turned me into a single mother, so there was really no point in having him under the same roof anymore.

"I yelled about feeling like nothing but a roommate and how he hasn't touched me in longer than I can remember. I broke down and started crying when I told him he makes me feel undesirable, that I don't feel like he wants me anymore. I told him that even if he hasn't cheated, it doesn't matter, because what we have isn't a marriage, that he doesn't even see me anymore. I'm just here, in the background like wallpaper."

My own eyes had welled up, the tears spilling free at my sister's sadness. "What did he say?"

She sniffled, wiping at her cheeks before looking to her lap and shaking her head. "The same shit he always says. He promised he'd do better, that the only reason he worked so much was so the kids and I could have this house and I could drive a nice car and have designer clothes and not have to work. Like any of that matters to me," she snapped.

"He swore he'd stop, that he'd be there for us more, and that he still loved me more than anything." She looked up at me, her chin trembling as a fresh wave of tears fell from her eyes. "But it's too late, Marin. I've heard it all a million times. His words don't mean anything anymore. I don't think he wants *me*. I think he wants someone to take care of him and make him dinner and wash his fucking underwear! I didn't sign up to be his maid. This was supposed to be a partnership."

On that, she broke down completely, and her words became a garbled mess. All I could do was hold her as she cried. My heart broke because it was so obvious hers was breaking.

I moved us into the living room and held her as she cried herself to sleep with her head on my lap, and I stayed right there until she woke up a few hours later, feeling a bit more in control of herself.

Our folks couldn't keep the kids away forever, but after that crying jag and nap, Tali was feeling much stronger, and was prepared to have the talk with Erika and Matt, explaining that Daddy wasn't going to be living at home for a while.

I stuck around as long as I could, but she wanted to be alone with the kids when she told them, so, reluctantly, I left, with orders that she call any time of the day or night if she needed me for anything.

It was already evening by the time I left, so I headed straight for my apartment, feeling the exhaustion of the night before and the emotional turmoil from today weighing me down like I had an anvil tied around my neck.

I waited until I was snuggled up in my bed, a happy

little rom-com playing as background noise on the TV, before I dialed Pierce's number.

"Hey. Is your sister okay?" he asked right off the bat.

What was it about his voice that made everything feel better? "No, but I'm hoping she will be in time."

I heard shuffling and figured he was moving away from Eli for a bit of privacy so he could talk to me. "Are *you* okay?"

"I will be after tomorrow."

There was a brief pause before he spoke again, and when he did, his tone dripped with trepidation. "What's happening tomorrow? Am I going to need to post bail?"

Man, he already knew me so well if that was his automatic reaction. "I feel like you really get me."

"Marin," he said in warning. "What's happening tomorrow?"

"I'm going to confront him at his office. It's obvious he's got his head jammed so far up his ass he can't manage to make the right choices, so I'm going to help him out."

There was a long, beleaguered sigh through the line. "I'd try and talk you out of it, but I'm pretty sure that's impossible, so I'll just say this: Please try your hardest not to get arrested. I'll be in court all day tomorrow and won't be able to get you out."

"Your concern warms my heart."

"Smartass," he muttered into the phone, but I could

hear the smile in his voice, and it made my lips curve up as well.

"Did Eli have fun at the botanical gardens today?"

"He did. He ran himself so ragged he's already starting to fade."

"Okay, then I should let you go so you can take care of him. I'm pretty tired myself. Give him a kiss for me?"

"I will, but where's mine?"

I puckered my lips and made an obnoxious kissy noise. "There. That should hold you over."

"Doubtful. Sleep well, baby."

"You too. Night, Pierce."

I hung up the phone and flopped back in my bed, staring up at my ceiling as I thought: *Uh-oh. I'm really starting to fall for this man.*

Chapter 23
Marin

I woke up the next morning with a text from Pierce reminding me not to do anything that would get me arrested.

Feeling the need to go into battle with every possible advantage, I donned my most professional outfit; a cream silk blouse tucked into a blush pencil skirt with nude pumps. I left my hair long and loose, but had tamed it with my flatiron, and my makeup was subtle with natural pinks and peaches.

I waltzed down to my car, a woman on a mission, determined to do whatever it took to make things better for my sister. It wasn't until I was parked at the meter outside Nick's building, that I stopped to think about what I was planning to do and thought maybe this wasn't the best idea.

Shaking off my uncertainty, I climbed out of the car,

fed the meter, and started across the street toward Nick's building. I headed for the bank of elevators that would lead me to his floor and hit the button, as I waited for the doors to slide open, I considered how I was going to get to his office without him knowing I was coming.

I pasted a smile on my face as soon as the doors opened onto Nick's floor. The idea was to treat the receptionist like we were old pals, warm her up so she'd have no problem just waving me on back.

"Hey, Cindy," I greeted the receptionist, a woman I'd never seen before in my life, like we were longtime friends as soon as I stepped off the elevator. I sent up a silent thanks that she had a name plate on her desk, because I wasn't sure 'girl' and 'babe' and 'sister' would get me through the door. "How's it going?"

She looked at me with a furrowed brow, and I knew she was scrolling through her memory bank, trying to figure out how the hell she knew me. "Uh, it's good . . ." she trailed off awkwardly.

"It's Marin. Remember? Nick Allen's sister-in-law?"

"Oh! Right!" *Bingo.* "Sorry, I didn't recognize you at first. You changed your . . . hair."

I hadn't but I wasn't going to tell her that. Instead, I reached up and gave it a fluff. "I did. Thanks for noticing. You like it?"

"Oh, yeah! Totally. Looks gorgeous."

"Cindy, you're the sweetest!" I leaned against her

credenza. "I'm just swinging by to pick him up for lunch since I happened to be in the city. He's expecting me. Is it cool if I just head on back?"

"Oh, um . . . yeah. Sure."

"Thanks, babe. You're a total doll." I started moving to the double doors that separate the reception area from the offices, looking back over my shoulder to ask, "Can we pick you up anything while we're out?" *Please say no. Please say no. Please say no.*

"No thanks. That's sweet though."

"All right, Cindy. See you around. Enjoy the rest of the day."

"You too," she returned as I pushed through the doors and headed in the direction I remembered taking the one and only time I'd come here with Tali five years ago, and prayed he hadn't moved offices.

If I had to, I'd walk through this entire place until I found him. I was a woman on a mission and I wasn't leaving until I did what I came here to do. Fortunately, I spotted his name plate on the door before I had to go on a search.

"Um, excuse me. Do you have an appointment?" a flustered little woman sitting at the desk just outside Nick's door asked as I bypassed her and grabbed the handle to Nick's office. "Hey, wait! You can't just go in there—"

I showed her how wrong she was by stomping across the threshold all *I am woman, hear me roar* and stopped in the middle of the room with my hands on my hips, striking a killer Pissed-off Female pose, if I did say so myself.

Nick lifted his eyes from his computer, looking like absolute shit that had been run over a few hundred times. "Marin? What's going on? What are you doing here?" His eyes went big and filled with fear. "Is it Tali? Is she okay?"

Instead of answering, I skewered the woman standing beside him, *behind* his desk, with a look so vicious, I hoped it melted the skin right off her face. Freaking *Eve*.

"No, Nick, she's not okay," I started snidely. "You and I need to talk." I pinned Slutzilla with a withering glare. "*Alone*."

"Excuse me, but we're in the middle of something here," she started, but I lifted my hand to silence her.

"Do you know who I am?" I didn't give her a chance to answer. "I'm his sister-in-law. You know what that means? That means my sister is married to the guy you're currently rubbing all over like you're hoping for a genie to pop out and grant you three wishes."

I'd forgotten all about Nick's assistant, and discovered that she was still standing behind me when I heard her snort. I turned and found her trying her hardest to cover up her laugh, and winked, feeling a sudden kinship to the woman.

"Nicky, do you want me to call security?" Eve asked, placing her hand on his shoulder like she was trying to offer him support when everyone in the room already knew the truth. She was trifling.

"No, Eve. It's fine. You can go now." He looked to the woman behind me. "Heather, can you please close the door on your way out?"

"Yeah, *Eve*," I sneered. Admittedly, it wasn't my most mature moment, but I gave myself credit for not plucking the hussy bald. "Get the hell out of here."

I glared at her the entire time she moved around the desk she had no business being behind and across the office until she reached the door. I caught a glimpse of Heather as she followed after her and returned the little finger wave she gave me. Apparently Nick's assistant was as big a fan of Eve's as I was.

I waited for the door to close before turning back to my brother-in-law, the man I'd considered family for the past several years.

He scrubbed at his face anxiously, and it was clear as day that this whole mess with him and Tali was seriously wearing on him. His face was unshaven, his hair was a mess, and his suit was wrinkled, like he hadn't bothered to iron it after Tali stuffed it in his suitcase.

"Look, Mar, whatever this is, I'm really not in the mood, okay? I've had a shitty few days, and I don't need you coming in here to jump on my ass."

I stomped to the edge of his desk and snatched up one

of the paper clips he kept in a bowl and threw it at his head. "Shut up, you idiot. I'm here to help you."

He rubbed at his forehead where the clip had just bounced off, looking up at me in bewilderment. "You are?"

I rolled my eyes like I was dealing with the dumbest kid in class. "Yeah, I am, stupid. You're my family, and as pissed as I am at you right now, I can't just sit back and watch you screw all this up." I held up my hand to stop him when he opened his mouth to speak. "First up, we need to address the problem that is your skanky little intern."

He collapsed back in his chair and pinched the bridge of his nose. "There's nothing happening there. I already told Tali all of this. I don't even see Eve that way. It's just a little harmless flirting."

"Does *she* know it's just harmless flirting?" I asked, pointing behind me toward the door. "Because I'm telling you right now, that's a woman biding her time. I can spot a chick like that from a mile away, and as long as she thinks there's even the smallest glimmer of a chance, she's not going anywhere. Which means she is most *definitely* a threat to your marriage."

"It isn't like that," he insisted. "I love my wife. I'm *in* love with her. I'd never cheat. When Eve gets like that, I don't even engage."

I arched a brow and crossed my arms over my chest.

"You don't stop her either. How do you not see that's a problem?"

"I don't—"

"I've seen you two together, Nick," I informed him. "Twice now. I was on a date at a restaurant here in the city when the two of you showed up together. She was all over you. Sure, you didn't engage, and maybe you pulled away, but you didn't tell her to stop. Then, the night I was staking you out—"

He held up his hands. "Wait. What? You were staking me out?"

"That's neither here nor there, and it's totally beside the point," I deflected. "As I was saying, you two were standing outside this building, and she was touching you in a way that was completely inappropriate. Whether you believe she's a threat to your wife or not, you have to at least see that her behavior is *beyond* unprofessional."

"You're right," he relented a second later, blowing out a weary sigh.

"Of course I am, dummy. I'm always right."

He nodded in complete agreement. "All right. I'll take care of the Eve situation."

I let out a sigh and moved to one of the chairs across from his desk, taking a seat. I needed to school the man, and that could take a while. Might as well get comfortable. Also, my super cute professional shoes were starting to pinch my toes.

"Unfortunately, Eve isn't the real problem in your marriage."

Leaning forward in his chair, he braced his elbows on his desk and let out a pained groan. "What do I do, Mar? How do I fix this? I know I fucked up. I let this get too far out of hand. I should have been home more, I see that. But doesn't she understand that the only reason I work this goddamn hard is *for* her and the kids?"

"You've known Tali a long time, Nick. You know her probably better than anyone. Why in the hell do you think she'd care about things like cars and clothes and houses? That's not my sister. That's not *your wife*. You know that. She'd be happy as a pig in shit living in a van down by the river if she had the three of you. She cares about you and Erika and Matt. You're her family, and family is all that's ever mattered to her. She doesn't want a caretaker, Nick, she wants a partner, and she wants to feel loved and desired by the man she's been head-over-heels for since she was fifteen years old."

"I just—" He stopped, looking at his lap and shaking his head in defeat. "I lost sight of what was important." When he lifted his gaze to mine, his eyes were glinting with sadness and tears. "I can't lose her, Marin. Without her, without our family, nothing matters. She's the only woman I've ever loved."

"Tell her *that*," I insisted vehemently. "Tell her all of that, and most importantly, stop making excuses for your fuckups. Own them. Until you do, nothing you say is going to matter. She needs to see how much you still care about her."

"I can't breathe without her, Mar. I have to win her back."

There wasn't much more I could say to help him out of this situation. All I could do was hope to God he took my advice and that Tali would remember how much she loved him. Rising, I hooked the strap of my purse over my arm and issued one more piece of advice. "Then fight for her, Nick. Let her see you still want her as much today as you did when you first met."

I turned and started for the door when he called my name. With my hand on the handle, I turned to look back over my shoulder. "Do you think I have a chance?"

"I do," I admitted. "But I'm afraid this might be your last one. Do me a favor and don't waste it, yeah?"

"You're a good sister, Marin. I love you."

"I love you too, dummy. Now make this shit right so you can go home."

With that challenge issued, I pulled his door open and stepped out. Heather was at her desk, staring up at me with inquisitive eyes.

"Can I ask you to do me a favor?"

"Yeah, sure. Anything you need. I think the world of Tali, so just name it."

Oh, I liked this woman. "Watch out for him, would

you? I think he might have finally extracted his head from his ass, but he's a man, so that means there's still a chance it could get stuck up there again."

"Don't worry, I'm on it. He might be a pain in the ass, but he's a good man." She chewed on her bottom lip pensively before finally saying what was on her mind. "It was all her, you know. *Eve.*" She curled her top lip like she smelled poo. "He would never—"

"I know," I assured her, and smiled when I saw her shoulders slump in relief. She liked Nick as a boss and a person, and maybe together we could help fix things. "Well, I'm off. It was lovely to meet you, Heather. I hope it happens more in the future."

My phone vibrated in my purse as I took the elevator back down to the lobby after saying goodbye to my new best friend, Cindy. I pulled it out and read the text as I stood at the crosswalk, waiting for the light to change.

Pierce: *You in handcuffs yet?*

I snickered as I typed out a reply.

Me: *Your faith in me warms my heart. Seriously. Stop. I might swoon. Also, shouldn't you be in court right now?*

Pierce: *We're on a brief recess. I wanted to see how it went. You save the day?*

Oh *man*, this guy. Even when he wasn't near he could make me melt.

Me: *Let's hope so. I did my best.*

Pierce: *Then I bet everything's going to be fine.*

Me: *Stop being sweet when I can't kiss you.*

I imagined his smirk as he read over that message.

Pierce: *Can't help it. You bring that out in me. By the way, you look beautiful today.*

I was being sarcastic earlier, but as I strode across the street to my car, I swooned so hard my knees nearly gave out. For safety purposes, I waited until I was in my car before responding back.

Me: *How would you know? You haven't seen me today?*

Pierce: *I don't need to see you to know you look beautiful.*

Yep, I thought to myself as I started my car and headed back toward Hope Valley. *I am most definitely falling for the Ice King.*

Chapter 24
Marin

I BIT my lip so hard I tasted blood as I struggled to keep from crying out. It was just too much, too good. My orgasm didn't just wash over me. It wasn't a slow, tantalizing buildup to the pinnacle. No, it slammed into me with all the force of a battering ram. In the past few days I'd been with Pierce enough to know he was a freaking rock star in bed, but somehow the intensity of my release always seemed to catch me by surprise.

"Fuck, I can feel you," he grunted from beneath me. I fell forward, bracing my hands on the solid wall of his chest as I drove myself down on him, riding his cock with all the strength I had as I urged my climax on, wanting to drag it out for as long as possible until there was absolutely nothing left. "Give me another, baby."

"Oh God," I breathed. "Pierce, I can't—"

My protest was cut off when he knifed up, grabbing

hold of me and flipping me onto my back. He took over, pounding into me with a relentless, unforgiving rhythm. "Yes you can, Marin. I want another one. You're so fucking close."

His hand came up just then and spanned the width of my throat. His fingers pressed ever so gently into my skin with just the slightest bit of pressure.

My eyes went wide, but not with fear, with amazement at the touch. It was something I'd never experienced before. He wasn't trying to choke me. It wasn't like that at all. As I looked up into his clear blue eyes, I saw him staring at his hand on my throat in a way that stole my breath, and I knew then what he was doing. The hold was one of ownership. He was making me his. Claiming me.

"Christ, so beautiful," he grunted as he drove into me again and again. "Always so fucking beautiful."

"Pierce," I whispered. That coil in my core tightened to the point I was actually afraid of how intense the release building inside of me was going to be. "It's too much."

"Never," he grunted, beads of sweat dotting his forehead. "It's never too much with you. It never will be."

At that declaration, I snapped. My back and neck arched, my nails dug into his back so hard I knew he'd have marks for days, and I swear to God, I felt like my body was levitating as I came harder than I ever had.

Sensing I wasn't going to be able to keep quiet for much

longer, Pierce slammed his lips against mine in a searing kiss, swallowing down every noise I made until he grunted with his own release, filling me with spurt after spurt until his arms finally gave out and he collapsed onto me.

I lay there, basking in the glow of some rather exceptional early morning nookie before reality came back to me.

"You have to get off me, honey. I need to clean up and get out of here before Eli wakes up."

Since the trial started, almost every waking hour of Pierce's day was consumed by it. Yet, as exhausted as he was, he still seemed insatiable when it came to me. I never in my life would have imagined he'd be such a tactile person, and after only a week and a half, I was already addicted to his touch.

With his crazy schedule, I'd had to stay late every night except the ones when I worked the club. Pierce would roll in, looking completely exhausted, but when I got up to leave that first Monday, he'd grabbed me by the hand and stopped me. "Stay." It had only been one word, a simple request, yet it was more powerful than when boyfriends in the past had told me they loved me. "I want you to stay with me."

"What about Eli?" I'd asked. My question seemed to pull him out of a daze, and I saw the indecision and unhappiness warring in his expression. So I'd said the only possible thing I could. "I can wake up early. Leave before he gets up."

"You'd do that?"

I gave him the God's honest truth. "If it meant I got to spend time with you, there isn't much I wouldn't do, Pierce."

And thus started the pattern. Each night I'd go to sleep with his long, solid body wrapped around mine in the comfort of his huge bed. He'd wake me up before the sun had risen, then he'd proceed to either make love to me in a way that almost brought me to tears, or he'd fuck me so hard it was up in the air whether or not I'd be able to walk once he was done. Either way, it was guaranteed I'd get off, and I'd get off in a *very* big way.

After we finished, there was the post-coital cuddle that he always seemed to initiate, then I'd have to clean up, get dressed, and sneak out like a thief in the night, going back to my own apartment that now felt horribly cold and lonely.

I'd usually catch another few hours of sleep before my day had to start, then it was wash, rinse, and repeat.

"Fuck, I hate this arrangement," he grunted into my neck.

My whole body went stiff as a board as those words washed over me. Was he ending this? Was he tired of me already?

A million miserable thoughts ran through my head in

less than five seconds, and when he lifted his head to look down at me, I braced for the inevitable heartbreak about to come.

"Obviously now isn't the time to discuss it, but once this trial's over you and I need to sit down and discuss what we're going to say to Eli so that you don't have to leave every goddamn morning before the sun's even all the way up."

"You—" *Wait. What?* "You want to tell Eli about us?"

"I mean, he's only six. It's not like he'll really grasp the nuances of what our relationship means, but yeah. I just figured it's time we stop sneaking around like we're doing something wrong."

Damn it, Marin! You will not *cry. Pull yourself together, woman!*

I cleared my throat and tried my hardest to keep my expression as blank as possible. "Y-yeah. Sure. I mean, that sounds good. If you want to. Cool. Cool, cool, cool."

Those glacial blues of his glinted as he grinned down at me. "I see you really like the idea of that."

I shrugged casually. "I mean, it's . . . whatever."

He wasn't buying my act, not even for a second, but he let it slide and bent down to rub his nose against mine before rolling off of me and moving to the bathroom. "All right, then it's settled. Monday's a federal holiday, so the courts are closed, how about we discuss it then?" he asked as he returned to the bedroom with a warm damp washcloth in his hands.

He proceeded to clean me up, wiping me with a gentleness I would never had guessed he was capable of. "Works for me. I'll pencil you into my calendar."

"Appreciate it, beautiful. Now give me one last kiss to tide me over until I see you again." He tangled his fist in my hair and used the hold to tip my head in the exact position he wanted before growling, "And make sure it's a good one."

I could definitely do that.

* * *

"You're in love." The statement was spoken by Ms. Weatherby, with Tali nodding in agreement.

I sputtered in my teacup, my eyes ping-ponging between my neighbor and my sister. "*Pfft*. That's ridiculous. I'm not in love. You need to go back to the eye doctor and have him check your prescription again; I think you may need to go up in thickness."

Ms. Weatherby narrowed her beady eyes. "Child, I've got the peepers of an eagle."

"You're blind as a bat!" I countered. "I had to put big fat labels on all your canisters so you'd stop poisoning everybody with that toxic lemonade you always made everyone drink!"

Bombshell

She waved me off like it was nothing. "Then call it intuition, but I know love when I see it, and you, missy, are in love."

"She's right," Tali confirmed. "Your cheeks are always this shade of pink that I now realize is whisker burn, and you've been walking around for weeks now with this dopey, glassy-eyed look. You were so out of it the other day that you walked into the wall." She narrowed her gaze speculatively. "I wonder what you were thinking about then. Or *who*?"

I threw her a withering look. "Remind me why I thought it would be a good idea to invite you to tea today?"

"Because you're a good sister and knew I needed to get out of the house today before I lost my freaking mind."

To say things had changed in the Allen household would have been a serious understatement. When Nick decided he was going to do everything he could to win his family back, he'd really pulled out all the stops.

At first, when Tali told me he'd informed her he had no intention of moving out of the house they owned together, I was certain that he was going to be found dead in a ditch somewhere and my big sister was going to be convicted of murder, leaving me to raise my niece and nephew all alone.

He'd been banished to their guest room, but apparently he didn't complain about it. He'd also taken some time off work, time that would end with him working from home two days a week to be closer to his family. For the time being, he was doing all the things around the house that had been neglected while he'd spent all his hours at work.

He'd cleared the gutters, replaced the rotted board on their front porch, painted the shutters around all their windows, and fixed that faucet that had been dripping in the master bath for months.

When he wasn't making repairs, he was making breakfast for the kids and packing lunches. He'd taken over the school drop-offs and pick-ups. But the thing that made me positively giddy was that, apparently, he'd taken to being as touchy-feely as he used to be. Tali called them his sneak attacks. If she was at the sink washing dishes, he'd come up behind her and kiss her neck. If he passed her in the hallway, he'd brush his palms along her hips. If there was a reason or an opportunity to touch her, he took it.

Tali liked to pretend like it was annoying the hell out of her, but I knew her better than that. She might not be willing to admit it yet, but she was softening to him. I had a good feeling that it was only a matter of time before all was right in their marriage again.

"Whatever," I grumbled, stuffing a chicken salad finger sandwich into my mouth then speaking around it. "I don't love him."

"Love who?" Ms. Weatherby asked.

"Her new man," Tali sing-songed. "He's the older, handsomer, more responsible brother of her ex."

Ms. Weatherby's attention whipped around to me. "The one who put his hands on you?"

I sighed and nodded.

She studied me closely, her eyes so shrewd I felt like she could see right through me. "And he's a good man?"

Ah damn, she wasn't going to let this go. "Yes," I said quietly, staring down into my teacup. "He's incredible."

"So what's the problem then?"

I looked up at her and finally laid it all out. "His wife died only a few months after his son was born. It was the most tragic, heartbreaking story I'd ever heard, and I'm the first relationship he's been in since she passed."

"Oh, wow," Tali breathed, her eyes going wide. "I didn't know that."

"We were only supposed to be taking it a day at a time, no expectations. I wasn't"— I swallowed down the lump that had suddenly formed in my throat—"I wasn't supposed to fall in love with him."

"Well, whether you were supposed to or not, you did," Ms. Weatherby stated plainly. "No sense in fretting over it. Your heart's already decided what it wants, and I'll tell you, child, it'll win out every single time. All you can do is sit back, enjoy the ride, and hope you don't fall off."

Another pearl of wisdom from my brilliant neighbor.

Tali looked at her with big, mystified eyes. "Wow, Ms. W. I really hope I'm as cool and insightful as you when I'm your age."

One bushy white brow went up as she looked my sister up and down. "You wanna be like me, then stop stringin' that man of yours along and forgive him already. I've known you two hours, and I know that's what you're gonna do. Your sister knows it. Hell, everyone in town probably does. Just admit it to yourself already and begin workin' to heal that breach."

We both sat in stunned silence at her brilliant dressing down. Then Tali burst into laughter. "You're like a crotchety psychic. I think I want you to be my best friend."

Ms. W snorted and sipped her tea. "Darlin', you and everyone else I meet. Go ahead and get in line."

Chapter 25
Pierce

I BENT to greet Titan who was waiting just inside the door when I got home. It was nearly midnight, and I was so fucking exhausted I felt it down to my bones. The only saving grace was that it was Friday night, and I had the next two days off.

"Where's our girl, huh?" I asked, mindful to keep my voice low.

As if he understood exactly what I said, Titan trotted back toward the living room. The television was on, the volume low, casting shadows on Marin's sleeping face.

Leaning over the back of the couch, I brushed the hair off her forehead and whispered, "Hey, baby. Let's get you into bed, huh?"

Her eyelids fluttered briefly before opening to half-mast. She let out a sleepy yawn and stretched her arms over her head. "Pierce?"

"Yeah, sweetheart. Come on, let me help you upstairs."

"Wha time's it?" she murmured as I picked her up off the sofa and carried her to my room.

"Late."

She hummed and burrowed her face into my neck, letting out the cutest little snore. She was dead to the world again before I even made it up the stairs. She stirred briefly when I laid her on the bed and undid the button on her jeans so I could pull them off.

"I can do it," she mumbled sleepily.

"I got it, baby. Just go back to sleep." Once I was certain she'd be comfortable, I pulled the covers over her and pressed a kiss to her cheek. "I'm gonna check on Eli and lock everything up. I'll be right back."

"Mm-kay, honey." She snuggled deeper into the pillow, her eyes closed as she whispered, "Love you."

Everything in my body stopped. My lungs seized. My heart froze in my chest, becoming nothing more than a worthless lump, just taking up space. My muscles all locked up as I hovered over her now sleeping form.

Love you.

Love you.

Love you.

Maybe she's just talking in her sleep, I tried to rationalize. Anything to keep my epic freak-out at bay. *Maybe she's dreaming you're someone else, like her sister or something?*

But the truth had been staring me in the face for a

while now, and I'd taken to doing what my mom was so good at, what Frank excelled at: I buried my head in the sand and ignored the truth of what I saw in her expression every time she looked at me.

The woman's poker face was so bad, she might as well have had hearts coming out of her eyes.

I ignored it because I didn't want it to be true. I didn't want what we had to end just because she had gone further than I was willing to go. I didn't want what we had to end because, other than Eli, it was the first time in six years that I'd actually felt happiness. I hadn't felt like this in longer than I could remember.

That's because you're in love with her too, asshole.

I stumbled backward at the thought, something in my chest squeezing so tight that every huff, every quick, desperate breath, felt like a thousand cuts.

No, no, no, no, no. That wasn't supposed to happen. We were just enjoying each other, taking things a day at a time. There were no expectations, and there was absolutely *no* love.

She stirred in the bed and a wave of panic set me moving. Heading out of the room and down the hall, I pushed my son's door open and quietly made my way inside. He was sleeping peacefully, so peacefully that just watching him for a few minutes calmed that storm inside of me.

I wasn't sure how long I stood there, looking down at

my boy, at the most precious thing I'd ever have, but exhaustion finally won out, making my legs weak. I dragged myself back toward my bedroom, back toward the beauty sleeping in my bed.

Moving on autopilot, I stripped out of my suit and climbed in beside her. She rolled into me, without conscious thought, her body, like mine, already trained to seek out the other.

I wrapped her in my arms and held her tightly to me, knowing this might possibly be one of the last times I would have this with her.

Because when she found out I would never be able to return her love, that what I gave her now was absolutely all I had to give, there wasn't a doubt in my mind that she'd leave me.

And as much as that thought hurt, I'd accept it, because she deserved a man who could give her everything.

It just couldn't be me.

* * *

Marin

. . .

Bombshell

I woke with a start, the sunlight coming through the bedroom window shouldn't be there. It should have still been dark outside.

I shifted in the bed, feeling Pierce's arm around me like a steel band as I tried to turn and look at the clock beside the bed.

"Oh shit!" I hissed when I caught sight of the white digital numbers. "Pierce, wake up." I put my hand to his shoulder and gave him a hard shake. "We slept in."

He grumbled and muttered unintelligibly, so I gave him another shove. That woke him up. "What? What is it? What's wrong?"

"We forgot to set the alarm. We slept in, it's already a quarter past eight."

He shot up to sitting in the bed, his panicked eyes shooting toward the bedroom door. "Oh, fuck."

"We have to hurry," I blurted, jumping out of the bed. I wasn't sure how or when I'd gotten out of my jeans, but I found them on the bedroom floor and quickly started pulling them up my legs, jumping in place to get them up faster.

Thankfully I still had my shirt and bra from the day before on, because as soon as I got the button on my pants done, the door flew open, and I whipped around, looking like a deer caught in the headlights of a semi.

"Daddy! Can we have—?" Eli stopped, taking me in,

standing in the middle of his father's room first thing in the morning. His gaze bounced like a ping-pong ball between me and the bed where Pierce was still sitting, the covers pulled up over his waist. "Did you and Mar-Mar have a sleepover?"

He sounded upset, like he was heartbroken that he didn't get to be a part of it.

"No, sweetie," I started, grasping at straws for something to say.

Finally, Pierce spoke. "Kind of, bud. She was asleep when I got home last night. It was really late, and I didn't want her driving home when she was tired like that."

That seemed to be a good enough answer for him, because his feet came unglued and he skipped the rest of the way to the bed, throwing himself on top of the covers and cuddling up to his dad.

"You can have breakfast with us, Mar-Mar," he announced, the picture of seriousness. "I'll even share my Fruity Pebbles with you."

"Thanks, kiddo. Fruity Pebbles are my favorite."

"Mine too!" he declared, bouncing on his butt on the bed until he reached the edge. He threw himself off and came to me, taking my hand in his. "Come on. Let's have some now."

"Oh." I turned and looked back at Pierce to see he was climbing from the bed and pulling on a pair of sweats that had been on the floor by his feet. I wasn't sure if I was overstepping by still being here when Eli woke. I looked up, trying to read his face to see if this was okay, but it was nothing but a blank mask.

There hadn't been enough time since waking up in a fright for either of us to say anything to the other, but I suddenly got a strange, unsettling sinking feeling in the pit of my stomach, like I'd just eaten week-old pizza.

"Pierce?" I called out, forcing his gaze to meet mine.

"It's fine. You two go on down. I'll be there in a minute."

"Come on, Mar-Mar. Daddy doesn't like Fruity Pebbles. He eats gross Frosted Flakes." Eli pulled a face and stuck his tongue out. "They taste like cardboard."

"All right, Cool Guy," I said on a laugh, casting one last glance over my shoulder at Pierce, but he wasn't looking at me. He was standing at the side of the bed, one hand on his hip, the other reaching up to rub at the back of his neck. He looked tense, but I wasn't sure why, and as I headed down the stairs with Eli, I pushed the feeling in my stomach to the back of my mind, telling myself that everything was going to be just fine.

Just fine.

Chapter 26
Marin

Everything was *not* fine. Not at all.

Pierce had returned to his former icy self all through breakfast Saturday morning. He wouldn't meet my eyes over cereal. Any time I directed a question or statement to him, he'd give me short, one-word answers or simply grunt. It was déjà vu. I was getting serious flashbacks of the Pierce I'd known back when I was with Frank, and I didn't understand why.

Needing an escape from the constant frigid chill, I'd made an excuse and booked it home. I'd piddled around my apartment. When that became boring—which didn't take long—I visited Ms. Weatherby. However, that didn't last long. The damn insightful woman sensed something was off, and when she'd started asking questions, I lied and said I needed to get my laundry done and shot out of there like a bullet.

I'd called Tali, but she and Nick were in the middle of some sort of battle that consisted of him trying to woo her and her giving him the silent treatment. Figuring my brother-in-law didn't need any interruptions when it came to winning his wife back, I'd turned down her offer to meet for drinks at our local bar, The Tap Room.

I'd lost count of how many times I checked my phone, hoping for a text or missed call or *anything* from Pierce.

When dinner time rolled around, I finally got sick of waiting and decided to take action.

Me: *I hope you and Eli had a good day today. Miss you guys.*

I waited and waited for a reply. An hour passed, then another, and still nothing. I could see he read it, which meant he was avoiding me.

Through the ball of dread taking up residence in my stomach, I shot off another one.

Me: *Is everything all right? Something's happened. Tell me what it is.*

I'd racked my brain all day long, trying to figure out what could have caused the Pierce I'd had for the past few weeks to revert back to the Pierce I didn't all that much like.

Another hour passed before he replied. However, what he had to say certainly didn't help shed any light on the situation.

Pierce: *Everything's fine. Would it be possible for you* to watch Eli on Monday? Turns out I need to go into the office despite the holiday to catch up on some things. I'll need you here by 7:30. Let me know if that doesn't work so I can make other arrangements.*

Was he serious?

Me: *Of course I'll watch Eli. You know that. Does this mean you and I won't be having that talk on Monday?*

He didn't make me wait with that one . . . the jerk.

Pierce: *Marin, you know how busy I am right now. I don't have the time. We'll discuss that later.*

That dread gave way to a knot of anger that grew bigger and stronger through the rest of Saturday and all the way through Sunday when I didn't hear a word from him. I wanted to cry. I wanted to rage. I wanted to track him down and punch him in the face, then demand he tell me what the hell was going on. Then I wanted to punch him in the face again for good measure, just because he'd put me through the emotional wringer.

When Monday morning rolled around and I returned to Pierce's house for the first time in two days, I wasn't sure exactly what it was I was walking into, so I'd braced myself, deciding to go in with my guard up, and it turned out that was the smartest option, because as soon as I used the key he'd given me and let myself in, I was hit with an arctic blast so frigid it froze the air in my lungs.

He was already dressed in another immaculate suit, his jaw was clean shaven, and the blue in his eyes was once again a wall of ice. The only difference between this man and the hard as stone one from months ago were the shadows that were smudged beneath his eyes. It looked as though he hadn't been sleeping. Well, that made two of us.

"Pierce," I started as I stood just inside the entryway. I'd barely moved into the house and he already had his briefcase and keys in his hands, ready to escape. Crossing my arms over my chest, I stayed directly in front of the door with my feet braced shoulder width apart. If he wanted out, he was going to have to go right through me. "What the hell is going on? And don't tell me nothing, because that's a lie and we both know it."

Something passed through his gaze, giving him the impression of humanity, but instead of feeling relief that the man I'd fallen hard for was still in there, the sadness I saw etched into his expression made my stomach sink.

With a deep sigh, he dragged a hand through his hair, ruining the style he'd accomplished. "Look, I'm sorry, but can we talk about this later?"

I shouldn't have pushed, but I couldn't help myself. I couldn't go another minute, hell, another *second* without knowing. "You're ending this, aren't you?" The question came out in a ragged whisper, and I was sure my heartbreak was written all over my face. When he didn't say anything for several long seconds, I asked, "Did I—did I do something wrong?"

"No," he said with a tenderness that only made the

pain worse. "You didn't do anything. But we were just having fun. This thing between us, it's run its course, Marin. That's all."

"Bullshit," I snapped. If he was going to do this, I was going to demand the truth. I wasn't going to let him take the coward's way out. "You're lying. At least do me the courtesy of telling me the truth."

"I can't give you what you want," he replied, his tone ravaged. "I don't have it in me. You deserve a man who will love you and build a life with you. I did all of that already with Constance, and I can't do it again."

Ignoring the white-hot blade that sunk into my chest at his confirmation that he didn't love me, I demanded, "Can't or won't?"

That frigid chill returned. "Won't," he said with a lifted chin and squared shoulders. "I won't, because I don't feel it."

God, he was such a liar. I knew, with every single touch, every look he gave me, that he loved me just as much as I loved him. But I wasn't going to beg this man to admit the truth. I was worth more than that.

"We can discuss this further later, but for now, I really have to go."

It took an act of God, but I somehow managed to suck the tears I wanted to cry back up and let out a bark of caustic laughter. "Discuss it further," I repeated bitterly. "You know what, don't worry about discussing it further.

You've said everything there is to say." I stepped to the side, out of the way of the door. "I hope you have a productive day," I spit acidly.

He didn't move from his place for several beats. "This isn't—you aren't going to—That is, Eli won't—"

That fucking coward.

"I'm not abandoning Eli," I clipped. "That boy has my love and he knows it. I'll be there for him in any capacity he needs me."

Pierce nodded, dropping his eyes to the floor. "Thank you."

I didn't watch him leave. I simply moved into the living room, carefully shutting off the valve to the feelings swirling around inside of me so I could get through the day without breaking down.

Chapter 27
Marin

EDDIE VEDDER WAS CROONING through my Bluetooth speaker as I laid on my living room floor, staring up at the ceiling, with an empty box of wine beside me. I'd officially become *that* girl, drowning her sorrows in cheap wine and Pearl Jam. It had been three days since that jackass Pierced had danced a jig all over my heart, and to say I wasn't handling it well was putting it mildly.

I'd been there for Eli when he needed me, but I'd fallen so deep into my wallow that I'd done something that I'd never done before. Not only had I bailed on rehearsals the past two days, claiming to have come down with the stomach flu, but I'd also called in sick to my shift at Whiskey Dolls the other night.

That had instantly put the girls on red alert, so I'd been screening worried calls from them for the past couple days.

I knew I was running out of time, that my reprieve

would be coming to an end sooner or later, but until that time, I fully intended to nurse this broken heart and go full on emo.

Unfortunately, my time was cut shorter than I'd expected when someone began banging on my apartment door.

"Marin? I know you're in there," my big sister called thought the cheap wooden door. "Open up."

"Do you think she's really sick?" I heard another voice that sounded suspiciously like Mac ask.

A third voice answered. "Doubt it. Someone told me they saw her at Muffin Top just this morning, buying up two boxes worth of muffins."

That was true. I'd hit Dani up earlier that morning, filling her in on my sob story so she'd feel sorry for me and make me *all the muffins*. They were mine, and I wasn't sharing them with anyone.

"Go away," I called out pathetically. "I'm extremely contagious. You could all die if you come in here."

"Yeah?" Another voice called back. "What do you have?"

"Tuberculosis." I deadpanned, then made a half-hearted attempt to cough.

"That's it," I heard Tali grumble. "I'm going in. This is ridiculous."

A second later, I heard her key scrape in the lock and

silently cursed myself for giving her a spare in case of emergencies.

At Layla's, "Oh God. It's even worse than I thought," I tipped my head back, looking at my sister and the girls from the club as they moved, upside down, into my apartment.

"Hey guys. What's up?"

Alma curled her nose up in offense and pointed. "Is that boxed wine?"

"It was buy one get two free," I answered just as Eddie started *do do doing* through the speaker. "Hey!" I lifted my head just high enough to glare at Tali when she hit the power button and cut the speaker off. "That was my favorite part."

"Sorry, babe. But I'm not gonna let you ruin Pearl Jam's "Black" for me." The room filled with silence as she headed over to me. "What the hell is going on, Mar? I've never seen you like this before. Did you really buy a dozen muffins?"

I briefly glanced at the one bakery box I had left. It was a foot from my head and now only held six maple bacon muffins "Yes. And before you get any ideas, I've already licked the ones that are left, so hands off or you'll get my cooties."

Sloane bent to pick up one of the wine boxes and gave it a little shake. "Oh, hell. How many of these have you polished off already?"

"Just that one," I replied in a monotone voice. "And maybe half of another, but that's been over the past two days."

Layla looked at me with big, bewildered eyes. "How did the lining of your stomach not burn off after that?"

"The muffins soaked everything up." That wasn't quite true. I was feeling a little indigestion-y, but I wasn't about to admit the boxed wine was a huge mistake.

Tali's hand appeared in front of my face, her fingers wiggling as she ordered, "Come on, get off the floor already."

I let her help me up, letting out a dramatic groan as I moved into sitting position for the first time in at least six hours. *Man*, I was pathetic.

"Now tell me what's going on," my sister insisted. "You're a disaster." She took in my stained sweats and ratty hair. "When's the last time you washed your hair?"

I had to give that some thought. "What's today?"

"Oh God," Mac whispered.

"That's it. Start talking," Tali clipped. "You're freaking me out."

"There's nothing to be freaked out about," I muttered as I looked down at my ratty t-shirt, picking at a mysterious stain with my fingernail. "I'm fine."

"You're absolutely not," Layla chimed in. "And for your sake, I hope like hell that stain is chocolate."

"Is it cancer?" Alma asked, earning an elbow to the ribs, courtesy of Sloane. "Ow! Jeez! What was that for?"

Sloane gave her a hard look. "Cancer? Really?"

Alma shrugged. "Hey, it was a legitimate question. I mean, look at her." She waved her hand at me like the state I was in said it all.

"I don't have cancer," I said with a roll of my eyes. "I'm just . . . sad."

"If you went out in public this morning dressed like that, I'd say your more than just sad," Mac insisted.

Tali plopped down on the floor beside me and placed her hand over mine, staring at me with concern. "Did something happen between you and Pierce?"

I leaned forward and snatched a muffin from the box, biting off a huge chunk and spitting crumbs everywhere as I replied sarcastically, "You mean other than him basically telling me he doesn't love me and never will? Nope, nothing comes to mind."

Everyone seemed to pull in a collective breath at the same time, sucking the oxygen from the room.

"He really said that?" Tali asked, her face going hard in that protective big sister way she tended to get when it came to me.

"Not in so many words, but that was the gist of it. He ended things because he said he couldn't give me what I wanted, which, to him meant anything more than us just *having a little fun.*" I added finger quotes for good measure.

"That son of a bitch," Layla clipped. "I have half a mind to go over and punch him right in the nads."

I let out a sigh and leaned back against my couch. "Don't do that," I said softly. "It's not his fault, really. I mean, he was up front about what we were before we even started."

But even as I defended him, the words didn't sit right, leaving a vile taste in my mouth. I knew it hadn't all been in my head. How him touching me seemed almost compulsive, how I'd catch him looking at me with a warmth that stole my breath. I hadn't made that up. The things he said and how he was with me, it was all there, clear as day.

He was just too big of a coward to grab hold of something that could make him happy. However, even thinking that, I couldn't bring myself to say it out loud. I couldn't stand the thought of my friends, of my sister, looking at him in a negative light. As badly as he'd hurt me—and it was *bad*—he wasn't a bad guy, and I wanted people to know that. God. What the hell was wrong with me?

"I'm so sorry." Tali looped her arm around my shoulders and pulled me into her side. "I know it hurts now, but I promise, it'll get better."

My mask slipped then, and I lost hold of my tears. They came spilling out before I could stop them. "Are you sure?" I whispered brokenly, looking over at my big sister. "Because it sure as hell doesn't feel like it will ever get better."

Her eyes grew wide as she studied my expression. "You really did love him, didn't you?"

I couldn't bring myself to tell her that I'd never felt for another man what I felt for Pierce, that whenever he laughed or smiled, it made everything seem better. How, when he was inside me, I felt complete, like the one and only thing that had been missing from my life had finally snapped itself into place. I couldn't say any of that, because voicing the truth would give it even more power than it already had, so I simply nodded.

Her face fell in a mask of sympathy. "Oh honey."

"Why would anyone ever want to fall in love if it hurts this bad?" I asked on a sniffle. "I mean, this *really* sucks."

"That's it," Alma spoke, spinning on her heel and heading toward the door.

"Where are you going?" Mac called after her.

"To the store to get some *good* wine while one of you calls and orders pizza. Tonight we drink, eat a million calories, and binge watch *Yellowstone* so we can pretend that men like Rip exist in real life." She pointed her finger at me. "Then tomorrow, you're going to pull yourself up, shower, and start living again. Got it?"

I nodded, feeling the corner of my lips tremble with a suppressed smile. Alma wasn't the mama-bear type of our group. She was more the let's-party-and-have-the-time-of-our-lives one, so seeing her like this was more than just a little heartwarming. "Yes ma'am."

She nodded resolutely. "Good. And if you find yourself slipping again, you *do not* slip into a black hole of 90's grunge music and bad hygiene. You call your girls and we'll come over and do this again and again, as long as it takes for you to feel better."

Okay, so maybe—definitely—I was heartbroken, but I still had some incredible women at my back. Despite how I'd been feeling the past few days, I started to think that, maybe, with their help, I'd be okay.

Eventually.

Chapter 28
Pierce

GOD, I was a fucking idiot.

It had been two weeks since I ended things with Marin, and that black cloud, those shadows that had followed me every single day before she came into my life, had returned, blocking out the light I'd had shining down on me the past several weeks.

I'd made a huge fucking mistake. But the worst part was, I couldn't bring myself to do what I needed to do in order to make things right.

Having to see her almost every day, even for just the short blip of time it took her to get from my front door to her car, and not being able to touch her or hold her was a special kind of torment. The few times I'd gotten a glimpse at those tawny eyes what I saw in them felt like someone had punched a hole right through my chest. The light in them was gone, darkened by sadness, and it was all my fault. I'd done that to her. I'd snuffed out that light, and I hated myself for it.

That hate had put me in a foul mood that I'd been taking out on everyone around me. My assistant had gotten to the point where she turned and ran in the opposite direction whenever she saw me coming. Not that I blamed her. I'd been acting like a prick.

The intercom on my desk phone buzzed, pulling me from my self-inflicted misery. "Mr. Walton?"

That spike of irritation coursed through me once more as I hit the button. "Abigale, I told you, no interruptions."

Christ, I was going to really need to pull out the stops come Christmas and get her something amazing, like a week-long cruise, or she was liable to quit on me.

"I know sir," she said, her voice small and shaky. "I'm sorry, but there's someone here to see you. A Tali Allen? She doesn't have an appointment, but she was insistent that you'd want to talk to her. I'll send her away if—"

My back shot straight at the name. "No!" I spat out quickly. "No, that's all right. I'll go get her myself."

"Oh . . . okay."

I shot from my chair and bolted out of my office, stopping to back-peddle to my assistant's desk. She looked up at me with no small amount of trepidation. "Abigale, I'm sorry for how I've been treating you the past few days."

Her eyes went wide with surprise. "Oh . . . um, it-it's okay."

"No, it's not," I told her, feeling like a piece of shit. "I've been in a bad mood that's all my own fault, and I've been taking it out on you. I'll try and do better."

I waited for her nod before I turned back around and headed for the reception area. A woman I could only assume was Tali was standing a few feet from the desk, looking around the lobby when I stepped through the glass doors and called her name. She looked so much like her little sister, it wasn't funny, and I felt my breathing grow choppy as her eyes met mine

She turned around and gave me a slow, appraising once-over, the expression on her face telling me she wasn't all that impressed with what she saw. "Swanky digs you got here. You guys must bring in some serious cash."

I felt a grin tug at my lips. She had the same fire and attitude as her sister, and while it was cute on the woman standing before me, it was even more adorable on Marin. "If we're good at what we do." I stepped aside and held an arm out. "How about we go to one of the conference rooms for some privacy. Are you hungry? I could get my assistant to order in some food."

God, I was nervous. I couldn't remember the last time that happened to me. But this woman here held a whole hell of a lot of sway with Marin, and if I had any chance in hell of getting her to stop hating me, I knew I'd need Tali Allen in my corner.

Her blank expression gave absolutely nothing away as

she started toward me. "That's not necessary. I won't be here long."

She let me lead her deeper down the hall to an empty conference room, spinning around to pin me in place with an unhappy scowl as soon as I closed the door behind me.

"So," I started awkwardly. "How are you—"

"Cut the pleasantries bullshit. I'll make this quick. I had to Google Pierce Walton, attorney, and Richmond to locate you, and the stupid internet gave me *two* freaking posibilities. So I've already gone through this whole thing with a poor, unsuspecting guy who nearly called the cops on me before I found the real you, and I'm a little annoyed I have to repeat myself. That said, I'm not here to be friendly," she snapped. "I'm here to tell you you're a dumbass."

I let out a sigh, lifting an arm to rub at the back of my neck. "I know."

"I can't believe you'd—wait. What?"

I looked up, meeting her wide, bewildered eyes. "I said I know. I'm a dumbass."

She shook her head, and I got the sense that she'd been expecting this conversation to start off much differently and was trying to shift her plan of attack since I'd caught her off guard.

She threw her arms out at her sides. "Well, if you already know that, why the hell haven't you done something to fix it?"

"Tali, it's not that simple."

"Do you love her?"

The word yes was on the tip of my tongue, desperate to be put out into the world, but I just couldn't make myself say it. "There are things you don't understand—"

"You mean about your wife?" My chin jerked back in shock at her question, and a small amount of that hostility in her eyes and body drifted away. "Marin told me. She wasn't gossiping or anything like that, but she knew she was developing feelings for you, *real* feelings, and it scared her." As if she'd sensed herself softening, she squared her shoulders and lifted her chin up, all hard and protective once more. "The difference between you and her, though, is that she was at least brave enough to put herself out there, despite being scared."

Fuck me, but that hurt. "How . . ." I had to swallow past the sandpaper grit suddenly filling my throat. "How is she?"

She gave it to me honestly, no matter how hard the truth was. "Not good," she snapped. "She's shattered. Truth is, I've never seen her like this. She's been hurt in the past when relationships went bad, but this time is different. She's not just hurt. You managed to devastate her. So congratulations, I guess," she spat hatefully.

That aching hole in my chest felt like it was getting wider and wider by the second. "I never meant to hurt her, Tali. I swear. I just . . . I can't."

At the way she looked at me just then, I felt an intense wave of pity drifting off of her and slamming into me. "I can't imagine what you went through, losing your wife like that," she said quietly. "I'm so sorry, Pierce. But what you don't get is that you're one of the lucky few. There aren't many people that get a second chance at that kind of love again. You have that right now, but you're wasting it. Marin can't replace your wife, no one can, and she wouldn't ever try. But she *can* make you happy. That's all she wants."

I struggled to pull in a breath, my chest tightening to the point it didn't feel like there was any room for my lungs as she continued laying it out for me.

"I've never seen her like this because she's never loved anyone the way she loves you. She has the biggest heart of anyone I know. Her capacity to love, to shine that light that's all her own down on the people she cares about . . . it's an extraordinary thing to witness, and even more so for those of us lucky enough to experience it firsthand. There will come a day when a man enters her life who gets all of that from her and so much more. Whether or not that man is you is your choice, Pierce. And I really hope you don't miss your shot at a second chance at that kind of happiness." She shook her head in disappointment. "It would be such a shame."

With that parting shot, she skirted past me and through the conference room door, leaving me reeling.

Chapter 29
Marin

THE PAST TWO weeks had been a test of my strength and sanity, to be sure, but I was determined to persevere.

After the come-to-Jesus with my girls, I'd gone about my days the same as I had before Pierce had gone and made me fall in love with him. I woke up, I attended rehearsals, I spent time with Ms. Weatherby and my family, hell, I even managed to feel genuine happiness when Tali informed me that she'd finally decided to give Nick a chance. They were taking things slowly for now and seeing a marriage counselor to help them talk through their issues. My heart might have been broken, but that didn't mean I couldn't feel happy for my sister.

I picked Eli up from school and soaked up every ounce of light he had during our hours together. Now that Pierce's trial was over, there were no more late nights, so as soon as I heard his car pull into the driveway, I'd have my purse in hand, and the moment he came through the door, I got the hell out of there without saying a word to him.

I performed at the club, faking a bright, cheery persona in front of the girls so they wouldn't worry even more than they already were. Now that I knew just how much I'd been giving away, I'd worked tirelessly to build a mask that I could wear in public, and I made *damn* sure that thing didn't budge.

I had a foolproof plan. If someone did happen to catch a glimpse behind the mask, I'd just avoid their questions all together. Okay, so maybe it wasn't foolproof, but it was what it was. If I could just keep pretending like my heart hadn't been ripped to shreds, then maybe I'd actually start believing it.

"Mar-Mar?" Eli called my name, pulling me from the melancholy that had been following me around like a black cloud for the past two weeks.

After I picked him up from school, I'd decided ice cream and the park were in order before I took him home. The vanilla cone I'd ordered had begun to drip down my hand, so I tossed it in the trashcan as we passed it during our loop of the park. After my muffin and wine binge, I hadn't had much of an appetite lately, and I was starting to worry that I'd done some serious damage to my stomach with that cheap, acidic alcohol.

I looked down at the little boy beside me, feeling my chest swell with love. He held my hand in his free one as he licked at his chocolate cone, getting more ice cream on his face than in his mouth.

"Yeah, kid?"

"I think my daddy's sad."

Oh God. My heart would not beat out of my chest. I wouldn't allow it.

"What makes you say that, sweetheart?"

He stared down the path, a little boy deep in thought. "He doesn't smile like he used to," he stated, proving once again that kids were so much more perceptive than adults gave them credit for. "And he doesn't joke around as much. He tries to pretend with me, but even his smiles seem sad."

How the hell was I supposed to navigate this situation? I didn't know what to say. "You know what, kiddo? Your dad is tough. If he's sad right now, there isn't a doubt in my mind that it won't last. He just needs to work through it, then he'll be back to normal."

He looked up at me with those eyes that were so much like his father's it wasn't even funny. Just seeing them sent a pang through my chest. Every. Single. Time. "You really think so?"

"Absolutely," I assured him. "On top of having the coolest dad, you also have the strongest one. So you don't need to worry, okay? He'll be just fine."

God I hoped like hell I hadn't just lied to my sweet Eli.

I distracted him from his worry by racing him over to the swings and making a bet with him on who could swing higher. We killed the rest of the afternoon at the park. My hope was to get Eli back after Pierce was already home so I could just drop him off and be on my way.

I'd just finished buckling him into his booster seat when I noticed *her*. Suzette Walton, Pierce and Frank's mother, was coming out of one of the shops across the square. She'd seen me before I saw her, and her eyes spit venom as she looked from me to Eli in the backseat of my car.

I raised my hand in a small wave and attempted a smile, but was frozen in place by the look of pure hatred on her face. Before I could move, she whipped around and stomped down the sidewalk toward her car, and I knew with absolute certainty that the shit was about to hit the fan.

I would have raced back to Pierce's house, blowing the speed limit out of the water, had I not had to be mindful of Eli's safety. His car was the only one in the driveway when I pulled up, but I had a gut feeling it was only a matter of time before Hurricane Suzette came rolling in.

Eli beat me into the house, running straight to his father who was standing at the kitchen island with a glass of what I assumed was scotch sitting on the marble countertop in front of him.

He looked completely wrecked. His hair was in disarray like he'd been running his fingers through it all day long. He was still in his suit, but at some point, he'd ditched the tie and jacket. His sleeves were rolled up, and the shirt looked more wrinkled than he usually allowed them to get. Those circles were still beneath his eyes, and they'd been getting darker and darker with each passing day.

"Daddy!" Eli crowed, plowing into his dad's legs for a hug. "Guess what!"

Pierce looked down at his son with love and adoration that would have melted the wall of ice I'd put up around my heart if I let it, but I refused to.

"What, buddy?"

"Mar-Mar took me to get ice cream, then we went to the park to see who could swing highest on the swings! And I won!"

"That's great!" He smiled at his boy, but I could see the sadness Eli had told me about. I forced that to the back of my head and looked to Eli. "Why don't you go put your backpack in your room and color a bit, yeah? I need to talk to your dad."

"Okay." He started toward the front of the house, stopping just long enough to give me a big squeeze. "Love you, Mar-Mar."

That lump in my throat that I'd been battling for the past couple weeks made a sudden reappearance. "Love you too, Cool Guy. I'll see you tomorrow."

He took off like a bat out of hell, running up the stairs and into his room with Titan on his heels.

I pulled in a fortifying breath before turning back to Pierce, and what I saw in his gaze nearly struck me mute. The longing in those clear blues was so obvious you couldn't miss it or possibly mistake it for anything else.

"Hi," he said in a low, husky voice. "Thanks for doing that with him today. I bet he had a blast."

"He did. But we need to talk."

He blew out a sigh and rubbed at his jaw that was covered in a few days' worth of stubble. "You're right. Marin, I—"

I wasn't sure what he thought we needed to talk about, but I *was* certain it wasn't something I could handle. At least not right now. "We have a problem."

At my blunt statement, his back shot straight and concern carved into his features. "What's wrong? Is it Eli?"

"No, nothing like that. When we were leaving the park, I saw your mother. Or more correctly, she saw me . . . with Eli. And she did *not* look happy."

"Fuck," he hissed, his shoulders slumping like the weight of holding them up was just too much.

"Yeah. And from what I saw on her face, I don't think you have much time before she gets here."

As if Satan himself had summoned her, the doorbell rang through the house, the normally melodic chime suddenly seeming like an ominous gong.

Pierce lifted his glass to his lips and threw back the entire thing in one gulp before wiping his mouth with the back of his hand. "Might as well get this shit over with."

"What do you want me to do?" I asked, my eyes darting toward the back door.

"You *are not* sneaking out," he grunted with a frown. "You have every right to be here. You're one of Eli's people, whether she likes that or not. Let's go."

Without giving me a chance to object, he started toward the front door just as the person on the other side began to pound on it. I stayed a few paces back as he whipped it open, the picture of calm as he greeted the woman on the other side.

"Mom, this is a pleasant surprise," he said in a deadpan voice. "What brings you by?"

Dun, dun, dun.

* * *

Pierce

The past couple weeks had been absolute misery. I couldn't eat. I couldn't sleep. My sheets still smelled like Marin, like sugar and flowers, and I couldn't bring myself to wash them or strip them off the bed.

It was a self-imposed punishment. I'd made the huge fucking mistake of throwing Marin away, and having to smell her every night, having that fragrance surround me, was my penance for screwing up one of the best things I'd ever had.

I'd been racking my brain the past few days, trying to think of ways to make it right and summon up the courage to actually do it, but every time I started, fear would clutch my chest in its icy grip, refusing to let me go.

What if I gave my heart to her completely and something happened? What if I lost her too? I couldn't possibly survive another heartbreak like the one I'd had with Constance. But I also didn't know how to live any longer without the light Marin brought into my life, and that talk with her sister earlier that day only made that more obvious.

Any attempt I'd made at talking to her the past two weeks had been shut down in an instant. She wanted nothing to do with me; she made that clear every time she walked out of my house, brushing past me without so much as acknowledging me.

I couldn't get a word in edgewise with her, not that I was putting my all into trying. That was on me. Just another example of my complete and total cowardice. I'd let her go without a fight, and I continued to do it again and again every single day, every time I let her walk away from me. But Tali had helped to pull my head out of my ass, and I knew it was time to act, really and truly act.

When she came in earlier and said we needed to talk, I

felt a niggling of hope bloom in my chest. This was my chance. Then she squashed that hope with what she said next.

Now I was standing in the doorway of my house with my mother on one side and the woman who held my heart in her delicate hand on the other.

This was the last goddamn thing I wanted to deal with.

"You know exactly what brings me by," my mother declared acerbically. Her focus shifted over my shoulder and her face pinched with so much anger and hatred it took me aback. "What I want to know is what in the hell is *she* doing here," she spat, jabbing her finger toward Marin. "And what in the world is she doing carting my grandson around town like it's her right?"

"*She* is here because it *is* her right," I stated in a flat, cold voice. "And she's carting *my son* around because, one" —I lifted my index finger in the air— "she's his babysitter. And two"—my middle finger joined the first— "because Eli loves her and enjoys spending time with her."

I felt Marin edge closer to me, and when she spoke, her tone was soft and soothing, attempting to ease the situation. "Suzette, would you like to come in for a cup of coffee? We can sit and talk about this like—"

"Don't you dare invite me into my own son's home like it's your place!" my mother barked. "You have some nerve, young lady, moving on to my other boy after what you did to my poor Frank."

What she did the Frank? What the hell was she talking about? Before I had a chance to ask, my mom's narrow-eyed gaze returned to me. "And as for you. I'm absolutely ashamed. Where's your family loyalty, huh?"

"My loyalty lies with that little boy upstairs right now," I gritted out. "That's the *only* place my loyalty lies. Frank's a fuckup. He's a piece of shit, and you've allowed him to remain that way. He thinks the world owes him something simply because he exists. Newsflash, Mom, the world doesn't owe him shit. I've got no loyalty for someone who's done nothing to earn it."

She jerked back, placing her hand on her chest in affront. "Do you even know what she did to him?" She seethed. "Your brother will walk with a limp for the rest of his life because of her!"

"Okay, that's enough," Marin said just then. "It's obvious you're geared up to do this, so let's do it. But we're moving this outside, because I'm not going to allow Eli to overhear what I have to say."

Marin shoved past me, a ball of fury and indignation.

Chapter 30
Pierce

She didn't give either of us a chance to speak as she stormed onto the front porch. My mother and I had no choice but to follow, and by the time we did, it was clear Marin was geared up for a fight. Her hands were on her hips. One was cocked, and she was tapping her foot in agitation.

"Who do you think you are, bossing me around like—?"

"Shut it," Marin snapped so sharply my mom went silent. "What happened to Frank was his own goddamn fault," Marin hissed. "He earned that shattered knee because of what he'd done to me."

"He got a little carried away," Mom defended like she always did, but I couldn't even be annoyed by that because what they were saying was starting to seep through my skin, turning the blood in my veins to sludge.

"He made a mistake and he took things too far, but he

didn't mean anything by it," my mother insisted, her voice sounding like it was coming from the end of a long, dark tunnel.

Marin reared back. "Are you kidding me? Suzette, your son beat the hell out of me because I told him I was leaving him!"

"He made a mistake!" my mother cried.

"He hit you?" My voice came out in a growl so ferocious the two women on the porch jerked their attention to me.

Seeing the rage simmering beneath the surface, Marin's face wiped clean of all her anger. In its place was worry. "Pierce—"

"Frank *hit you*?" I repeated, barely hearing my own voice over the blood rushing through my ears.

"He was just upset," my mother started, but swallowed the rest of her pathetic excuse when I cut my eyes to her.

"There is *never* a reason for a man to put his hands on a woman. Not. Fucking. *Ever*. There is no excuse, and the fact that you would stand here and attempt to make one for him blows my fucking mind."

"Pierce, sweetie—"

"Get off my porch."

She staggered back at the impact of my words. "What?"

"You heard me. I want you off my porch and off my property. Your relationship with Frank is toxic, and I'm done sitting back and watching it. The fact that you'd not only excuse him taking his hands to a woman, but place blame on the woman he hit?" I shook my head, completely dumbfounded. "That makes me sick to my fucking stomach. I don't want that shit near me, and I *definitely* don't want it around my son. I'm busting my ass to make sure I raise my boy right, and it's clear you and I don't share the same opinions on what that means, so until you get your head out of your ass and see what a monster Frank really is, I'm done."

She attempted to lift her chin in indignation, but the tremble in it gave her away. "I hope, for your sake, when you call me to apologize I'm in the mood to be forgiving."

I let out a bark of laughter that sliced through the air like a knife. "Don't count on that happening, Mom. You'll be sorely disappointed."

I watched in silence as she stormed down the front steps to her car. It was only once her taillights disappeared that I felt calm enough to turn around and face Marin again. The storm was still raging inside of me, but I had a lock on it, at least for now.

"How often?" I demanded.

"Pierce, listen—"

"How often did that fucking piece of shit hit you, Marin?" I clipped. "Was it just that once?"

The way she curled her lips between her teeth was all the answer I needed.

I didn't realize I was moving until her voice slashed through the air. "Pierce! Where are you going?"

I didn't stop. I still had my keys in my pocket, and I was in my car, peeling out of the driveway before my brain engaged with what I was doing.

I was moving on autopilot, not registering the drive through town until I was pulling up in front of Frank's house.

I barely had the car stopped before I was out and storming up his front walk, my fist pounding on his door so hard it was a wonder I didn't crack the wood.

"Dude, what the fuck?" Frank barked as he whipped the door open. As soon as he saw it was me, he narrowed his eyes into hateful slits. "What the hell do you want, asshole? You here to tell me again I need to grow up and get my shit together? Is that it? Well you'll be happy to know the bitch was never really pregnant. Just wanted to trap me."

I didn't register a single word he said over the blood rushing through my ears. Placing my hand in the center of his chest, I shoved so hard he went stumbling backward, the backs of his legs slamming into the coffee table. I moved inside, shutting the door behind me.

"Motherfucker," I seethed. "You *hit* her?"

Frank puffed his chest up, trying to look big and bad. "What the hell are you talkin' about?"

"Marin," I growled. "You put your fucking hands on her?"

"Is that what that bitch is sayin'?"

"Yes or no, Frank. Answer the question. Did you put your goddamn hands on her?"

"It's not that big a deal!" he shouted. "Besides, what her cunt friend did to my knee is worse than anything I ever did."

I was seeing red. There was a beast under my skin clawing to get out, and like the dumb fuck he was, Frank didn't notice.

"What do you care anyway? You barely even know her." His eyes turned shrewd and a twisted grin pulled at his lips. "Wait. Are you fuckin' her now?" He let out a brittle laugh. "Man, that's classic! How do you like my sloppy seconds, big brother? I wrecked that snatch before you even had a chance—"

His words cut off of a garbled shout of pain when I plowed my fist right into his face.

"Jesus Christ!" he bellowed, cupping his hands to his nose as a guiser of blood spurted out. "You broke my fuckin' nose."

I was too far gone to care. I hit him again. And again. And again. My knuckles split and I couldn't tell what was his blood and what was mine.

He was on the ground, my fist in the collar of his dingy shirt so I could hold him up as I continued to pummel his face into pulp. By the time I was finished, I was breathing like I'd just run a marathon, like a dragon ready to spit fire and burn the entire fucking world down.

"You will never go near her again. Do you understand me?" He made a pathetic noise, choking on his own blood. I gave him a violent shake. "Confirm you get me, asshole!"

"I get you!" he rasped.

"If I ever find out you so much as *looked* in her direction, I'll end you. Fuck blood. Fuck being brothers. I will. End. You. Tell me you understand."

"I understand!"

Dropping him to the floor, I wiped my fist on the front of his shirt and stomped out of his house while he writhed on the floor in pain. Not that I gave a single shit.

* * *

Marin

It had taken everything I had not to lose my grip on the panic attack that was clawing at my chest, desperate to get out as I waited anxiously for Pierce to return from wherever the hell he'd gone.

By some miracle, Eli hadn't heard the exchange between me, his dad, and his grandmother, and when he came downstairs after Pierce had taken off, he was none the wiser.

"Where'd Daddy go?" he asked, hopping up on the barstool across from where I'd been pacing in the kitchen.

I don't have any clue, I thought. But instead of letting him see I was freaking the hell out, I smiled and lied. "He had to run a quick errand. He'll be right back." *I hope.*

It was getting late, so I made Eli a sandwich for dinner with a handful of his favorite chips on the side. He ate in front of the television while I resumed my pacing and dialed Pierce's cellphone number every five seconds.

All of the calls went to voicemail, but that didn't matter, because five minutes later the front door swung open and Pierce came walking through.

I started in his direction, feeling my eyes go wide the closer I got. "Holy shit," I hissed, keeping my voice down so Eli wouldn't hear. "Pierce, you're covered in blood!"

He looked down, seemingly in a daze, like he hadn't noticed until just then that his button-down was completely ruined.

"It's not mine."

Well that certainly didn't make me feel any better.

"Jesus Christ. Get upstairs," I ordered. "Change out of that before your son sees and freaks the hell out."

He did as I commanded, and I went back into the living room to make sure everything was good. Eli had finished his sandwich, so I hustled him into the shower before going to check on his father.

I made sure the shower was running before I inched Pierce's bedroom door open. He was standing in the middle of the space, wearing nothing but his slacks, holding the shirt in his hands like he was inspecting it closely.

"Whose blood is that?" I asked as I closed the door behind me.

"Frank's."

"Oh my God. Have you lost your mind?" I screeched. I stormed over to him and snatched the soiled shirt from his grasp, then I headed into the bathroom and stuffed it in the wastebasket. There wasn't a drycleaner on the planet talented enough to get that shirt clean again. "What the hell were you thinking?" I snapped as I stomped back into the bedroom.

"He had to pay," he grunted, a look in his eyes I'd never seen before.

I drilled my finger into his chest. "Maybe so, but it's not your place to dole out his punishment."

"It absolutely fucking is," he grated, the ice completely gone from his eyes as fire flashed so bright it melted everything.

"No. It's not," I barked. "I don't know what kind of savior complex you have going on, but I don't need rescuing. What happened with Frank was over and done with a long time ago. I've moved on with my life. I don't need you swooping in to avenge me, or whatever the hell you're doing. You and I are nothing. You saw to that."

He grabbed my wrist before I could pull my hand back, placing my palm flat on his chest, directly over his heart. I could feel it beating wildly beneath his breast and pulled in a stuttered breath.

"You're mine, Marin."

Oh no. No way in hell. I couldn't do this. "I'm not," I whispered, feeling that burn behind my eyes.

His voice changed all of a sudden, dropping low and going so tender I lost my battle with my tears. "You are, baby." I slammed my eyes closed, feeling them leak out and spill down my cheeks. I lowered my head and gave it a shake. "Yes. You are," he continued, his gentle voice battering at my defenses. I felt his fingers beneath my chin as he pressed my face back up to meet his. What I saw in his eyes when I looked up at him stole my breath. "You're mine, Marin. But more importantly, I'm yours."

"Don't say it if you don't mean it," I said in a barely-there whisper.

"I mean it, sweetheart. I love you. I'm *in* love with you. I have been for a long time now."

"Pierce—"

"I hate that I hurt you, but you have my word, I'll never do it again."

This couldn't be real. I had to be dreaming, because this was too good to be true. "But you said—"

"I lied. You knew it all along. So did I, but I was scared. I lost something I cherished once already, and I've been terrified that if I let myself love someone like that again, I could lose her too. I told myself I couldn't love you because I wouldn't be able to survive losing you. But it doesn't matter, because I love you anyway. Lying to you and myself is never going to change that, so I'm done fighting it."

I pulled at my hand, trying to break his hold on me. "Stop it."

"I want you, Marin. I want everything. I want to wake up with you every morning and go to bed beside you every night." He took my face in his hands, leaning in so close his lips brushed against mine as he spoke. "I want you to keep loving my son with all your heart and giving him something I thought he'd never have. And I want you to keep loving me, because I'm so crazy, stupidly, insanely in love with you, I can't breathe if you aren't near me."

He closed the last miniscule bit of space and kissed me. "Say you forgive me, baby, because I'm done living without you."

"Is this for real?" I croaked, my heart lodged in my throat. It couldn't be. I couldn't believe it was possible that I'd melted the Ice King.

"Nothing will ever be more real than this. Let me have you forever, Marin."

I wasn't sure there had ever been a more moving, more romantic declaration of love. I was pretty sure Pierce just took first place in that. "O-okay."

His lips smiled against mine. "Really?"

"Yeah. Really." My forehead puckered into a frown. "But if you ever hurt me like that again—" I started to warn, but he cut me off.

"Never again, baby. I swear. Tell me you love me. Please."

God, this man. "I love you so much, Pierce. You have no idea."

He laughed and kissed me again. Over and over. Speaking through kisses. "I think I might have some idea. After all, you've got the shittiest poker face on the planet."

I pulled back in an attempt to scowl up and him, but he wasn't having any of that. His lips were on mine again when the bedroom door came flying open. Eli stood there in his little man pajamas, looking up at us with his face twisted in disgust.

"Eww! Are you guys kissin'?"

I leaned into Pierce and giggled into his chest as he rounded me with his arms. "Yeah, buddy. That's what two grownups do when they love each other."

He gave that a think, his little brow furrowing and making him look even more like his father. "If you guys are kissin' and you love each other, does that mean Mar-Mar can be my mommy down here on earth?"

I honestly wasn't sure how much more my heart could take at this point. Breaking away from Pierce, I moved toward the little boy who owned my heart so completely, I knew I'd never get it back. And I was totally fine with that. As far as I was concerned, the Walton men could keep it forever.

I crouched down in front of him and took his hands in mine. "I'll be whatever you want me to be, Eli, Eli, the coolest guy. It doesn't matter what you call me, because I'll always be your Mar-Mar. You will always have me. Does that work for you?"

He scrunched his little lips to the side in thought, then eventually shrugged. "Yeah, that works."

Three little words, and suddenly everything in my world was right.

I might not have been looking for love when I met Pierce, and he certainly hadn't wanted it, but it found us anyway. As Ms. Weatherby said, the heart always gets what it wants.

I was just lucky that mine wanted someone so amazing.

Epilogue
Pierce

THIS WAS SO STUPID. I couldn't believe I'd let her talk me into this.

I felt the eyes of every single person in the room staring at us, waiting with bated breath. Waiting to see if we were going to fail or succeed.

Christ, even Tali and Nick had gotten in on the action. They were currently at the station beside ours, looking way too damn smug. *Bastards.* Sure, yes, I was thrilled they'd worked their shit out and were now happier than ever, but did they really need to come here every week just to rub mine and Marin's faces in our lack of skill?

When Marin had suggested we sign up for a couple's cooking class a few weeks ago, I'd initially felt my balls shrivel up inside my body at the thought of it. But she'd just looked so damn adorable, all sure of herself and excited to share something like this with each other, that I couldn't say no.

I'd regretted it from the very first class. But we were in this now. No backing out . . . unless of course, the instructor kicked us out of this one too.

Ignoring the curious looks from everyone else, I turned to Marin. She was anxiously chewing on her bottom lip, gnawing away like crazy as she stared at the stove, waiting for the timer to ding.

Leaning over, I whispered in her ear. "You know what they say. A watched oven never dings."

She turned to me and glowered. "That's not the saying, dummy. It's a watched pot never boils. That damn oven is going to ding no matter what. I'm just worried what's going to come out of it when it does."

Before I could reassure her that it didn't matter, that I'd love her anyway, the sound of the timer going off at the station beside ours caught our attention.

As a couple, Tali and Nick pulled the oven door open and slid out a perfectly roasted chicken.

But seriously, what kind of cooking instructor had their students doing a roasted fucking chicken on week three? It was like she *wanted* us to fail.

"Look, baby!" Tali said much louder than necessary, shooting a snide look toward her sister. "We cooked it perfectly!"

"You know what you can do, Tali?" Marin started, her

tone one I recognized all too well, a tone that meant I was going to need to hold her back or hit up an ATM for bail money. "You and Nick can take your perfect chicken, grease it up nice and good, and shove it right up—"

"All right." I grabbed her by the arm and pulled her back against me, slapping a hand over her mouth so she couldn't finish. "You're letting them get in your head, baby. What did we talk about, huh?" I spun her around to face me, placing my hands on her shoulders and crouching so we were eye to eye. "Keep cool. Keep calm. And whatever happens, happens."

She closed her eyes and steadied her breathing. "You're right. It doesn't matter. Even if that chicken is a block of charcoal when it comes out of that oven."

"Exactly."

"But I *really* want to win this."

"It doesn't matter—wait, what? Win what?" She smiled sheepishly, giving me those freaking doe eyes she knew I couldn't resist. "Marin," I said in warning, "what did you do?"

"Nothing major."

"Why don't I believe you?"

"Hey, Mar?" Tali called. "Don't worry about bringing your own cleaning supplies. You can use ours."

I turned back to my woman with an arched brow. "Cleaning supplies?"

She let out a huff before speaking in rapid fire. "If we

screw this chicken up, we have to clean Matt's bathroom every Sunday for the next two months."

I stumbled back, bracing on the counter to keep from falling to my ass. I'd been over to Tali and Nick's house plenty of times now, so I knew for a fact that their son Matt's bathroom was literally a hell pit.

"Why would you do that?" I cried. "You put way too much faith in us!"

"I know! I just get so excited when I'm watching those cooking shows, and I think, if they can do it, then I can too, right? I mean, they make it look so easy it gives me a false sense of confidence! It's all *Food Network's* fault!"

The timer on our oven dinged just then and we both turned to look at it like we were waiting for Satan himself to climb out.

"Well, I guess it's now or never," she mumbled before looking back at me. "No matter what happens, just know I love you."

I glared at her. "You're just saying that because you don't want me to stick you with that bathroom all by yourself."

"This is partially true. But I *do* love you."

I sighed in exasperation. "I love you too."

"Oh for the love of all that's holy!" our cooking instructor, a normally congenial woman named Nancy, yelled. "Just take the damn bird out of the oven before you burn my classroom down!"

Bombshell

I slid the oven mitts on my hands and bent down next to Marin as she pulled the oven door open.

I held my breath as I carefully pulled the roasting pan out. The chicken *looked* good, but that didn't necessarily mean anything.

I sat it on the worktop cautiously, and Marin and I took a step back so Nancy could come over and shove the meat thermometer in the bird's ass—or wherever you were supposed to put a meat thermometer.

A hush fell over the room, so quiet you could hear a pin drop. Then, "It's at the perfect temperature!" Nancy announced, and the whole class started cheering.

"Yes! I did it!" Marin yelled, throwing her hands in the air. "I did it! Suck on that, Tali! Your son's bathroom can stay a pit until the end of time!"

"Babe, I think you mean *we* did it."

"Yeah, of course. That was implied, wasn't it?"

Christ, just when I thought I couldn't love this woman any more, she went and proved me wrong.

"You know how I think we should celebrate?" I asked, looping my arms around her waist and pulling her into me. I burrowed my face in her neck, inhaling her fragrance before pressing a kiss to her lips.

"H-how?" she asked as she melted into me.

Pulling back, I looked down at her, smiling bigger and brighter than I had in years before she'd come into my life.

That was just the effect she had on me. She made life better.

"By packing up your apartment and moving you in with me and Eli."

She beamed back up at me. "It just so happens, I bet Tali that if we pulled this meal off, she and Nick had to come over and box up my entire apartment by themselves."

"Ah," I chuckled. "So you already knew I was going to suggest it."

She snorted loudly. "Of course I did. I'm a very smart woman."

"Yes you are. I love you."

Her arms banded around my neck, her fingers sliding into the hair at the nape of my neck. "Good, because you're stuck with me forever."

"Promise?"

I wasn't sure I'd ever seen a more beautiful smile than the one my bombshell gave me day after day. "Absolutely."

The End.

Thank you so much for reading!
Keep reading for a sneak peek at ***Wrong Side of the Tracks***

Enjoy an Excerpt from Wrong Side of the Tracks

Wondering where the idea for Whiskey Dolls came from? After writing **WRONG SIDE OF THE TRACKS**, I couldn't help but wonder . . . where are they now?

Keep reading for a peek at the book that started it all.

Enjoy an Excerpt from Wrong Side of the Tracks

PROLOGUE

Gypsy

Those stunning hazel eyes stared down at me, the intensity in them penetrating the shield I kept around my heart at the same time his perfect cock stroked that place deep inside me.

It was like pouring gasoline on a fire.

Dangerous.

Explosive.

So. Incredibly. *Hot*.

The power behind his thrusts was scrambling my brain and making it impossible to think. All I could do was feel as he drove in and out with the perfect rhythm.

"*Marco*," I moaned, throwing my head back as my body strung tighter and my nails dug into his back. *God*, it had never been like this.

So good. So sweet.

It was perfect.

He was perfect.

"That's it, *girasol*." The rich, husky cadence of his voice forced my eyelids open. The greenish brown of his eyes was nearly swallowed by lustful black. "Give it to me. Let me hear how much you love what I'm doing to you."

I was about to. I could feel my release growing, building into something so powerful it scared me.

Enjoy an Excerpt from Wrong Side of the Tracks

I let out one last whimper as Marco slammed in deep, grinding against my clit. That was all it took. My mouth fell open and—

The shrill buzz of my alarm clock sounded and I shot up, panting and gasping for air. A clammy sweat coated the goose bumps that covered my skin, and it took several seconds for me to get my bearings and realize it was just a dream.

"Shit," I whispered, flopping back on my mattress as I tried to calm my frantic heart and shallow breathing. That was the third sex dream I'd had about the undeniably sexy Marco Castillo, and each one was more detailed and vivid than the last.

All it took was one word. One *freaking* word and a sultry look at my friend Nona's backyard barbecue a few weeks ago, and I was done for.

On the few occasions I allowed myself to daydream, to *hope*, I could still feel that look from him like a physical touch. I could hear him calling me *"girasol"* in that smoky voice, and it never failed to elicit a shiver from me when I thought about the smooth way his tongue rolled on that *r*.

But it wasn't just the word said in that beautiful accent that turned me into an achy, needy puddle of desire. It was the meaning behind it. I'd looked it up about a million times. Partly because I was hoping the more I saw it, the more desensitized I'd become, but mainly because I loved the way it made me feel. As ridiculous as it sounded,

Enjoy an Excerpt from Wrong Side of the Tracks

having him call me "sunflower" as opposed to "babe" or "sweetheart" or something equally innocuous made it seem like I was... special.

See? Ridiculous!

"Shit," I repeated, then again with more passion as I kicked at the mess of tangled covers around my legs. "Shit, shit, *shit*."

This was bad. So, *so* bad.

I couldn't afford to let myself get hung up on Marco Castillo. A man like him wasn't for the likes of me. And as much as I didn't want it to, that realization depressed me. My life was all drama and baggage and constant headaches.

And speaking of my life....

The slam of a door sounded through the paper-thin walls, quickly followed by a loud pounding and my sister Sunshine shouting, "Rhodes, get outta the bathroom! I need to do my makeup!"

"No way in hell!" he yelled in return. "You'll hog it all damn mornin'!"

As the two teenagers in the house, fifteen and seventeen respectively, both kids were infamous bathroom hogs.

Lifting my arms, I pressed the heels of my palms into my forehead, hoping to stave off the inevitable headache. I knew what was coming next. It was the same thing every freaking morning.

Like clockwork, the Sunny and Rhodes shouting

Enjoy an Excerpt from Wrong Side of the Tracks

match was quickly followed by a sharp squall from my youngest brother, two-year-old Raleigh.

After that, it was full-blown chaos.

My bedroom door crashed open, and my six-year-old sister Holiday stood in the doorway, rubbing the sleep from her eyes and pulling off an unhappy glare at the same time.

"Morning, doodlebug," I offered with a smile at my adorable little sister.

"Rhodes and Sunny woke the baby again," she grumbled, moving into the room and climbing into my bed.

Seeing as there wasn't nearly enough room in our house, Holly was forced to bunk with Raleigh and Sunny, while Rhodes and my nine-year-old brother Raylan shared another room. So when Raleigh woke, Holly woke. And my baby sis was *not* a morning person.

"You got a few more minutes, honey," I said softly, reaching up to brush her thick, shiny blonde hair from her face. "Rest your eyes, and I'll come get you in a bit."

And just like that, she was out like a light again.

Heading out of my room, I crossed the narrow hallway into Holly and Raleigh's, moving to the crib to pick up my screaming brother.

"Hey, punk," I cooed, propping him on my hip and brushing the tears from his chubby pink cheeks. "What's all that noise about, huh?"

Wrapping his arms around my neck, he burrowed his

Enjoy an Excerpt from Wrong Side of the Tracks

face against my shoulder and rubbed it there, still half asleep.

"That's it, punkin," I whispered as his cries turned to whimpers, then stuttered breaths. A second later, he was my calm, sweet baby once again.

"Gypsy!" Raylan yelled. His tone was laced with an anger I understood the moment he added, "Rhodes ate all the Cocoa Pebbles again!" To say my brother was a finnicky eater was a massive understatement, so if we happened to run out of one of the only foods he was willing to eat, it was DEFCON 1. Luckily, I was prepared.

Brushing off the frustration I was all too familiar with, I jumped into action and headed back down the hall toward the kitchen. "Relax, little bro. I got you covered." With Lee still perched on my hip, I used my free hand to open the cabinet where I usually kept the spices and reached to the very top shelf where I'd stashed a box of Cocoa Pebbles no one else knew about.

Raylan gave me wide eyes before twisting his lips into a pleased grin. "Sweet!"

Wrangling the Bradbury clan was like trying to herd cats. However, I had *years* of experience, so I was pretty damn good at it.

Our folks hadn't been good for much other than pushing out kids and gracing them with embarrassing names, so the moment Rhodes had come into the world, the responsibility of raising him had fallen on my own eight-year-old shoulders. Sunshine came two years later, and it was the same gig. Over and over again for years.

Then something in Danny and Peggy Bradbury changed when Raleigh came into the picture. They decided they weren't the type of people who wanted to be parents after all, and I woke up one morning to discover they'd bailed.

That had been a little over two years ago, and as far as I was concerned, it was good riddance. We didn't need them.

Hell, *I* hadn't needed them for twenty-five years, and the way I looked at it, I'd been the only parent my siblings ever had, so we'd get on fine without them.

I'd only been seventeen years old, barely into my senior year of high school when, thanks to my parents being worthless blobs who refused to work or be responsible in any way, I'd had to drop out so I could get a full-time job to care for the kids and myself. Unfortunately, there weren't a lot of options for a girl without so much as a GED, so I'd been forced into multiple jobs that paid shit money. Shit money that our worthless folks stole whenever the need for beer or vodka came over them. And the need came *often*.

Without them there to mooch off me, things got a little easier. Then one day I saw an ad in the paper for a strip club two towns over. It wasn't something I'd ever wanted to do, but to keep a roof over my kids' heads and food in their bellies, I did what needed to be done.

Enjoy an Excerpt from Wrong Side of the Tracks

I'd been a dancer two to three nights a week at Pink Palace for a year and a half now, and the headlining act for the past eight months. I hated every second of it. Pink Palace wasn't exactly a classy joint, but it paid the bills. Barely.

To supplement my income and make sure there was enough cash for the unexpected—and there was always something unexpected—I worked as a checker at Fresh Foods, the local grocery store in Hope Valley, five days a week.

Most days it was a struggle just to keep my eyes open, and I lived off coffee and energy drinks more than was probably healthy, but this was my life, and I'd learned a long time ago that feeling sorry for myself didn't solve my problems. All it did was waste time and make me feel miserable.

Truth was, my siblings needed *all* of me, so time for pity parties was out of the question. My whole life was those kids, and that was just fine with me.

With each one that came, my heart swelled bigger and bigger. Each and every one of them was *mine*. I'd go to the mat for them. I'd fight and bleed and die for them if that was what it took. I just wished I could give them better life than the one they had.

The shitty three-bedroom double-wide we lived in sat in the middle of a trailer park in an even shittier part of town.

Enjoy an Excerpt from Wrong Side of the Tracks

The place was meant for a much smaller family, and we were constantly stepping on each other's toes, but it was the best I could do. I had to admit, I hated myself a little for that.

I wanted to give those kids everything I never had. Unfortunately, life wasn't always fair, and good things weren't a guarantee. Especially for a girl who'd grown up on the wrong side of the tracks.

It always managed to surprise me, but just like every morning before, I somehow managed to get four kids dressed and out the door for school with their teeth brushed and bellies full.

I might not have graduated high school, but I fully intended to see to it that all my brothers and sisters did. And because of that, I insisted they fuel up with breakfast every morning so they had enough energy to make it through the day.

I had a little while of just me and Raleigh before I had to pass him off to our neighbor Odette so I could get ready for my shift at the grocery store, so we went about our morning routine. I clicked on a playlist I made just for him. Fast-paced, high-energy Top 40 songs he loved, and I spent the next hour dancing and singing loudly as I made us breakfast. As usual, Raleigh spent the whole time squealing and clapping at my antics with the biggest, happiest baby grin on his face.

That grin was all I needed to pull me out of my earlier

Enjoy an Excerpt from Wrong Side of the Tracks

funk. As long as the kids were happy and healthy, nothing else mattered.

So what if a man such as Marco Castillo wasn't for the likes of me, a high school dropout stripper who lived in a trailer park? I had the love of the five most important people in the entire world, and that was more than enough for me. I didn't need anything else.

Or at least that was what I was determined to make myself believe.

CLICK HERE TO KEEP READING

About Jessica

Born and raised around Houston, Jessica is a self proclaimed caffeine addict, connoisseur of inexpensive wine, and the worst driver in the state of Texas. In addition to being all of these things, she's first and foremost a wife and mom.

Growing up, she shared her mom and grandmother's love of reading. But where they leaned toward murder mysteries, Jessica was obsessed with all things romance.

About Jessica

When she's not nose deep in her next manuscript, you can usually find her with her kindle in hand.

Connect with Jessica now
Website: www.authorjessicaprince.com
Jessica's Princesses Reader Group
Newsletter
Instagram
Facebook
Twitter
authorjessicaprince@gmail.com

Made in the USA
Columbia, SC
30 October 2022